# PRAISE FOR SON OF A SERIAL KILLER

"Straddling the line between true crime fanaticism and f*cked up fever dream, Adams doesn't just throw a twist into the serial killer fiction subgenre: He powerbombs it."

—Rebecca Rowland, Shirley Jackson Award nominee of *White Trash & Recycled Nightmares*

"Propulsive and provocative, Adams's *Son of a Serial Killer* takes a magnifying glass to our society in the grips of true-crime obsessions and serial killer fandoms. In Glenn, we encounter a lost soul protagonist, a proverbial cog in the machine, and then witness his bloody journey to find his true identity. It's not just his story we're reading, it's the story of America—body count and all."

—Patrick Barb, author of *JK-LOL* and *The Children's Horror*

"Adams pulls you into a story where paranoia, ghostly warnings, and a town's buried fears collide—leaving Glen Overton questioning whether Brock Blackwood's nightmare ever really ended."

—Mason Marks, author of *The Serpent's Call*

"Adams crafts a well paced story using beautiful words under a sinister guise. We've got likable and relatable characters, the echoes of a bad bad man whose presence looms heavy throughout the story, and an interesting direction in the third act that left me guessing as I turned each page."

—David Washburn, author of *DIY Exorcism*

# SON OF A SERIAL KILLER

## ANDREW ADAMS

MADAXEMEDIA.COM

Published by Mad Axe Media

madaxemedia.com

Cover & Interior Design By Joey Powell

Edited by Nico Bell

Print ISBN: 979-8-9906858-6-4

E-Book ISBN: 979-8-9906858-7-1

"Whatever in creation exists without my knowledge exists with-

out my consent."
-from *Blood Meridian* by Cormac McCarthy

To my better half.

# SON OF A SERIAL KILLER

# CHAPTER ONE

"Hands up, motherfucker! On your knees!" the young cop shouted. His right hand gripped a service pistol with white knuckles while the other shakily grasped for his radio. "This is Officer Baker requesting back-up near the intersection of Second and Stafford. I have the suspect in custody about a mile off the main road."

The man smirked under his thick mustache with a satisfied sigh and turned to face the rookie cop. The freedom of the mountain air at his back is inviting. "Do you? I don't feel very confined."

"Shut up! Get down right now, or I'll shoot!"

"Don't make threats, just do it."

"I'm warning you!" Baker stammered as he tried to steady his grip with his other hand.

"You already warned me. Either kill me or don't." They shared a brief stare down as the man flipped the cigar from atop his ear and the officer fired a warning shot into the asphalt between his feet. He cackled. "Easy there, cowboy, I was just yanking your chain!"

"Get on your knees right fuckin' now!"

"Of course, officer. I am a law-abiding citizen after all."

"None of that funny stuff, you hear me? I've heard all about your tricks and the next round goes through your skull!" Officer Baker took several shuffles forward and reaffirmed his intentions by dropping the revolver's hammer for another shot.

The man grinned sharply again and dramatically stretched his thick and heavily tattooed arms behind his neck. The white tank top he was wearing revealed an entire torso full of ink-covered skin. "So, it's glory you want, is it? You want to be the one who brought down the boogeyman."

"I want to do my job and get you off the streets. Get down so I can cuff you, then we're going to sit right here and wait for backup."

"Everything happens exactly as it should. Did you know that? You were sent here for a reason."

"Stop talking, I don't want to hear any of it."

"Think of the news articles about you, young officer Baker. You can kill me now and take sole credit before your comrades arrive and rob that from you. I can make your whole career with one pull of the trigger!" The man spat to the side of the road and dropped to his knees with both hands still tucked behind his head. "There you have it, ready for execution!"

"I need you to put these cuffs on your wrists and remain quiet. No more funny business!"

"Of course, officer ... or should I say *Lieutenant* Baker? Think of all the opportunities."

"That's enough!" The young officer stepped gingerly around the man's back with the cuffs in one hand and his revolver in the other. He slapped one of the steel restraints around the suspect's wrist and shifted the gun to his off hand.

"Such a waste." The man flipped his cuffed wrist to grab the officer's and yanked him forward into a backwards headbutt that broke his nose. Baker fired an errant shot into the meat of his thigh then writhed around on his back in pain with blood and tears stinging his eyes. The man leapt on top of him and bit the officer's lower jaw within his own, clinking teeth on teeth and tearing the bone structure from its place with a few savage shakes and pulls. He cast the mandible aside like a dilapidated boomerang and retrieved his loose cigar that had fallen to the asphalt. "I offered you everything and you took it for granted. Pity."

Baker tossed about the road in existential agony as the man stood above him and removed a lighter from his pocket to light the cigar at last. He took only a few drags then grabbed a half-pint of whiskey from his back pocket and took a couple swigs. He gave his final evil grin and dumped the remainder of the liquor on Baker's restless corpse-to-be, then flicked the cigar onto the accelerant.

Police sirens swarmed from afar as he stood next to the burning body and held tight by the rising flames with his tank top soaked crimson red from blood. He limped forward and stared into the distance as his demonic blue eyes reflected their siren lights and he drank the last few drops of whiskey with a deep sigh of relief.

# CHAPTER TWO

"**G**len. Glen!"

He shoots up from the desk and looks around in bewilderment before peeling off a sticky note that adheres to his cheek. "Hi, Monica. Lovely day in the office, isn't it?"

She glares down at him over folded arms, tapping her elbow impatiently with all four fingers. "You tell me, although I'm sure it's a rather charming existence in that empty little head of yours." Monica points her index finger in Glen's face but stops just short of jabbing his forehead for fear of another HR blow up, then walks away fuming instead.

A mousy woman pokes the top half of her face over the dividing wall between their cubicles. "Don't get yourself in trouble again, Glen. You're the only thing I like about working in this terrible place."

He rubs his eyes and stares at the blurry computer screen for a moment before responding. "She's nothing but talk, Dana, everything will be just fine. It isn't the first time she caught me sleeping."

"Just be careful, alright? Monica would love nothing more than to fire you in front of everyone just to make a point." She lightly bites her bottom lip as he stares blankly ahead. "Hey, are you doing anything tonight? Want to get coffee after work?"

Glen takes three hard blinks to focus his vision and notices the sticky note sitting atop his desktop calendar. *Don't forget Mom's birthday!* "I don't think tonight will work for me, Dana. Sorry."

She opens her mouth slightly to respond but instead drops her chin onto the cubicle wall between them in equal parts disappointment and embarrassment.

"But how about a rain check?" he continues. "It's Mom's birthday today, and she doesn't have anyone else to celebrate with. Otherwise, I would love to go."

"Sounds good. Just ... try not to get fired before then because I don't know if I can afford to pay for both of us."

"In that case, we had better go tomorrow because I can't make any promises against falling asleep again. For now, I should catch up on my work to at least remain employed another day."

"Yes, you should." She nods before disappearing.

Glen yawns and gazes at the keyboard as if it will eventually type for him, then begins to tap his pencil eraser on the table, careful to not make too much noise. "Hey, Dana."

"Yes?" She pops up again.

"You're my favorite part of working here too."

She stares for several seconds with only her spectacled eyes visible. "Took you long enough."

"Yeah, well, I—" Glen turns to see that she has retreated again from their shared wall. "I'm just having a tough day, that's all," he grumbles, clicking on his mouse and keyboard with malaise. Mixtures of murky musings swirl in his brain to distract him from accomplishing much of anything at all. The energy required to respond to even one more stupid, nonsensical email cannot be found, deadlines be damned.

Intrusive thoughts force their way through his racing mind. The job is horrendously boring and devoid of meaning aside from collecting an undersized paycheck. *Much like yourself, boring and useless.* He twirls a company-provided premium roller ball gel pen effortlessly between the fingers of his other hand—their gift to the hard-working employees as a token of appreciation, which is ironically a tool meant to drive production forward. He procrastinates and flips it around like a toy instead. Being a corporate data clerk never crossed his mind as the answer back in high school whenever a teacher would ask what he wanted to be when he grew up; there never really was an answer, but clicking arbitrary numbers into digital spreadsheets certainly wasn't at the top of the list.

His computer lights up after nearly entering sleep mode, accompanied by a slightly obnoxious musical jingle sound. Another email atop the inbox pushes the rest down a slot as Glen bites his tongue not to release profanities at the screen. This one, however, is from Dana next door. She sends a video of a dancing dog, her favorite brand of humor, along with matching clipart. *Thank you, I needed that,* he types before leaning back in his chair again. He glances at the small dog figurine on his desk that she gave him when they first became friends because she said it would brighten his days there. Everyone in the office could use the same bit of cheer, yet none of them seem to have much of a sense of humor left after spending years in the corporate graveyard. *I need to get out of here at five on the dot today, so I am going to slip out. See you in the morning.* He types his response to the email and clicks send.

"Happy birthday," Glen says as he pushes the front door open with his foot, holding the cake he bought on the way home and a last-minute gift dangling from his right pinky. "Mom?"

Their home is quiet and still aside from the low volume of a television commercial playing in the living room. The light flickers off the walls and pours into the hallways and kitchen. Glen walks in the room cautiously to find a plastic liquor bottle resting on its side and dripping rhythmically onto their end table. His mother sits slumped over in the old reclining chair with her arm dangling and the remote rests on the floor next to her slippered feet.

"Oh, Mother ... what else is new?" Glen gently props her upright against the cushions and uses his shirt to wipe away the small puddle of vodka, noticing that it has already begun to dissolve the protective varnish on the wooden table next to many more similarly faded blotches.

"Brock? You're finally home," she whispers as he squats down to grab the television remote.

"It's Glen, Mom. Your only son ... Hell, your only child."

"So good to see you again, Brock," she slurs as her eyes roll back.

He places the remote back on the end table, which wobbles unevenly as he releases it from his grip. Glen discovers a broken white pill beneath it. He takes a deep breath to berate his mother for falling into the abyss again but knows she won't be listening anyway. And not only due to inebriation. It's her birthday for Christ's sake, and he can try pointlessly to save her from herself another time.

"We should try to get you into bed upstairs." He shakes her feeble shoulders gently but with enough force to make a solid attempt at waking her. Even if only to say he did. "Mom."

She begins to snore slightly and rocks like a rag doll as he tries again without enthusiasm to bring her back to consciousness.

"Forget it," he grumbles. Glen stares at his mother once more with a conflicting push and pull between rage and pity. He then glances at her bottle of booze again and shrugs, plopping down on the couch with it before taking a few swigs himself.

A tiny voice in his brain fights back against the notion that he *needs* to be here on her birthday when she is already unconscious and thinking that he should try and see if Dana would still like to get coffee. Glen is now thirty years old ... Why waste any more energy on a woman that has been mostly absent for the majority of all three of those decades?

It's her fiftieth birthday today, and she didn't even make it to dinner time. Not that she eats much anymore regardless. His mother has always been guarded, secretive, and deceptive about her personal life and feelings, reaching for the false securities of compressed powder and booze instead of facing herself in the mirror. The woman is essentially a complete stranger, like the many co-workers he never speaks to but sees daily in a forced capacity. Glen secretly wishes he could feel a similar level of detachment toward her, even though the moral compass tends to point toward forgiveness time and time again for the woman who raised him. Even if she did a shit job.

He tips the bottle back and downs what little liquor she left inside before passing out. Lowering the vodka and plunking it on her end table, Glen truly pays attention for the first time since sitting down and notices they are watching a VHS tape instead of a live broadcast. The light on Mom's VCR is lit up with the timestamp beside it on the display. This particular video appears to be from the late eighties, at least, judging by the grainy video quality and dated production. Not to mention the hair.

*Welcome back and as always, we hope you are enjoying the show.*

"How the hell should I know?" Glen mocks. "All I've seen is commercials so far."

*In case you haven't been following along at home, we will now return to the final interview with famed serial killer Brock Blackwood before he is put to death.*

"THAT Brock?! You really thought I was *the* Brock Blackwood sneaking into your living room? Jesus, Mom, you're even further gone than I thought."

*Brock, would you care to introduce yourself to our television audience? It will be your last chance to do so.*

The killer turns and stares directly into the camera with an overwhelming darkness hidden behind his sparkling blue eyes. He stares nonchalantly with a sarcastic expression above his slight cleft chin and unsuspectingly masculine jawline. "(Bleep) your audience!" Brock cackles with the rabid expression of a caged animal.

Glen watches his mother's VHS tape for a few seconds longer as the pressure within builds. Even Brock's analog presence from over twenty years in the past is enough to make him squirm. The serial killer continues to smirk through the television set and locks eyes with him from a time period that has long-since passed.

Glen shivers involuntarily in his seat, still watching the devil's every move with a chill of morbid curiosity. Brock Blackwood was the most unfortunately famous of all serial killers who wrought absolute havoc across the western states throughout the seventies and eighties, though his influence carries on well into the new millennium.

"Before we get going, Brock, is there anything you would like to share with your fans? The majority of our audience is rooting for you, by the way."

Glen watches with bated breath as the legendary killer turns to stare at him once more from the low quality faded and overplayed VHS tape. He lowers his head and looks up at the camera as his mouth curls into a sharp smirk. "Yes ... I hope you all die."

# CHAPTER THREE

A knocking sound within the house pulls Glen from a deep sleep. His heart pounds in the darkness, though it wouldn't be the first time his mom dropped a glass from the top of the stairs and it bounced all the way down. Their home is silent again, and Glen allows himself to relax into the mattress, nearly falling back to sleep right away.

Another knock, more closely resembling pounding, resonates throughout the old house from somewhere outside his bedroom door. He bolts upright in a fright as his heartbeat crescendos, and the sound echoes again, seemingly shaking the wooden floorboards where they lie. Glen hesitates with a deep breath and pauses before getting out of bed to investigate.

"Mom?" he asks sheepishly with only his face poking through the doorway, thinking she might have woken up and moved herself to the bedroom in a stupor. No answer. Another bang from down the hall frightens him, and he swallows his heart back into his chest. There is nothing to see. No burglars, no stray animals that made their way inside, no middle-aged inebriated women stumbling over thin air.

Glen exits the room fully and walks out to inspect, if nothing else for the peace of mind, figuring it must be a shutter clattering outside or something similar. The hallway curio cabinet always frightened him as a child with its glass doors reflecting strangely in the darkness when he would be unable to sleep and wandered the house. Now it sits quietly with both doors closed and nothing smacking around to terrify him at least once more.

Now convinced he was only having a strange dream, Glen scoffs and dismisses his fears as simply paranoia. He steps forward toward the hall closet to prove to himself that nothing is there, with his mind already focused on getting back to bed and preparing for work in the morning. He pulls on the door and a young woman falls out into his arms scrambling with the side of her head caved in and covered in boot print-shaped bruises. Blood drains from her sunken ear onto his shirt sleeve as she drops the crescent side of her skull into the crook of his arm. She reaches out for Glen with frayed ropes swaying from her friction-burnt and bleeding wrists. The sleeves of her denim shirt have been torn open to reveal the rope burns and lacerations.

"You have to help me! He's coming back!" she pleads as she rises, though her jaw dangles loosely and detached and the words spill out in warbled mumbles. Glen gasps sharply and recoils as an adrenaline shot electrifies his chest. "He did this to me! Tied my arms to two different posts and stomped his boot into my head until it all went black! We have to get out of here!"

Glen swallows his fear, still numb from shock as he continues to stare at her crooked, dangling jaw. "Who ... Who did this to you?"

"Why aren't you more scared?! He stomped my face in ... just imagine what will happen to you!"

He steps backward with quivering legs and slips on the edge of the top step then falls to one knee as he grasps for the railing to avoid a tumble. "Let me call you an ambulance ..."

"It's too late. Blackwood is here and we all must suffer."

"What's your name? I can still help you!"

"Abby, my name is Abby! Help me ... HELP ME NOW!" she shrieks, causing Glen to jump and slide down the steps in a half prone position, skimming the edges of each stair with his bent knee. He reaches the bottom floor and leaps up to watch for her next move, but the woman is gone. "Abby? Abby! Mom!" No answer from either.

Glen rushes for the hanging house phone and dials 911, knowing that his mom is done for if she moved to her bed and passed out, although how can Brock Blackwood attack them? The three rings seem to echo forever before an operator finally answers.

"911, what's your emergency?"

"There's a strange woman in my house that says she has been attacked. She's bloody, and her jaw has clearly been broken. Blackwood. She said it was Blackwood."

"Blackwood? As in Brock Blackwood?"

"That's what she told me, yes! She's in terrible shape and needs help right away!" he shouts.

"Is this a prank call? Brock Blackwood has been dead for twenty years."

"No, it's not a prank call! It doesn't matter what she said. There's a young woman in my house that needs help right now!"

"I have your address and first responders will be there as soon as they can. Please hang tight, as it seems you aren't in immediate danger." The line goes dead with a lingering dial tone as Glen smacks himself in the face to ensure that he is awake. No, definitely not dreaming.

The upstairs remains somber and silent, with no sign of his mother or Abby. Feeling guilt building up for leaving his mother behind, he grimaces amidst the panic and pounding heart and calls for her once more. "Mom!" Glen turns toward the front door to ensure that it is still shut and locked when he sees her still unconscious in the chair as the television glows with a blank blue screen. "Wake up! We need to get out of the house!"

Her eyes begin to stir behind her eyelids as she leans forward awkwardly. "What? Where are we?"

"At home, but we have to get outside! Someone is in the house with us!"

"Huh? Who is it?"

Glen rolls his eyes and grabs her frail wrists to lead them outside until the police arrive. She stumbles with her eyes barely open and leans against his body for support as they stand in the brisk night air. He continues to glance back over his shoulder in fear of the battered woman or her attacker running after them.

"What are we doing outside, Glenny?"

"Just be quiet and wait here for a few more minutes. We're safe on the porch." He shakes his head to repel the burrowed images of Abby's dilapidated jaw dangling loosely and the embedded boot prints that appeared to reshape her head structure as if the skull was fractured inward ... it's almost unfathomable that she survived.

Sirens in the distance greet their street, followed by red and blue flashing lights painting houses on both sides of the neighborhood, undoubtedly disturbing many of the sleeping residents. "Why are they coming here?" she asks.

"Hold tight, let me talk to them." Glen jogs to the sidewalk and waves his arms for the vehicles to stop. Four police cars lead the charge, followed by an ambulance and two fire trucks that line the sidewalk in front of several houses in both directions. He quickly realizes the situation to be much more than he bargained for as several news vans approach only a few beats behind.

An older officer with a gray mustache exits one of the police cars and his mannerisms would suggest that he is the lead on this case. His partner exits the passenger seat as the inhabitants of the other three cars join them. "I hear tell there's a woman that was found here severely beaten, is that correct?"

"Yes, she was hiding upstairs. I was the one who found her."

"My name is Lieutenant Steele. Am I right to assume we have your permission to search the premises?"

"Yes, of course." Glen nods. "I was walking down the hallway, and she jumped on me from a small closet right at the top of the stairs."

Steele motions toward the house with two fingers and six officers charge inside with their weapons drawn. "My team will take care of that for you, but

I hope you don't mind waiting here with me to answer a few questions in the meantime. Protocol."

"Of course ... I mean, no I don't mind."

"Name?"

"Mine or the girl's?" Glen stammers as he glances toward the news crews unloading camera equipment and approaching the scene posthaste.

"Yours. I want to know a bit more about you first before we move on to the girl."

"It's Glen. Glen Overton."

"And who else lives in this house with you, Glen?" Steele asks as he scribbles information on a small notepad. One end of his mustache twitches.

"My mother, it's just me and my mom here." He turns and points to her as she stands bewildered in the front yard. "You'll have to excuse her. She is quite drunk."

"I see. So, you walked down the hallway and saw this woman. What was her name?"

News cameras approach as closely as they can and shove their microphones outward to record his words for later. "She said her name is Abby, that's all I know. Her jaw was ... it was clearly broken and dangling diagonally, and she told me that Blackwood did it. That's it."

"Brock Blackwood?"

"I guess. It all happened in a flash."

"Ah. No wonder the media vultures showed up so quickly." Steele spits off to the side and grimaces at their pointed cameras.

"Why?"

"We don't say that name around these parts anymore, son, and when you do, this is the sort of backlash that happens. Saying *Brock Blackwood* on a recorded phone line is like screaming *bomb* on an airplane."

Glen looks perplexed and his vision narrows to that of a pin-sized tunnel. "But I said it on a 911 call."

"How do you think they knew where to show up? The people in this area still remember Blackwood's atrocities vividly, and those that don't … well, they should. So, your mysterious woman had her head caved in by a serial killer who was electrocuted twenty years ago? Have you been drinking too?"

"No, I haven't, and that's what she said. I was too shocked to process it at the time." Glen glares at the vans as each reporter declares to their respective camera operators that a murder has occurred in a shockingly similar modus operandi to that of the deceased Blackwood. "Do they *have* to be here?"

"I'm afraid there's nothing I can do about them. People in a paygrade much higher than myself have made it illegal to deny access to a crime scene from outside our established perimeter. Off the record, Mr. Overton, are you under the influence of any other controlled substances?"

"Me? Never! Is that what you think this is?"

"Keep your voice down if you don't want them to hear you. I only ask because I've been on the force a long time, and it just so happens that a young woman by the name of Abby was bound and had her head stomped to bits within this very house … back in 1980 by none other than Brock Blackwood. So, this is either an elaborate rouse or you are on some seriously good shit. Off the record, of course," Steele scoffs.

Glen's face falls frightfully pale and tingly as his tunnel vision shrinks to nearly complete blackness. "I'm sorry, what?"

The officers exit the home behind him and walk toward Lieutenant Steele. "All clear, sir. We didn't find anyone, nor were there any signs of forced entry, burglary, or any genetic evidence left behind. No blood."

"I didn't think there would be. We're done here. Mr. Overton, Officer Jackson will stay behind to take an official statement, and I'm going to recommend that an EMT gives you a thorough medical examination. I will complete the rest of the paperwork back at the station."

"Mr. Overton are you with me?" the EMT asks. She appears to be in her mid-thirties and already hardened by the job.

"Yes, I'm fine."

She pulls her rubber gloves tight and shines a flashlight into his eyes. "Follow the light, please. So, I hear this case has something to do with Brock Blackwood?"

"Apparently. All I know is that I saw a woman in our house, and it seems to match the details of an old murder case."

"I keep telling you it was only a nightmare, Glenny! There's nothing to talk about!" his mother adds from the front yard.

"It wasn't a nightmare. I know what I saw."

"Regardless, I'm required by law to perform a quick drug test to ensure you aren't under the influence. You would be surprised at how many people call 911 after doing drugs and thinking they're seeing demons and all sorts of things. I'm sure you can imagine how expensive it is to have us all out here."

"I have nothing to hide, so go ahead. Just out of curiosity, what happens to the people who test positive?"

"It's a misdemeanor and a small fine, that's all, but the test is required as part of your evaluation. Open, please."

Her eyes shift back and forth as she takes two cotton swabs and rubs one on the inside of each cheek, then places them into separate plastic evidence bags.

"Why did you do two?"

"It's standard protocol in case we need to run another test later for clarification. I will take your blood pressure now and continue to ask you a few more questions." The EMT hands one bag to a co-worker and discreetly stuffs the other into her pocket.

"I'm fine, really. Abby didn't hurt me."

"It's not a big deal, Mr. Overton. I have to follow procedure very closely for this type of call. Besides, it is not every day that we get calls about *Brock Blackwood* in 2011."

Glen feels his blood pressure spike beneath the cuff. Something about the way she phrased that statement felt accusatory and rubbed him the wrong way. "Well, I'm only repeating what I heard. Obviously, the facts might be interpreted differently by those who actually make the decisions."

"I sure hope so. Blackwood decimated many families in this area that still haven't fully healed decades later."

"So, I've heard. He's been dead for twenty years, though, so I doubt he's hurting anybody else now. The girl Abby was clearly deranged, and I should have kept that part private."

"You never know, everything happens for a reason." The monitor beeps as she scoffs at the reading and readjusts the cuff. "Your blood pressure is significantly elevated, but I would be surprised if it was normal after the night you've had. We'll check it again in a few minutes."

"He always was a nervous boy," his mother asserts herself. "Is there anything else you need from him? We would like to get back to sleep now."

"I don't *need* to take his blood pressure a second time. The cheek swab for controlled substances is the most important factor."

"Great, you've got that. Goodnight." She grabs Glen by the shoulders and leads him back inside as the EMT smirks behind them. "You've got to learn when to simply say nothing, Glenny. Sometimes silence is the smartest option."

He walks through the door and shuts it to silence the outside world. "I saw what you were watching earlier, Mom. I came home when Brock's interview was playing on the TV."

"Oh, you know how I enjoy my true crime," she dismisses while sitting back in her armchair. "Hey, maybe that's why you had the nightmare? Just an unfortunate coincidence."

Glen bites his bottom lip to avoid engaging in an asinine argument at this hour. She exists in her own limited plane of consciousness and wouldn't acknowledge logic if she drowned in it. The one thing he knows beyond a shadow of a doubt is that the vision of Abby was no nightmare.

# CHAPTER FOUR

Glen anxiously taps both index fingers on either side of his coffee mug as he waits for Dana to get off work. This is their favorite coffee spot to frequent about a block away from the office and somewhere that they often visit on their lunch break. Something about the familiarity of routine makes him feel like himself even when everything else in life seems to simply be off.

Dana walks in the door like a ray of sunshine amidst a torrential storm. "I hope you know what kind of trouble you stirred up at work today by staying home."

Glen stands and hugs his best friend, shocking her with the uncharacteristic act. "I already got your latte for you, just how you like it."

"Thank you. Are you alright? You look terrible ... No offense."

"None taken. Haven't slept in thirty-six hours aside from my quick nap at work yesterday."

"Jesus. Health conscious as ever, I see," she chides. "And is that whiskey I smell in your coffee?"

"Yes."

"Nice. So, what happened? Monica is on the warpath to find even a sliver of evidence against you."

Glen grasps his cup with both hands and stares at it intently while his left eye twitches continuously. "I think I might be going crazy, but I need you to keep this secret."

"I keep all your secrets, like when you take naps in the bathroom."

"Yeah, but this is *secret*. Nobody can know, as in not even having a conversation with your cat about it sort of thing. *They* might be listening."

"Who is listening?" Dana asks with a raised eyebrow.

"I don't know, but it could be anybody ... Any of these people around us might be spying."

"Okay ... My interest is piqued, and you're also beginning to scare me just a bit. I won't tell a soul, not even the urns of my departed cats. My lips are sealed."

Glen scrunches his face in what appears to be a glare, but then the eye twitch reveals itself. "Alright, but just know you are the only person I can trust, and I mean that ... Do you remember Brock Blackwood?"

"Of course, I do. Every family within a thousand miles shudders when you mention that name."

"Well ... last night, a young woman named Abby appeared in my house, but I had the most eerie feeling that she was *dead*. Her jaw was broken, and the side of her head had been caved in by a boot. She insisted Blackwood did it, and I called the police which turned out to be a huge mistake. The lieutenant said a woman was murdered in my house the exact same way and that her name was also Abby. He said Brock did it."

"But how?" Dana asks. "Are you sure you weren't dreaming? Or hallucinating?"

"She woke me up from a dream, so it couldn't have been a nightmare. I suppose hallucination isn't out of the question, but I have never felt more present in my entire life than when she was talking to me. Everything felt *too* real. Anyway, I looked it up online and the death of Abigail Finley was often attributed to Blackwood, but a lack of hard evidence has left it legally unsolved to this day. I just learned about her for the first time, but many enthusiasts believe she was murdered in my house over thirty years ago."

"I'm sorry, but I am certain I didn't hear that correctly."

"Yes, you did." Glen inhales deeply and stares into her eyes. "Brock Blackwood seems to have beaten a young woman to death in my home, and the poor girl's spirit is unable to move on. That probably doesn't even make sense, but I have no other explanations."

"How do you know? So, the woman wasn't real after all?"

"I can't be absolutely certain either way. Mom got drunk again last night and was passed out downstairs while this was happening. This girl, Abby, approached me in the hallway and nobody else ever saw her after that. Police and ambulances were at my house all night looking for her and running tests on me."

"Hence why you weren't at work today, yes ... Wait a second, why were they running tests on *you*?"

"The EMT said it was a drug test to determine the legitimacy of the 911 call. Something about a new law that would penalize people under the influence for making fake calls."

"Hmm." Dana raises an eyebrow again.

"It's not like I have anything to hide." Glen scratches his twitching eye with the shaky finger of a man on the edge. "She swabbed my cheek a couple of times and that was it. I assume I would have already heard back by now if there was something of note to report. They all left the house thinking I was completely crazy, I know it."

"Well, I hope you got plenty of rest today because the work situation isn't good. Monica was being even worse than usual, and other people are starting to catch on because of it," Dana sighs.

"Catching on to what? We don't have much to do in our department anyway."

"Yes, Glen, that is exactly what they are learning. She is using your absences as an excuse to turn people against you and, by extension, me."

Glen stops tapping the coffee cup and stares at his hands, then forces his eyes shut. "I'm just exhausted and suddenly feeling rather ill."

"Then go to the restroom, please, because you know how I get."

"No, not like that. It's up here, inside my head. It feels pretty bad at the moment, like my mind is sick, and I really don't like it."

"That tends to happen when you drink whiskey lattes after thirty-six straight hours of crisis and stress," Dana whispers, placing a hand over Glen's to stop his shaking. "You need some sleep. Take your mind off everything for a while and do something else. I'm sorry for throwing more problems on top of the pile."

"I'm having trouble relaxing inside the house after what I saw. Abby's jaw was completely *detached*, Dana, held on only by skin. Her head had been stomped into almost half its normal size."

"I'm sure that was traumatizing to see, but ... is there any possibility that you really were hallucinating? Think about it—a girl turns up matching the *exact* description of a Blackwood murder from thirty years ago and she just so happens to tell you he was the one who did it? Can you think of any reason why that would be in your mind?"

He forces his eyes shut for several seconds and rubs them desperately. "My mom was watching Brock's final interview when I got home, the famous one before he got the electric chair that was televised when we were kids."

"See? Blackwood was in your mind already when you went to bed, and it ended up giving you a nightmare about it, for whatever reason."

"But if she was only a dream, then how does that explain me knowing her name and the way she died? My mom said the same thing about it all being in my head, but I doubt I could have pulled all that information out of a nightmare."

"Probably not worth asking too many questions right now until your mind is able to process what happened. I'm sure you saw something subconsciously at some point about Abby, and then your mom watching Brock's interview brought it back out. She is obviously a fan and must have exposed you to the story at some point." Dana nods.

"But that's what I keep thinking about ... When would I have heard about something so horrendous without vividly remembering it?" Glen sighs. "What a shitshow of a family we have, eh? You're right though ... I'm not in the proper state of mind at the moment to make sense of this mess but thank you for trying to help me, Dana, just like you always do. I'm sure everything you said will stick tomorrow."

"Of course, it will. You're Glen Overton, the greatest soon-to-be fired data clerk in the state, and you're a good guy. Say it."

"I'm a good guy," he repeats.

"No, all of it, from the beginning. Trust me, it will make you feel better."

"I am Glen Overton, the greatest soon-to-be fired data clerk in the state."

"Damn right, you are," Dana laughs. "And you *are* a good guy. My best friend, in fact, and we'll get through this tornado together, then the next one, and so on."

"You're my best friend too. Really, thank you for everything. There is literally nowhere else I could have turned to explain."

"I know, and I'm happy to fulfill my duty whenever called upon."

Glen and Dana share a brief moment of comfortable silence and smile at one another, knowing fully well there is nothing else to add that wouldn't be repeating the same thoughts over and over again in feeble desperation. Glen is beyond exhausted and under more stress than he has ever had to shoulder, not feeling much like himself since bumping into Abby the night before. Hell, *something* has felt wrong deep inside him for some time now anyway.

Dana takes the last sip of her latte and scoffs internally. She and Glen are the most boring people in the office, while everyone else has personal lives, kids, spouses, hobbies, and outside interests. The two of them commiserate daily over idiosyncrasies and television shows to pass the time, sending each other goofy emails and text messages throughout their days at work. There is something alarmingly ironic that the two most plain people in the company have become best friends. "Hey, I'm going to go get myself a refill. Not that you need any more coffee, but do you want another? I'm buying this round."

"Sure, you know what I like."

"Yes, I do, but no whiskey in this one. I don't think you need any more."

Glen waits at their table as the echoes of Dana's voice dissolve and fade away. He can't hear anything outside of the endless chatter in his own mind, a dozen different sources of noise all competing to be heard at the forefront. *Yes ... I hope you all die,* he hears Brock's voice boom above the rest. Glen feels the urge to run but doesn't know where to find shelter when all those blaring shouts are drowning him from within. The familiar coffee shop walls and table morph into something unfamiliar and malicious. How can something as comforting as their friendly neighborhood stop suddenly feel so evil? He has to escape ... must shed his own skin if necessary to flee the thoughts of Abby and the treachery of what happened to her. Even slightly more jarring is the fact that an identical murder was supposedly committed inside the house before they moved in.

"Glen? You're sweating."

"Yes," he snaps back to cognizance. "Whiskey, remember? It's also rather hot in here."

"Never mind you're drinking toxic amounts of coffee on top of it. Here's your refill."

"Thank you. This will at least get me home, and God knows what happens then."

"Any thoughts on work tomorrow?" Dana clears her throat, finally broaching what is somehow the most uncomfortable subject so far.

"I'm not sure, honestly. I think I will try to get a good night's sleep and go from there, although at the moment, I can't even wrap my mind around going into the office."

"Maybe ... Maybe a bit of normalcy might do you some good? You wouldn't want to entirely flip your life upside down, right? Monica—"

"I don't give a shit what Monica has to say," Glen snaps and sighs quickly afterward. "Sorry, that was directed at her, not you."

"I know. I just think you might fall into an even worse place mentally without a job or routine to keep you steady. I would imagine your thoughts have been running wild in there."

"Yes, they have been … That's why I'm finding it difficult to focus on returning to work where our lovely boss has made a cozy home for herself up my ass."

"If you at least show up, there isn't much she can do to you, although today she tried everything possible to get you in trouble. I hate to keep harping on the same subject, but eventually, she will find more and more ways to make your life a living hell. Sorry, *more* of a living hell." She winks.

"Thank you for the distinction. Honestly, I think I'm dreading everyone else's reaction more than anything else."

"Why would you think that?"

"There were news cameras shoved in my face last night while I explained what happened because I mentioned Blackwood in the 911 call. I'm sure many of them already saw me on TV and think I'm insane," Glen laments. "Not that they ever thought I was normal to begin with."

"It isn't exactly legally binding information just because you muttered the words *Brock Blackwood* over a telephone. I'm sure everything will be fine."

# CHAPTER FIVE

*B* *rock Blackwood is back in the news today for the first time since his death in the early nineties, as a 911 call claiming to have found one of his victims—*

*The state of Washington is in an uproar this morning as local resident, Glen Overton, is in the hot seat—*

*Communities across Washington are filled with dread as Brock Blackwood's name enters homes again, bringing with it the unease and anxiety—*

Glen stands in front of the television and aggressively flips through news channels with a shaky hand. "Not a big deal, Dana? Really?" He throws the remote down at the ground, forcing the batteries to pop out and scatter across the living room. "This is a disaster! A God damn disaster!"

"Glenny? What's all that yelling for?"

A cold sweat accompanies his trembling body as her voice echoes from atop the staircase like the final nail being driven into his existential coffin. Throughout the whirlwind of the previous day and a half, his mother had been largely hidden away following her private birthday party with Brock's ghost and the Abby event. He was hoping to escape the house before she returned to the realm of the living and make an attempt at going in to work.

"Yes. It's me."

"What's going on down there? Why are you making such a fuss?"

A lump hardens in his throat. *How dare she?* The desire to scream even louder rises ... the urge to smash her beloved television and kick a hole in the wall ... but instead he pauses and takes a deep breath into a sore chest from breathing deeply so often the past few days.

"Sorry, I dropped the remote, and the batteries rolled away. I was already running late for work and got frustrated." It is not worth the fight to confront her right now. He still hasn't slept much, and the slippery slope of his fragile sanity seems to be growing ever more slick by the second. Dana is correct, per usual, and he should try to go to work and put on a plastic smile for the sake of normalcy, no matter how fake it may be.

"Don't worry about it, Glenny! We have plenty of batteries! I will take care of the remote. You go on to work!"

"Yeah, one of us has to," he mutters under his breath as he walks through the front door and climbs into his dilapidated old car. Yesterday's gloomy clouds have carried over into today, stifling him further as he tries harder and harder to reclaim a sense of routine. That's right, beneath the rumors and controversy, he is still just good old Glen Overton, the vaunted data clerk.

*I'm on my way. If anyone asks, tell them I'm talking to HR*, he messages Dana. Staring at the phone screen with a final pass over his words, Glen sighs and shifts the car into park again. *Actually, don't. They don't need to know every single detail about me. I don't care.* Send.

This will be the most difficult part of creating a new normal, going back to work and facing those judgmental cretins, most of whom Glen never cared for even on his best days. Maybe he shouldn't bother ... Take the day off and regroup, then return for another shot at it tomorrow. Although Dana will be waiting, and she is the only person that ever truly cared for his wellbeing. What's the worst that could happen?

Glen trudges down the everlasting hallway toward his company's office space. Working in the corporate world means every employee is dressed the same, acts the same, and follows the same routine of arriving at the office to rot in cubicles identical to everyone else's. The titles and job descriptions all essentially mean the same thing; generate more revenue for people high above themselves to enjoy. Needless to say, he dreads every last step down this hall each morning, but today takes the cake as the worst one yet by a mile.

*I can't cover much longer.* Dana's message comes through with a vibration that nearly causes Glen to drop the phone from his sweaty palms. *Yes, Dana, I know, that's why I'm fucking here,* he mouths without speaking and slams the top half of his cell shut. He needs to gain control of himself.

Glen stands outside the frosted glass door and inhales deeply before stepping inside. What horrors lie in wait? Then again, could this really be worse than any other day dressed up to play the role of an enthusiastic and motivated data clerk? Years of working in the building and he still isn't entirely certain what it is he does for a living.

*Take another deep breath and walk in. Get it over with. They're all going to laugh at you anyway, chastise you, call you names. Everybody hates you.* "That's not true," Glen mutters as he shuts his eyes. "I haven't done anything wrong." *Since when does that matter? They all saw you on the news and think you're a freak.*

Shaking and perspiring, he feels woozy but remains steady. *You can do this,* a voice of positive reasoning takes over. He hopes it is right but secretly believes the opposite. *You are fine. You are safe. Nothing can harm you here.* The first hints of a smile overtake him, something he has not felt for quite some time.

"Glen! So glad to have you join us! Are you here to work today or just stand outside my door like an invalid?" Monica snarls as she stands blocking the entrance.

"Good morning, Monica. I didn't realize you owned the company. I was searching for the words to ask you the same thing; are you here to work today or just stand by idly and stare at the door while collecting a free paycheck? Excuse me." Glen pushes past the boss with his head down but smirking secretly.

Her jaw drops and hangs loosely for a moment as she tries to formulate a retort. "Who the hell do you think you are?!" she responds finally, but Glen is already too far gone.

He scurries to his cubicle to hide for the rest of the day, rounding the final corner toward safety when the most sinister words he has ever heard announce his position.

"Good morning, Glen," the woman says sarcastically in a cold tone.

He freezes, unable to remember her name. *Is it Rita?* "Hi," he squeaks.

Dana rises from the cubicle next door, as do dozens more within earshot. Soulless eyes glare at him from every direction as all sound falls silent. Glen cannot move aside from his eyes darting around the room at their inquisitive gazes, each of them simultaneously asking themselves questions and forming unsolicited opinions.

"Glen ... you should sit down and ignore them," a soothing voice whispers, yet all he sees is their searing hatred.

"LUNATIC!" a man shouts from the distance as scores of other workers begin to whisper amongst each other. Their voices create a buzzing frequency that paralyzes Glen as he wonders what they could all be talking about, yet he knows well enough.

*You aren't welcome here,* the darker voice returns. *You will never be safe, run away quickly.*

"Glen!" Dana tugs at his wrist again and pulls him down into his office chair. "You have to ignore them," she advises above the chittering. "They obviously have nothing better to do than to cause trouble for you. Just ignore them."

"I need to go home; this was a mistake. I'm not safe here."

"Glen, just think about what you're saying ... Everybody here is scared that you might have some paranormal connection to Blackwood, but *you* aren't safe?" she cackles. "If anything, they all feel nervous that you might hex them or something."

"But you said it yourself, I'm a good guy. I can't explain what happened in my house the other night, but there's nothing normal about it, and they know too much."

"Yeah, well ... I guess I'm the only person here that has half a brain and can think rationally beyond reactive gossip. That part shouldn't be surprising to you."

"Glen! My office right now, wherever you are!" Monica shrieks as the hushed conversations fall silent.

"I should have never come in today."

"Shh, stop it. Repeat after me," Dana whispers.

"What?"

"Tell Monica exactly what I say, bozo. 'I do not consent to a meeting without human resources present.' Tell her."

"I do not consent to a meeting without human resources present!" Glen shouts from the safety of his tiny cubicle.

Monica audibly scoffs from across the office. "If you insist, but even they can't protect you forever!"

"Okay, now say, 'In that case, I would also like my union representative to join in on a conference call.' Say it."

"In that case, I would also like my union representative to join in on a conference call!" A pin drop could be heard clearly throughout the office, though nobody dares to make such a sound. "Wait, we're in a union?" Glen whispers privately to Dana.

"I believe so, yes. At the very least, it will keep her guessing. Oh, throw this one in there too. 'My lawyer would also be glad to join and answer any further questions.' That should shut her up for good."

"I don't have a lawyer, Dana."

"And? Do you think she wants to find out either way? Just say it," she nudges.

"My lawyer would also be glad to join and answer any further questions! Please allow me a few moments to get him and my union representative on the phone and then we will meet you in your office!" Glen recites from a piece of paper that Dana scribbled on after he had already begun speaking.

They can hear their boss's nerves vibrate through her silence and inability to respond. At the very least, Dana's quick thinking put Monica on the spot with all ears awaiting a response. "How about tomorrow then? That will allow you plenty of time to speak with your representative and legal counsel before we move forward." Without waiting for an answer, Monica slams her door shut like she usually does after a conflict that doesn't go in her favor.

"What am I supposed to do now, Dana? I have to find a lawyer by tomorrow?"

"That was a bluff. She won't mention it again, at least not any time soon. You are clear for now." She grins.

"But how can you be so sure? And how do you know all this stuff?"

"My dad. He was a lawyer for the union, and I always wanted to follow in his footsteps. He used to tell me about all his cases, or rather, I would bug him to death about them. I hate when people like Monica are allowed to treat people however they want without consequences."

"Well, thank you, that was brilliant. I would have just walked in her office and taken the beating because I thought I had to," Glen sighs.

"I know you would have; most people think the same way. The truth is managers and supervisors typically have far fewer rights than the people they oversee."

"Wait, if you know so much about this sort of thing and obviously love it, why didn't you become a lawyer yourself? Why are you still working in this dump?"

"Same reason you are, I guess. Lack of motivation, money, convenience, lots of factors." She shrugs.

"You're still here because you don't have enough money to get a new job?"

"Yes, it's expensive to become a lawyer, in case you haven't heard. Tuition alone can cost more per year than my annual salary here, not to mention all of the other expenses. My dad didn't exactly leave me a goldmine either."

"Don't you always tell me anything is possible? Where there's a will there's a way, make it happen, never give up ... That sort of thing? You can get a loan or a scholarship still," he nudges.

"I'm not sure colleges are incredibly eager to hand out free money to thirty-year-olds that already have jobs, Glen, but thank you for the ideas. I don't know, maybe something will come up one day."

"Well, we aren't getting any younger, that's for sure."

"What about you, butthead? What sort of failed dreams led you to work in this hellhole?" Dana fires back.

"I never had any dreams like that. I never knew what I wanted to do with my life, same as most people here, I'm sure. I've worked in jobs like this by default since I was eighteen because I didn't know what else to do."

"When you were a kid in school and they asked what you wanted to be when you grew up ... what did you say?"

"I lied. I would write down astronaut, or veterinarian, or whatever else they wanted to hear so they would leave me alone. I learned a long time ago that it's usually easier to just give the 'right' answer as opposed to what you're really thinking. Less trouble." He nods.

"You just never wanted to be anything at all?"

"It's not that I aspired to be *nothing*, although I didn't ever have an idea of what I wanted to do. But it all worked out fine, just look at me now ... I'm a successful mid-level data technician at one of the largest corporate offices in the Seattle area."

"Don't pump yourself up in front of me, buddy ... You are a data *clerk*," Dana responds as they share a quiet chuckle. Telephones ring in the background and low voices return to work after the spectacle a few minutes before. "So, you never had any hobbies that you thought to pursue? What did you do for fun as a kid?"

"Nothing in particular. I spent a lot of time outside by myself while my mom was sleeping or gone, but there was never anything I *loved* doing, at least not that I can think of now. We used to just call stuff like that exploring, you know, being a kid and walking through the woods, throwing rocks, stuff like that. I found a hollow tree one time and would go there almost every day to clean up the inside and make it like my own hiding place. That's what I remember most from those days, going there daily for over a year and pretending I could be someone else. Nothing existed outside of that tree, and it was pretty small even back then, but I felt safe and fell asleep there a couple times. I used to think my hiding spot was so good that nobody would ever be able to find me in my little tree house, but now that I'm an adult, I realize there just wasn't anybody looking. Anyway, that's what I did to pass the time, although it was more of a need than something I enjoyed doing."

# CHAPTER SIX

"Have a good night, Dana. See you in the morning," Glen says.

She probably responded with something nice, although Glen's incredibly fatigued brain has entered emergency power mode and is in danger of shutting down entirely. He is certain she understands anyway, given the circumstances.

What a day ... What a week. At the very least, Glen is almost positive that life can't get much more strange in the short-term, although he feels slightly foolish for tempting it to do so. He walks down the elongated hallway and takes an elevator down to the exit, feeling quite disheveled and like the last several minutes didn't happen at all. It is time for sleep, he concludes, having faced scrutiny for the first time since embarrassing himself on the news, yet still he lives. "What a day," he repeats out loud with a shake of his head.

It's possible that he blew his own situation out of proportion, something that would typically be his mother's forte. Dirty looks and hushed whispers don't bother him, so why did he allow the hypotheticals of such to create so much chaos before it actually happened? In time, this will all blow over and become just another hiccup in the life of Glen, another nondescript entry in an extraordinary series of them.

Exiting through the glass doors of their office building, a gloomy overcast early evening sky greets him. The sun has nearly disappeared already, a reminder that summer has come and gone once again and autumn is upon them. The cool breeze lifts his spirits slightly, and for the slightest of moments, everything seems like it might turn out okay.

Glen trudges to his car with every last bit of energy he has left, wanting nothing more than to get home quickly and recuperate by the morning. A young woman stands behind a car in the parking lot, staring at him as he steps onto the blacktop. She wears large, dark glasses and a sun hat that shields her face, though there is no doubt that she is staring directly at Glen. The paranoia of fatigue regains footing and returns even more harsh than before. It has begun ... citizens taking it upon themselves to seek Glen out and harass him for uttering those two words.

He takes another step forward and pauses in the road as the woman continues to stare without moving. They remain trapped in a stalemate for several more seconds before she turns and climbs into the car. It's *definitely* time for a deep sleep.

"Glenny?" his mother calls out when he cracks the door as quietly as he can. "Is that you?"

*Damn it*, he mouths. "Yes, I'm home, Mom. It's late in the afternoon, what are you doing awake at this hour? That's unlike you."

"Oh, I couldn't sleep. You know how it goes ..." she trails off as Glen rolls his eyes from the front door. He tries to slip by in the hallway without her noticing and make his way to bed. If she's still awake at nearly six o'clock, it won't be the case for much longer. "Glenny, can you *believe* what they're saying in the news?

These crazy reports, they think *you* have some sort of spiritual connection to *Brock Blackwood*! Who ever heard of such a thing?"

He pauses at the base of the stairs as his blood runs cold. Of all the manipulation, lying, deception, and outright psychological abuse she has put him through, the years of negligence, narcissism, and selfishness ... *this* takes the fucking cake. "No, Mother. I hadn't heard."

"How could they have ever gotten that idea? I saw the news myself and just couldn't believe it!"

"Then what's the truth? Why are they telling me a girl named Abby was murdered inside our house the same way I described?" Glen asks as he turns to face her at last. They lock bloodshot eyes.

"I don't know, Glenny. It's all so strange to me too! Must have happened before we moved in, but nobody told me."

He hesitates again, previously wanting to hold off on having this conversation and now choosing to finally get himself the recovery he requires. A string inside his mind pulls a bit too tight and snaps under the tension of deeply buried secrets; a lifetime of stifled lies boiling over. "It *is* odd, don't you think, that a complete stranger would know everything about the murder? A police officer at that, someone who has no knowledge of our family secrets, would tell me that Abby's death actually happened here in our hallway exactly as I saw it?"

"I don't understand why you're acting like this, Glenny! I said it before; you simply had a bad nightmare! You know, people say that it's possible to have dreams of things that happened a long time ago?"

Patches of his face begin to tingle as his lower lip quivers. "Regardless of whether it was a dream or not, how would I have known everything about the murder if she didn't tell me? Show me?! And how does everyone in the fucking city seem to know the truth except for *you*?!"

She stares at the television set for a full minute without speaking another word as the news report plays over again: "Local resident, Glen Overton ..."

She turns toward her end table and pours the last of a bottle of vodka into her glass. "I wouldn't expect you to understand."

"What? What the hell is that supposed to mean?!"

"It means I don't expect you to understand why I had to lie about certain things I know, but that was a long time ago, and I have had to carry those horrible secrets with me ever since."

"Are you kidding me? You're the victim here, is that right?! I forgot it's your name plastered across the news! You must have had a horrendous day at work because of it too!" he screams, unleashing thirty years' worth of suppressed rage on the drywall with the side of his fist.

Perhaps because she feels deserving of the lashing, or maybe it's the vodka holding her hostage, but his mother remains still in her chair, enraging Glen even further with unnerving silence.

"I was promised the world, though it never happened. And no, I wouldn't expect you to understand a mother's point of view, Glenny, because I was a stupid eighteen-year-old girl at one time and found myself in way over my head."

Glen glances at the empty bottle as a single eighty proof tear rolls down her cheek. Finally, at long last, she lets the truth slip for the first time, but his scars are now buried too deep to be reached by remorse.

"I prayed this day would never come," she continues. "I prayed for it all to not be true, for me to forget about Abby entirely, and to protect you from ever finding out. I prayed that it was all a nightmare and tried to convince myself it didn't really happen. I'm sorry, Glenny," she sobs. "And the worst part of it all ... I did it because I loved a man."

Glen feels his insides shatter from the gut outward. Never in his life has she told him she loved him or at least not that he can remember ... not on birthdays, holidays, or during the more raw moments when he needed comforting the most. Her only take away from the absolute shitstorm unleashed upon him, his name, and public safety, is that it's unfortunate anyone found out the truth. The image of Brock from the interview flashes over Glen's vision again, that sinister and mocking smirk hung below his thick mustache. "What did you do to Abby? Why are you still keeping these secrets?"

"Nothing with my own hands, but I was silent when I could have saved her life. I didn't say anything after because it allowed us to get this house."

"Of course, because who would want to move into a home where a woman had recently been bludgeoned to death? Jesus Christ, Mom, I don't have time for your shit anymore. I'm going to bed. One of us has to get up and face the world tomorrow." He turns to stomp up the stairs and keeps an ear open for any sort of retort from her, but the living room stays silent. There is no, "Hold on, Glenny, let me explain," coming, and there never will be. He will put the pieces together later. None of it matters now. The damage has long been done, and his blood will always run sour with venom because of it.

Glen rips his work clothes off and tosses them in a crumpled pile on the floor then collapses atop the mattress. His body is shutting down rapidly, though his mind continues to roll like a runaway train headed for a guaranteed wreck. He is angry at himself for feeling even the slightest bit sorry for her; no matter how much damage and destruction his mother has unleashed like a wildfire on the loose, he still feels the last tugs of fraying heartstrings for her ... the way a parent *should* feel for their children. Although he grimaces with resentment to admit that she can't change the past any more than he can.

Will he ever understand why Abby visited him from the grave with a stern warning? Children told stories in school to terrify each other about the *boogeyman* coming to get them, inspired by haunting news reports and true crime shows aired endlessly after his arrest and death throughout the late eighties and nineties. They had plenty of source material to work with and even more unproven rumors. This corner of the country will be wary of the name *Brock Blackwood* for generations to come, but no other area was hit harder or for a longer period of time than Seattle, their hometown.

*Just go to sleep, you clearly need it.* More than anything else, yes, yet the searing thoughts continue to haunt him just as he begins to slip away. Glen Overton, public laughingstock and enemy of the people for simply stating a name. That poor Abby, her agony must have been unfathomable.

# CHAPTER SEVEN

"**G**ood evening, darlin'. How are you doing tonight, pretty lady?" the man asked from the side of the brick building. He leaned against the wall and struck a metal lighter to re-ignite a cigar then flipped it closed.

"You startled me!" she laughed. "Sorry, it's just that there usually isn't anyone back here."

"Yes, ma'am, that's why I'm here myself. You need a light?"

"Please." She walked over as the cigarette dangled loosely in her mouth and craned her neck forward for it to be lit by the man. "Can you do me a favor and not tell anybody you saw me? I'm not supposed to be here."

"I was out here smoking alone, no pretty young ladies in sight to my knowledge. Although, since I now have to carry this dark secret with me for life, and I'm happy to do it for you, but maybe you can answer a question for me."

She took a drag from the cigarette and exhaled a glorious cloud into the murky sky. "Sure thing." She smiled.

"What's a nice girl like yourself doing in a bar if you ain't supposed to be here?"

"Oh, um ... I'm tending bar tonight to make a bit of extra money so I can finally get out of this shit town. The problem is I'm only eighteen and I lied to the owner, but I have experience, so he brought me in."

"Well, I already promised I would keep your secret, although I never imagined it would be so *nefarious*," he smirked. "Where are you headed?"

"Anywhere but here. I've been saving up cash to get a new start somewhere else."

The man allowed the cigar to hang beneath his thick mustache as the billow of smoke continued to rise in front of his face. "Lucky for you, I'm only passing through and don't have anyone to ride with. My passenger seat is open for you."

"Oh, really? Where are you headed?"

"Washington. I have business to attend to in that area and plan on staying there for some time."

The girl blushed as she looked at the man's rugged face between puffs. He was strikingly handsome and a good amount older than herself, maybe even as much as fifteen years or so. "I like your tattoos," she said at last.

"Thank you. I plan on filling out my entire body at some point."

"What do they mean?"

"All sorts of things, but every one of 'em has a story behind it. What's your name?" he asked.

"Penelope, but I haven't been called that in years. Everyone calls me Penny. What's your name?"

"My name is Brock ... Well, Penny, should we hit the road?"

"Us? Now?" She raised her eyebrows in shock but also showed a glimmer of interest.

"So, you're saying you don't want to get out of town after all?"

"I do ... but what about my shift? All my stuff?"

"Aren't you only working tonight so you can get out of town? I have money. You won't need any more. I can buy you new stuff, don't worry. All I need from you is to come with me, and the rest will be sorted out along the way." He offered his hand toward her as she smiled ... Penny suddenly felt safe. A way out, a new start, a second life ... all she had fantasized about finding for years. "Well? What do you say?"

"Yes." She nodded gleefully after a brief delay. "Let's do it."

"Excellent ... Go grab your purse and hurry back. I'll be waiting out front for you, Pretty Penny."

Glen leaps from his bed in a cold sweat and tries desperately to shake off the confusing dream. The last thing he remembers is a flurry of vivid visions, yet he is relieved to have finally slept for several hours in succession.

The dream remains at the forefront of his thoughts for a few more seconds before every detail begins to dissolve like ink in water. It seemed important at the time, whatever it was. Even though it's still rather early to go to work, he rises regardless and begins to get dressed for the day ahead before trying to convince himself to go back to bed. The house is dark and quiet as expected at this time of morning, though he is glad to not hear a television playing downstairs. His mother's schedule is sporadic and chaotic in general, but this is one time in particular that he is incredibly happy she isn't awake. There's not much left to say to each other after their confrontation last night.

The darkness is peaceful at least, if he were to pick out one positive from being awake so early. Finally, an opportunity to sit quietly amongst his very loud thoughts with some coffee and a light breakfast before getting a head start to work to try and beat the crowd. It would be fantastic to already be sitting in his cubicle, or rather hiding there, when everyone else enters the office. Glen saunters into the kitchen and turns on the coffee maker as he waits in blissful silence and several moments of lazy reveries. He removes the pot as a drop of black liquid hits the burner below and sizzles. The small stream of smoke rises and brings back faint memories of his dream ... before drifting away and disappearing in a cloud of brain fog.

* * *

He pulls into the parking lot and sees only one other car there, which was the outcome he hoped for when arriving an hour and a half early. He spots a woman standing beside an old sedan as he leaps from his own car then hurries by without looking up at her.

"Glen Overton?" she asks with a hushed sense of urgency as he scurries by.

He stops in his tracks, unsure of whether to answer the question or double down and rush inside. Hot shame flushes his face to think of being a cowardly and panicky shell of his former self. Glen has devolved into the anxious, fidgety sort who is apparently afraid of his own shadow and absolutely terrified of a woman who knows his full name.

Glen steals a quick glance and recognizes her to be the same person he saw yesterday after work, wearing the same hat and standing by the same car. She must work in the building and is probably hoping to seize an opportunity to chastise and berate him. Not happening today, especially not this early in the morning. He picks up his pace to the door and greets security halfheartedly without waiting for a response.

The office door is already open, as Monica arrives at seven each morning. Glen is not concerned about running into her since she spends her first hour drinking coffee or in the restroom or sleeping or otherwise pretending to be working harder than everyone else. As a lifelong neurotic creature of dysfunction, this morning is not Glen's first time sneaking into the office early to avoid waiting around at home.

He slides into his cubicle and sits down quietly, hoping a smooth start to the morning would help him feel a bit more "normal", whatever that means. The best possible outcome now is for the storm to blow over in due time, allow everyone their moment of outrage, then resume a boring and traditional life as Glen Overton, the glorified nobody.

# CHAPTER EIGHT

"You're sleeping already?" Dana asks as she shakes the back of his chair. "What are you doing here so early?"

He snaps to attention and looks around in shock. "I couldn't sleep, so I decided to come here before I didn't make it. The office was so quiet and boring, I guess I couldn't hang on anymore. What time is it?"

"A little after eight."

"I wasn't out for long, in that case. Wait, what are *you* doing here so early?"

"I always come in about thirty minutes to an hour before work starts." She shrugs. "It gives me time to prepare, make coffee, or whatever else. Speaking of, do you want a cup?"

"Please. You know how I like it."

"I sure do, two creams and sugar, but I'm afraid we're fresh out of whiskey." She winks. "I'll be right back."

"Thanks, Dana." Glen relaxes into his office chair and stares at the blank computer screen as flashes of Abby's stomped face and dangling jaw stare back in place of his own. The feelings of fear and helplessness as she lunged for help resurface as five more minutes pass without him moving physically, paralyzed inside his own mental prison.

"Here you go. Drink up, seems like you need it."

"That was quick."

"Monica had the pot on already. I probably stole the last of her batch," Dana snickers.

"Oh, good, so I can savor it twice as much now knowing it's hers."

"Enjoy. You've earned it, having dealt with her for this long. So, do you care to share why you couldn't sleep? No offense, but it isn't like you to want to spend any more time here than absolutely necessary."

Glen nods with his nose deep in the coffee mug. "Because of a bad dream I had, but I don't remember much about it now. Something involving a girl."

"A girl? Like Abby?"

"Well ... maybe. I have been thinking about it throughout the morning, but I'm having a tough time recalling any of the important details. A man and a woman were talking and smoking, but it's one of those things where just as you feel like you've got it, the whole dream disappears."

"It seems logical to think the girl was Abby with all that has been happening. You don't remember what she looked like?" Dana asks.

"Not clearly, no. I think she said she was eighteen and they were dressed in old clothes that were probably from the seventies."

"Glen, it might have been Abby and Brock! Of course it was, you're having dreams about them together because of the whole situation. Did the guy look like Brock?"

"I don't know. I never paid much attention to his appearance," he says. "I've only seen him a few times."

"He was everywhere. There were books, television specials, the trial, his botched suicide attempt, the execution ... His face was hard to miss."

"Yes, well, I suppose I missed a whole lot back in those days. We only had one TV set, and my mom would either be watching something or asleep in the chair, and I couldn't change the channel. She used to ... not respond well to being woken up. I knew all about Brock but mostly through exaggerated stories from other kids. They would tease me and say that Blackwood was coming to get me. Strangely enough, Abby told me the same thing."

"That's actually pretty funny in hindsight. They have these websites nowadays where people make profiles and connect with old friends. You should try and look them up and see what they have to say about it now. You could make a veiled threat that *you* will come after *them* now that Brock is dead, since people think you have some weird connection to him." Dana grins from ear to ear.

"I'm pretty sure that my phone and online activity are already under heavy watch."

"It was a joke, bozo. I could only imagine how it would feel to get your revenge, though, even if it was only implied."

"Implying that I want to murder them?" he scoffs.

"Not necessarily murder, no, but imply intent and leave them wondering if you are joking. Something subtle."

"That was over twenty years ago. They probably don't even remember teasing me."

"That's the problem, they might not remember it, but you do. I'm just joking, obviously, but I have a few people from my childhood that I wouldn't mind giving a good scare like that. Twenty years or not, I still think about the bullies," she scowls.

"So, why not do the same thing? Make an online profile and threaten their lives. Subtly, of course."

"You know I'm a sissy. I talk a good game but as soon as confrontation begins, I can't handle it. That's why we're such good friends."

Glen grimaces and opens his mouth but pauses to find the right words. "I have a lot of good counters to that, but I will be the bigger person and—"

"What, run away?" She laughs.

"I was going to say keep it to myself but fine."

"It's okay if you can't handle it, wimp. I'm kidding. You know I wouldn't even be able to pretend like this with anyone else."

"I know, that's why we're both data clerks. We don't want to fight for any reason, even if it would help us to find success," Glen deadpans.

"Oh, a double burn, nice. And I can't even offer a retort since you insulted yourself too, so I won't."

"Good, because it was my best burn, and I don't want to try and top it. There's something else that's been bothering me too, Dana."

"Oh, yeah? What is it?" she asks with her eyebrows raised.

"Like I mentioned before, when I got home Monday night on my mom's birthday, she was watching an old VHS tape of Brock's final interview. It's all just such weird timing."

"It is, and I don't even have anything reasonable to offer. Wait a minute, I thought you didn't know what he looked like?"

"That was the first time I have ever really watched any video of him, but it was old and grainy." He shrugs. "Did you know about his tattoos?"

"What about them?"

"He had one for every person he killed, but his body was absolutely filled with them. How could he have escaped capture for so long with such a distinctive look? Wouldn't the tattoos have made him much easier to identify?"

"I'm not exactly the world's leading expert, but I think it boils down to the fact he just didn't care about being caught, and it seems sometimes apathy can actually be beneficial in that respect, for a while at least. Luck favors those who don't need it. He never stopped going and never looked over his shoulder which led police on an erratic path that made zero sense to them at the time since they couldn't predict where he would turn up next. Brock traveled to new states frequently, where he might have killed ten people, or maybe only one. Then he would skip a few states over and do whatever he did there. You also have to remember that the seventies and eighties were a much different time. It was difficult to track someone back then without the internet as we know it."

"Oh ..." Glen scratches his eyebrow as he stares at Dana. "You're not an expert, eh?"

"That's really all you got out of my speech? What if I pretend to be Abby and talk to you about Brock that way instead?"

"Ouch, take it easy with that. I've just now begun to stop feeling sick whenever I think about it."

"Then don't bring it up if you can't handle the truth." Dana stands with her empty mug and walks toward the opening of the cubicle. "Hurry up and finish your coffee. Don't forget about the meeting at nine."

Glen freezes in his chair as a prickly sensation crawls up his arms and torso. He had absolutely forgotten about the weekly staff meeting that he already dreaded every week even before developing crippling fears of public shaming. Every employee in the company will be piled into an undersized conference room and eyeing Glen like judgmental hawks. It also doesn't help his case that he never got along well with his co-workers to begin with. All their social mixers, happy hour gatherings, and poker nights that he made mass excuses to skip undoubtedly cast a shadow on him as the office weirdo to most of them. His status as a pariah is now undeniable.

"The meeting?" he squeaks at last.

"Yes, you know, the same hour-long staff meeting we have every week?"

The noose tightens around his neck as the hypothetical hangman begins to tug at it slowly. "Of course. I'll be right behind you."

Glen forces himself to remain steady while wanting to erupt inside. Dana takes a final glance at him then disappears as he loses the internal battle and starts to shake violently. He should run away, leave and never come back, escape from this suffocating prison and begin anew somewhere else as an anonymous stranger.

Glen rings his hands and pulls at his shirt collar for relief, knowing all too well he won't feel any better until the meeting is over, and even then, there will only be minimal improvement. The cracks in the foundation have spread rapidly and without control.

Maybe he could fake an illness or injury by throwing a pencil on the ground and slipping over it. No, that would only bring even more concentrated attention. *Better come up with something stellar*, the voice of ancient instinct reminds him, followed by a repeat of Dana's nudges to threaten a revenge murder against those who have crossed him. While that is not the route he wants to take, it is a solid reminder that their whispers and gossip are only signs of fear, and Glen should not cower to those who are wary of *him*.

He regains enough confidence, if only momentarily, to rise and catch his breath. "Thanks again, Dana," he mutters and trudges toward the meeting room with a sigh.

"I'm just going to cut the bullshit; this fiscal year has not been kind to us. If you would, please turn your attention to the screen behind me, and you will see that our expenses have skyrocketed further as we continue to navigate the aftermath of the recession. Revenue has decreased at a minimum ..."

Glen tries his damnedest to pay attention to the droning of Monica's grating voice, but the void of thoughtlessness pulls him deeper. He spaces out and fades away far enough that the room falls into the void of a shadow. This meeting has nothing to do with his job anyway, discussing finances and sales figures, while he only files the data of the scraps left over from the big wigs' irresponsible spending. The fiscal year has been poor due to overindulgence more so than an economic downturn, though Glen lets the thought go as he returns to the fleeting comfort of his errant daydream.

"Now, let's move on to status updates regarding our several ongoing contracts. We have a multi-tiered plan to reach each milestone within the allotted time frame agreed upon by our suppliers and buyers. On the next slide, you will find ..."

Glen drifts again and glances to his left where Dana sits. She smiles at him quickly and returns her focus to Monica as he tries to do the same but feels his eyes flutter several times. The first wave of darkness lasts only a second, though each successive bit of solitude grows progressively longer.

"Psst ... Don't fall asleep or you might never wake again. Like me."

Glen straightens up in a jolt and looks to his right to see a young woman with poofy permed hair mostly contained beneath a headband and wearing a neon crop top. Her face is heavily bruised and bloodied with both eyes blackened.

"Excuse me, but what did you say?"

"I said ... you don't want to fall asleep and end up like mghghg." The woman chokes as her tongue flops out through a massive slit in her throat, and she tries frantically to push it back inside.

Glen leaps up and knocks his chair over as he releases a shriek. The meeting comes to a screeching halt while Monica glares at him mortified. His co-workers turn quickly in their chairs to stare and sneer in varying degrees of disgust.

"Sorry ... I'm really sorry, I just ..." Glen begins to hyperventilate as his eyes dart around in circles, eventually landing on Dana beside him, who silently pleads for him to sit down. Small patches of muttering pick up around the room as their eyes burn holes in his body. Dana finally tugs on the side of his pants to force him back into his seat. Another awkward moment of silence follows before the meeting continues.

"You know, I always liked you. I knew you were stalking me for a reason," the woman continues from Glen's right, licking her lips and teeth with a bloody tongue to leave red streaks behind as she grins.

"What the hell are you talking about? I've never even met you," he whispers in a panic from the corner of his mouth.

"Don't try to deny it now, Brock. You picked me for a reason. You wanted me to be your special girl."

Another wave of nausea hits Glen as he takes several shallow breaths. "I'm not Brock ..."

"Then who are you? Oh, that's right ... the only begotten bastard of Blackwood's whore." She begins to chant in baritone, sounding as though multiple people are speaking at once through the echoes of her gashed throat. "Blackwood's whore, Blackwood's whore ... the sins of the father have now become yours ..."

"Glen ... Glen ..." Dana nudges, tapping his left hand. "People are starting to stare again and it would be nice if you could return to normal now ..."

The young woman pinches the two halves of her neck skin together to release a booming guttural bellow. "Blackwood's only son must pay forever more!"

Rows of co-workers continue to glare with black, sunken eyes as the room appears to darken under an encroaching shadow. "Blackwood's only son must pay forever more," they repeat with layered voices that cause the walls to tremble.

"I didn't ... I didn't do anything wrong ..." Glen chokes out.

The young woman's eyes descend into their sockets as if unseen hands dig their thumbs into them, leaving empty, sunken pockets in their place while thick, black blood begins to pour down her cheeks. She removes the hand holding her skin together and extends the thumb sharply, running it along the incision in her throat as the slit reopens beneath. "Blackwood's only son must pay forever more", they chant again.

Glen drops to his knees and releases a scream of despair. The walls swirl around him in a cyclone as a dozen bodies rush toward him. The world spins loudly for a moment more before finally falling silent.

# CHAPTER NINE

*It's okay, Glen! Really!* Dana reassured him, though her words meant nothing. *I'm sure everybody understands that you have been under loads of stress recently!*

All he remembers is feeling short of breath before the weight of the world leaned upon him and his mind popped like a champagne cork. Some people rushed toward him, whoever they were, and then his memory resumed again inside his cubicle. That's it, and the rest is a giant mystery that is best left to woeful speculation.

He *has* to leave now, that much is non-negotiable, even though Dana begged him to wait it out for the rest of the workday and make his final decision later. She cited medical protection laws or some such shit that would prevent Monica from discriminating or retaliating against a condition or ... *disability.* The official labels have begun to be slapped upon him after already being known as the local lunatic and office psychopath. Keeping co-workers on edge with unpredictability can be fantastic as long as the implication of instability remains just that—implied. Otherwise, he is undeniably a bona fide weirdo with a growing habit of speaking with dead girls.

*But Glen … think of your job!* Dana had pleaded with him. *How well will you be doing without working? A paycheck? You need this!*

*Like a hole in the head*, he wished to respond, though to no fault of her own. She continues to be not only the ideal friend but a model person as well, who doesn't deserve the inevitable backlash for only trying to help. Again. *And again.* Obviously, work is a net negative that is currently draining him of more life than it is providing. *But thanks, Dana.*

He angrily packs a few personal items from his desk while preparing to leave. This is not a permanent resignation, but Glen is not at all fit to be here for the time being. He is a walking disaster that needs to get home immediately before another episode, or worse, occurs.

Exiting the cubicle with purpose, he rounds a corner and marches onward as scores of eyeballs stare from above their respective cubicle walls. Glen ignores them, knowing the only path to restoration is escaping before any more corpses reappear, clearly only a figment of a fragmented imagination. It's time to run; he has already tried resisting. Let them stare; let them whisper because they will do so regardless at any chance they get.

Few truly cared for his wellbeing as he collapsed, while the majority only watched out of morbid and vicarious curiosity. A sizable chunk probably even wished him dead—or at least he reassures himself to justify fleeing the building. There is no time for allies, unfortunately true for both serial killers and social pariahs. He will attempt to hang on to Dana for as long as she dares remain by his side, but Glen's darkest impulses scream that she will immediately abandon ship when his own circumstances grow to be too much of a burden on her. And why shouldn't she? Being smart, a good and moral person, selfless, thoughtful … she doesn't deserve the backlash that will inevitably swallow her up for being friends with the wrong person. Loyalty has its limits.

The glass doors to freedom enter his view as Glen kicks the right half open and exits into the morning light. Obliging instinct against his better judgment, he turns to glance back at the windows of his office floor to see dozens of eyes peering shamelessly down at the parking lot. News will spread rapidly throughout the company that the outcast they had all gossiped and whispered about did, in fact, turn out to be a lunatic. *Fuck 'em.* Glen waves facetiously and marches toward his car once more, feeling simultaneous relief and embarrassment at doing so.

"Glen Overton!" a voice shouts from the rows of parked cars.

He continues on, wanting nothing more than to escape the premises as quickly as possible before something else unfortunate happens.

"Glen Overton!" the feminine voice repeats from much closer this time, standing in the shadow of a tall passenger van where the nosy eavesdroppers upstairs won't be able to see her, conveniently parked next to his own car. "Come over here. We need to speak with you."

"With me? What do you want from me?" Glen looks around the parking lot to see at least three others approaching. There's no point in running. They will only follow and make it worse in the end. There are surely people waiting around every corner that want to give him a beatdown for simply existing. So be it. He is cornered and outnumbered.

"We only wish to speak with you. It won't take much time. We'll return you to your home safely after."

"My house? What about my car?"

"I wouldn't worry about that." She smirks. "Hop in and do so quickly before your friends see you."

Glen looks at the office window once again as half a dozen heads duck quickly and out of sight below the windowsill. In a week full of only the strangest events, what's the weirdest thing that could happen now? How could it get worse? He hasn't even begun to process the girl with her throat slit and what implications that would have toward his own mental state. Glen sighs and allows his shoulders to drop as he begins to walk toward the woman. She slides the side door open and gestures for him to enter while two men and another woman rush toward them and leap inside. The first woman slams the door shut, and the person in the driver's seat accelerates.

They stare at him for a moment, all four in the back section, plus the driver who eyes him constantly in the rear-view mirror. Glen watches their hands intently and wonders if he will be stabbed, bludgeoned, shot, or some combination of them all, conceding it would only be a fitting end if that is what fate allows. "Well? What did you want to talk about?"

The four that surround him grow giddy before the first woman shushes them at last. "Glen, you do not know how long we have been looking for you. It had been rumored that you existed, but there are millions of people in Washington. I can't tell you how ... ecstatic we are to finally be in your presence."

His head begins to swirl. "I'm sorry ... What? Why the hell would you be looking for me?"

"Glen ... you are the only living heir of Brock Blackwood, and the only one that will ever be! There had been whispers that you were out there, but it was the news stations that found you for us! What a joyous day!"

"I'm ... what?! Who are you? And why would you think something asinine like that?! Brock Blackwood was a horrendous man!"

Gasps and vitriol roll through the van as the first woman calms them. "Hush, all of you. He has only been brainwashed and is not yet aware of his own importance. My name is Kathleen, and I am here to serve you, Glen Blackwood. We *all* are here to serve you." She places a hand over her chest and bows her head as the other three do the same.

*Glen Blackwood ...* Sounds absolutely filthy.

"Do not be rude, everyone, introduce yourselves to The Only Son," she snaps at her compatriots.

"Thompson, sir."

"Carol."

"Reginald."

Glen gives a collective nod to the three of them in return. "I don't mean to be difficult, but I'm afraid I still don't understand ... Who are you? What is this?"

"We are Blackwood's Babies," Kathleen replies in a soothing cadence. "We began as a group of children whose mothers and grandmothers were killed by Brock during his reign of power in the seventies and eighties but have since expanded to accept members that properly demonstrate their devotion. We are thousands, Glen ... A full legion at your service."

He stares at them for a moment longer, hoping to make sense of her words. "I ... I'm very sorry, but I just can't comprehend ... Why am I important to you?"

"It's perfectly understandable. You must be in shock having to carry this heavy weight alone, and what a weight it is to step into Brock Blackwood's shoes. Think about it, Glen ... All of our mothers were seen as unfit to carry the Blackwood gene, but *you* ... You are the last of his bloodline. Brock was a spiritual stepfather to all of us, but you are the only living person with his blood pumping in your veins."

"You are ... The Only Son," Thompson follows in awe.

"But I didn't do anything to earn it! Shit, I didn't even know my father's name! I've never met him!"

"Doesn't that strike you as odd? Glen, the annals of history are littered with kings and deities who received their titles by simply showing up! You are the last Blackwood; that is as good as royalty."

"I will take your word for it. Sorry, but this is all very foreign to me. I woke up on Monday morning like it was any other day to go to my boring job, then I ended up on the news for all the wrong reasons. I'm nobody."

"There is no need to keep apologizing. You will adapt to your new life soon enough; that is why we are here, after all, to assist you." Kathleen smirks. "Now, if you have nowhere else to be, there is someone else who would be absolutely thrilled to meet you."

A vibration in his pocket pulls him from the altered reality inside the van with his new ... friends? *Where did you go? Is everything okay?* Dana asks in the message.

Where to even begin? *Yes, I am fine. I will call you after work and explain.* He flips his phone closed and places it back in his pocket. "So, this person ... Did he or she also lose their mother to Brock?"

"She. Her name is Eleanor, and she will explain everything else herself. We do not speak for Eleanor."

Thompson, Carol, and Reginald continue to stare excitedly at Glen, while Kathleen turns and speaks to the driver. Their ages vary wildly from Kathleen, who can't be any older than mid-twenties, to Reginald, who is seemingly in his forties.

"We will do anything for you, sir," Reginald whispers.

"Yes, sir. Anything," Thompson follows as Carol nods in solid agreement.

"Thank you." Glen clears his throat uncomfortably and nods at them in return. They all grin and straighten up as Kathleen turns back toward them.

"We are almost there. Prepare to meet Eleanor."

"Glen ... I cannot even express how delighted I am to be staring at you after all this time." A regal woman of about fifty waits by the front door to a large, old looking house and approaches him as he exits the van. "Welcome home." She embraces him in a hug as if they have known each other all their lives.

"Thank you. You must be Eleanor."

"I am. You clearly have gotten an earful already." She chuckles.

"Yes, well, really more like an overview."

"Fantastic, then I will fill in the rest. Please let me know if any of our members give you trouble and I will have them executed."

"No, really, they were ... *ahem*, they were great."

"Good. Very good." Eleanor grins, holding the position for quite some time. Her teeth are unusually white for someone of her age. As Glen inspects further, everything about her is perfect, from her hair to her clothes, and otherwise. "Please. Come in."

Two more men stand by the door and nod wholeheartedly at Glen as he walks through. Eleanor leads him into a living room, which has been remodeled recently, judging by the state of the house's exterior. The walls have been painted black to cast a certain comforting gloom over them even at the height of daylight outside.

"This is it. Do you remember?" she continues.

"No, I don't think so ... Should I?"

"This is the birthplace of all that we represent; Brock's childhood home, the house in which he intended to butcher me to death, according to the police."

"Oh, um ... I'm sorry to hear that." Glen fidgets uncomfortably.

"Nonsense, it was an honor to have been considered and meet him face to face, however briefly. They said he was in pursuit of me for weeks and that's how they caught him, yet I never knew it at the time. Rumor would have it that the only other target he left alive ... was your mother."

"My mom?"

"Yes. He had been watching closely with the intent to gut her like the rest, but something about her left him so smitten, he couldn't go through with it, although we don't know the precise details. She is the victim that never was." Eleanor grins once more, immediately both a soothing and eerie sight. Her voice floats through the air with a velvety drawl and a clear vibe that she is never in a hurry for anyone.

"I'm sorry for asking so many questions, but I just don't understand why you seem to think Brock was my father? And why is he so important? He nearly killed you, and he definitely did kill dozens of others."

"Or more, yes. And please do not apologize, as we are here for you now. The answers to those questions are rather complex, Glen. Your father was simply the apex predator at the absolute top of our food chain, but there was much more to him than that. He was frightfully handsome, clever, and enigmatic. He was the counterculture icon we so desperately craved. Those of us that were lucky enough to meet him felt captivated beyond our control, and it was *exciting*. Brock Blackwood was not of this world, and a select few were lucky enough to witness the magic in real time. As for your lineage, it was foretold within our circles that a true Blackwood would eventually begin to see the visions. Once we heard the story on the news, I pulled a few strings for a bit of information. The evidence appears to be undeniable."

"Did he not kill many of your mothers? How can that be a good thing?" Glen panics as a fretful feeling rises in his gut. "And how can you rely upon a wild hunch that he was my father? Wouldn't the police be kicking down my door if it were true?"

"You do not understand, not yet, although that is okay. And no, the police would not suspect you to be Brock's son if they weren't specifically looking for that to be the truth. They are also bound by legal channels and due process, while my team knows how to ... be a bit more creative in getting what we need. Do not worry, though, we have already prepared for every possible angle. I want you to think for a moment; what kind of wolf is worried about consuming a couple sheep along the way? I digress. You do not need to understand the *why* because you are the *what*. You have devoted fans, Glen, even if you don't yet realize it, and they will do anything that you ask. *We* will do anything you ask."

"I apologize for ... Sorry, I mean ... *ahem*, this is honestly overwhelming. I'm nothing more than a corporate data clerk for Christ's sake."

"Yes, we have been watching, and you have certainly been under duress. You feel such stress because your entire life has been a lie. You are not Glen Overton, the data clerk, but Glen Blackwood, the heir to the throne of a demigod."

Eleanor straightens her suit jacket proudly and stares at him with a triumphant expression.

"I have never felt comfortable a day in my life ... I never felt like I fit in anywhere or like I was doing what I should. Nothing ever felt ... right."

"Of course not, because you were living a lie. You have not heard of me, but I am the CEO and president of EcoHarbor Solutions, and my success was directly inspired by Brock. His actions brought me to the brink of death, but his strength taught me a lesson that I was weak and had no time to waste in growing powerful and building influence. As such, our resources are vast and all available indefinitely to you, as well as being the driving source of funds behind Blackwood's Babies. This house is also yours by birthright, should you ever need it, though we have been utilizing it as our base of operations in the meantime. This is our church, if you will, but it is all yours. You will never need anything again, Glen."

"Thank you. I think I'll be fine at home for now, but I will keep all of that in mind. I wouldn't want to take your church away from you." He chuckles awkwardly.

"I know you are only being funny, but it is yours at any time. Would you like a drink? Soft or stiff."

"Um, stiff, please."

"Stiff drink, it is. Thompson, please bring us both a double from the top shelf. Glen, regardless of how you may be feeling right now, you are going to need us in your corner. We have acquired information that one of the enemies has already attained a DNA sample and run a test to confirm your identity. There will be people out there that wish you dead, or worse, simply for your heritage. Take my information and be sure to call if you ever need anything at all." She unclasps a small brass case and passes a business card across the table.

Glen picks it up and admires the fancy lettering of her name: *Eleanor Windsor*. "I appreciate the offer, but how do you know that someone has already run a test? How is that possible? I think at this point, what I need most is a bit more sleep. It's been a strange week."

"We have eyes and ears everywhere. The EMT woman that visited your house after your 911 call, it seems that her mother was murdered by your father, and we have already ... questioned her extensively to understand the extent of the damage. The cheek swab she took from you was used in an at-home test, although, fortunately, those are not legally binding. Please be careful in the coming days, as we don't yet know how deeply her connections run or who she has already told. Anybody outside of this group is conceivably a suspect."

Glen stares at them all as his head spins in a typhoon of questions and emotions with too much information to process at once and too little left in the tank to try. Is this all a huge ruse, or are they exploiting his weakness after being exposed as a weirdo on the news?

"Can I have a refill over here?"

# CHAPTER TEN

Glen struggles with his keys before stumbling through the doorway and nearly falls flat on his face. He holds tight and regains his balance with bated breath, hoping his mother does not beckon for him after hearing the noise. *So far, so good.* All signs point to her being in bed.

It is already four o'clock in the afternoon, and Dana will be out of work soon, though the couple drinks he had with Eleanor have hit much harder than expected, surely only exacerbated by fatigue and stress. The house is dim and quiet, which is all he could have hoped for after the day he had.

Glen stumbles into the kitchen and decides to put on another pot of coffee. The armchair beckons for him to rest at last, and he floats to it sleepily. His mother's end table rests beside her chair, and her bottle of vodka sits tall and tempting atop the wood surface.

Perhaps it's the relaxation of his willpower from Eleanor's drinks, or a loosening of his own arbitrary restraints, but Glen finds the bottle to be irresistible in the eerily silent home. *Just a taste*, he promises to nobody in particular as he unscrews the cap and knocks back a hearty swig. The coffee maker indicates that the pot is finished, although he tells himself that he'll rise after another little sip, which he finds odd, being that he is not much of a drinker.

The will to stand entirely disappears. His current spot, sunken into the old and broken armchair, is simply and suddenly more desirable than anything else in the world. The false shelter and warmth feel so nice, in fact, that Glen decides to pour himself one more big glass to keep the good times rolling longer. If a handful of drinks is great, then another couple must feel even better, he decides.

Glen chuckles with a drop of vodka clinging to his lower lip, realizing he has been drinking today to escape his own shadow, and instead has stumbled directly into his mother's. Drinking booze by the pint, melting into her armchair like an invalid, and avoiding responsibilities at every turn; yes, he has turned into Penny today, but it is still preferable to the rather nasty rumors that have begun to swirl ... though, by that logic, it is worrisome that he has adopted some of her personality traits because there must also be a bit of his father in the mix. What could possibly be next?

Another drink before anything.

"Glen, wake up. Glen." Gentle hands softly shake him as he begins to stir from a faraway place. Dana stands over his slumping body, still in her work clothes.

"Dana? Is that you?" One of his eyes opens fully while the other fights to stay closed.

"Yes, it's Dana. You left the door ajar. Gosh, have you been drinking? It reeks in here."

"That's your mom I'm smelling, I mean ... whatever. Hi, Dana. How was work?"

"It was odd without you there. The vibe in the building was incredibly strange after our meeting. I just came by to check on you, like you mentioned earlier. You said you would tell me what happened."

"What happened?"

"Yes, after work. You said you would explain everything."

Glen gestures with a hooked finger for Dana to lean in closer, which she does. "I went out for a couple drinks with strangers," he whispers into her ear. "Then I had a few more. I'm honestly really upset to be drunk like my mom because I *fucking hate her*."

"It's okay ... it happens to the best of us, Glen. I think you just need some sleep and you'll feel ... well, not better tomorrow, but at least on the road to recovery. Can I get you anything?"

"No ... you're right. I just need some sleep."

"So, what happened when you left?"

"It was nothing, really ... I just ... I needed a break, that's all."

"Needed a break from who? From work?"

"From everyone. I hate everybody."

Dana scoffs and stifles a grin. "Everybody? Even me?"

"*Especially* me. I hate me the most. I despise everyone else for being happy, but I hate me even more for being unable to be happy."

"What do you say, Glen? Time for bed? Come on, I'll help you upstairs."

"No, I'm fine right here," Glen argues as he swats at her hand and misses, falling back into the armchair like a sack of bricks.

"Okay. I just wanted to ... are you doing alright, Glen? I mean, aside from being super drunk, but are you *really* doing fine? That was pretty scary at work today."

"Yes, I'm fine ... Thank you for asking, *Dana*."

"That's good." She pauses, fidgeting nervously. "But what ... what happened, though? You were screaming like you saw something, Glen ... Something dark."

He leans forward shakily with his eyes nearly bulging. "I DID. The woman next to me began speaking with her throat slit wide open in the meeting. And she was talking crazy to me ... This dead woman. But everyone else was dead too. All corpses around me," Glen slurs as he tries to hold his composure but falls back in defeat.

"That sounds terrifying, no wonder you shouted. I don't mean to overstep any boundaries, but have you thought about seeking a professional's opinion? You've obviously been under levels of stress I don't think most of us could possibly understand. Again, maybe now isn't the best time."

"The best time for what?"

"To talk about ... Nothing, Glen. You go ahead and enjoy whatever planet you're currently on." She laughs with the slight twinkle of a tear in the corner of her eye. "I just wish I could help, that's all, because I know you're going through it in the worst way right now."

"Yeah. Me too. Dana ... I don't have anyone else. It's just you to talk to ... please know that."

"I do, Glen ... I do. It's a responsibility I don't take lightly."

# CHAPTER ELEVEN

"Look at me. I told you to look at me, and please don't make me repeat myself, sweetheart. I absolutely fucking loathe saying the same thing twice. You wouldn't want me to lose my good nature, would you?"

"No ... No, sir." The young girl cried as streams of eyeliner-tinted tears ran down her cheeks. She sniffled a few times and looked upward at the rugged, inked man who took her captive, knowing all too well she fell victim to the infamous Blackwood charm.

"That's good ... Good girl. You look nervous, little lady. What's wrong?"

"I just ... I want to go home."

"Oh, you don't want to be here anymore? Is that what I'm hearing?" he asked with a voice of stone.

"No, I mean ... I just really miss my family and want to see them again."

"Do you? I have a deal that will get you out of here and headed back home within the next few minutes. How does that sound, my dear?"

"Good! It sounds really good!" she wailed through tears and sloppy inhales.

"Excellent, that's what I like to hear, although I am just a bit disappointed you don't want to spend more time with me. You didn't mean to disappoint me, right?"

"No!"

"Good ... In that case, here is my bargain." Brock's eyes changed as he removed a revolver from the back of his belt and handed it to the young woman. "You've heard of Russian Roulette before, yes?"

She hesitated before taking the gun with a shaky hand and inspected the side of it quickly. "One bullet, right?"

"Oh, dear, no ... Allow me to assist you. You see here?" He took the revolver and released the cylinder to reveal five loaded shells and one empty chamber. He spun the metal drum emphatically and smacked it back inside. "There you go. Your odds are great to leave here alive, one in six!"

"Don't make me do this! Please, just let me go!"

"Oh, sweetheart ... You know I'm not going to do that. You know too much and have already seen my face. I wouldn't be very good at my job if I allowed every sniveling little shit to walk away just because they asked nicely."

"But I don't even know who you are!" the woman shrieked between sobs.

"Yes, you do ... Say it."

"B-Blackwood?"

He closed his eyes and inhaled deeply. "Say it all."

"Brock ... Blackwood ..."

"Yes ... Now aren't you special? It isn't every girl I take this kind of liking to."

She stared with a quivering lip and eyes that darted back and forth. "But what if I just turn the gun on you and shoot?"

"Do you really think I would hand you a loaded revolver without having another by my side? The difference is, there are no empty chambers in mine, and I can assure you I won't miss. Go on now, take your shot. Earn your freedom."

"And if I live? If I get the empty chamber, you'll let me go then?"

"Of course. If the chaos of our universe declares it ... then so shall it be. Go on."

The woman trembled as she raised the chrome barrel to her lips and streams of tears ran down her cheeks. She blinked hard and winced before removing the revolver and screaming, "I can't!"

"Oh, but you will ... Do not feel bad, stupid girl, as you are not the first to mistake me for an ordinary human and enter my vehicle, although I can promise you this: none of the rest of them got off so easy. That's just how much I *like* you. Either we play my little game, or I go grab the claw hammer, baseball bat, and pickaxe to do a bit of *open face surgery*. Do it. Now. Don't try me."

Without hesitating a second longer, she jammed the gun in her mouth and pulled the trigger. The shell ripped through her throat and blew out the back of her head with crimson showers of brain matter as Brock leaned back and cackled.

"Ha! You got the hollow point!" He walked around the woman to inspect the gruesome exit wound, leaning in close and cracking another smile, which shined through the open hole in her head as if it were her own maniacal grin.

Glen jumps out of bed and slips over a pile of clothes. He can't remember the previous night at all, nor how he got back into his room, but the image of that woman's mouth agape with Brock's Cheshire grin through it will be burned in his mind forever.

It's still dark outside with a misty early morning fog floating by the window. Since this will apparently be his new sleeping schedule, he rises from the heap on the floor in a sickly sweat and is greeted with a pounding in both the front and the back of his head.

*I guess I didn't get Mom's drinking gene*, he thinks as he staves off an encroaching spinning sensation. *At least it's Friday.*

A sense of panic sets in, realizing it is indeed only Friday morning. So, the dread begins as he anticipates a rocky reception from the co-workers who witnessed his freak out yesterday, meaning basically the entire company.

Dana will be disappointed if he misses work again, but so what of it? She doesn't have to show up and be Glen Overton. Monica will be livid if he skips again ... but when is she not? The rest of the office, including Glen, will be relieved if he doesn't make it, which sets the boulder in motion for him to take yet another personal day. Although there is very little that is *personal* about his life anymore ... It has become the public traveling shit show.

*So shall it be.*

Glen winces with a wave of nausea after repeating Brock's words from the dream. How horrid. He fires up the desktop computer and loads the company's absence reporting system, which is perfect for avoiding speaking to Monica or having to feign illness over an answering machine message.

The monitor's bright light nearly knocks him out of the chair and brings with it the next level of pain in his eyes and forehead. After wincing for a solid ten seconds, Glen slowly allows one eye to open and notices the time is still only 4:49 a.m.

He opens the website and begins filling in his information, beginning with employee ID number, name, and date, when that woman forces her way into the front of his attention and Glen begins to feel quite ill.

"*What's the matter? Scared?*" she taunts, appearing normal for a moment before allowing her mouth to dangle open and reveal the gaping hole inside. "*Here, it's your turn next ... I even took one of the bullets for you, so your odds are better than mine were. I only have half a brain left, but I would say your chances of survival are ... about thirty-three percent! Here you go, don't blow it!*"

Glen smacks his face to remove the woman from his mind as quickly as possible, but the image is etched too deeply into his eyelids. "No ... no, thank you." Glen clears his throat to avoid gagging from fear and hangover.

"What's the matter? Too *good* to play your own daddy's game?"

"No, it's not that, and he isn't my dad. I just don't want to play. What's your name anyway?"

"Tiffany. Why? Are you interested? Brock sure was." She turns and whips her fluffy hair around seductively, spraying droplets of blood through the air. Glen shoves himself backward from the desk to avoid any spatter showers and stares through the hole in her head.

"Tiffany what? What's your last name?"

She rolls her eyes and places a hand on her hip. "Fine, if you gotta be such a buzzkill, it's Schwartz. Tiffany Schwartz."

Glen reaches to grab a pen sneakily to avoid being chastised for not paying attention and scribbles down *Tiffany Schwartz* between pounding heartbeats with his writing resembling a shaky EKG reading. "Thank you," he mutters, looking for the woman but finally seeing nothing aside from the glowing computer monitor.

He opens a new tab in the browser and types 'Tiffany Schwartz + Brock Blackwood' into a search engine, tapping his fingernail on the desk anxiously as the results begin to populate his screen. The first hit, "Tiffany Schwartz, Age 22, Found Dead In Her Seattle Area Home" seems to be the logical starting place. Glen moves the cursor over the hyperlink and clicks before waiting for the page to load.

Uncomfortable memories arise from the nightmare, though they are quickly stifled by opening his eyes and accepting the truth. Tiffany Schwartz was found dead on May 21st, 1979, with an apparently self-inflicted gunshot wound inside her home, evidenced by a mostly loaded revolver found next to the corpse and no signs of foul play.

Other, more obscure websites and discussion forums reveal the conspiracy theory that Brock was responsible for her death, along with several more 'forced suicides' scattered around the Pacific Northwest area. Many posters seemed to think that Tiffany perfectly fit Brock's bill for murdering young, petite woman of a certain facial complexion. No note was found, while friends and family were reportedly absolutely shocked. Go figure.

Falling into the rabbit hole of Tiffany Schwartz conspiracy theories, Glen loses himself in related cases and feels a familiar tugging within to do his due diligence and examine the Brock situation further. The basement is the only logical place to check for information, hopefully putting an end to the ridiculous rumors that he is Blackwood's son along the way, denial be damned. But first, finalize the absence. He clicks submit and scoots the desk chair back to finally head downstairs armed with nothing but a trusty flashlight and a growing list of questions.

Boxes, trinkets, and junk galore inside the basement line his vision as Glen scrambles through the grungy cellar in search of the one thing that might answer the absurdities; his mother's keepsake box that she vehemently guarded from him when he was a child. Glen isn't entirely sure where to begin, but the repeated and invasive visions of Brock's victims need an immediate answer.

Containers of raggedy old clothes and outdated household decorations are stacked from floor to ceiling in all directions with only a narrow walkway available between the aisles. Brock's face continues to reappear in his mind through the musty shadows; the devilishly handsome features, mustache, and long hair in the back verging on a mullet. They are haunting ... and even more so when observed through Tiffany's blown out skull.

Another stack of boxes and three more strikeouts, unearthing nothing but ancient junk and dead spiders. He hadn't thought of his mother as a hoarder before, but the collections of damaged silverware and vintage newspapers might suggest otherwise. Glen flips the lid from a container of her old art supplies and vividly remembers scattered time periods when she was utterly obsessed with painting to the point of neglecting her motherly duties when inspiration would consume her. The art ... Brock's heavily tattooed body forces its way into Glen's thoughts, how he looked during that final interview in a tight white tank top with zero blank skin from the neck down.

"One of your most famous attributes is your tattoos, Brock. Tell us a bit about them." The interviewer gestured.

"I get a new tattoo for each victim to keep them with me at all times. I travel lightly and don't have space for physical trophies."

"Yet you are absolutely covered in them."

"Yes. One for each victim."

Brock stared forward, perhaps deep in thought or waiting for another conversational cue to follow, but Glen can't seem to blink it away now.

Tucked in the back behind the tallest stack and covered by a wool blanket, he finds a well-worn shoebox with 'Brock' written across a strip of masking tape atop it. Glen quivers upon reading the name as the back-and-forth battle of *is he* or *isn't he* takes another turn for the worse. After a hard, dry swallow, he carefully moves the box to a smaller stack in front of him, then lifts the lid and places it off to the side. Several newspaper clippings, a pocket watch, black comb, and two Polaroid pictures rest inside. The top one is a photo of Brock standing alone, something his mother could have possibly bought from a novelty store, proving nothing ... though the photograph beneath it is much more damning. The crazed, psychopathic serial killer stands with his arm around her shoulder as she kisses his left cheek. Those same intense eyes and stoney expression, although with noticeably fewer tattoos at the time. Simultaneously enthralling and revolting.

Glen stares for an unusually prolonged second, trying to remember to simply breathe as he releases a long and deep exhale. His mother has made a separate career of lying and can't be trusted any more on the subject, though hopefully the evidence will bring undeniable vindication. A brief flash of emotion strikes from somewhere in the back of his racing brain. He has spent three decades trying to figure out his father's identity and now must either continue the search in vain or own the fact that he is the only known offspring of a historically violent and malevolent figure. His tunnel vision elongates further as he decides what to do with the rest of the shoebox.

Glen notices a black bandana wrapped around another unseen object laying beneath the rest. How had he missed that before? It stretches across the length of the box but otherwise doesn't seem to be out of place. He reaches inside and grabs one half, feeling a cylindrical handle in his grip. Relief floods him after manufacturing multiple escalating far-fetched theories as to what the hidden item could be, but of course ... it is the matching brush to Brock's comb. He unfolds the top half of the bandana like a banana peel and reveals a crimson coated steel knife blade.

Glen succumbs to tremors as he grasps the dagger, catching a shadowy reflection of himself in what little area of shiny steel is still clean and exposed. A drop of dried blood stretches down further than the rest and sits between his bulging eyes on the blade. A sudden sense of panic seizes him as he hurls the weapon upward and begins to cough between a choke and regurgitation. It spins end over end in the air and punctures the bottom of the shoebox, standing on end triumphantly. Beads of sweat coat his body and run freely down every appendage as he slumps defeatedly against a pile of stacked containers and tries to catch his breath.

*I just held a murder weapon ... A knife that actually killed someone ... Or a bunch of people.* He gasps, feeling like he might be sick or pass out. Glen can only focus on the tall two-tone blade standing upright as it looks down upon him with disgust ... or is he staring up at it? The divinity of an object that has been misused to end lives and shatter dreams looms large overhead like a beckoning icon. Is it an omen of what's to come or echoes of the past that call to him now?

In the confusion of a hangover and even further shock after finding the knife, Glen realizes he sliced his middle finger open on the blade's edge as blood drips onto the concrete. Concerns of exchanging fluids with an unknown victim send him into a tailspin of worry about contracting pathogens, and ... and ... and what? Is that the worst thing to happen this evening? Finding out his mother was at best a hoarder of a serial killer's memorabilia and at worst his secret lover? Discovering the most prolific and evil murderer in modern history may be his genetic father? What is a bit of blood-borne disease compared to a tainted bloodline?

"This is why you've always been so secretive?" he scoffs, looking up at the ceiling beneath their living room floor. "That's why you wouldn't even tell me my father's name, or where he went, or anything about him. You're just as twisted as he was."

*There is still no hard evidence.* Factually, there is more evidence in this basement to convict the late Brock of murder than to determine a familial link and no amount of fear, or conversely paranoia, will be able to convince him otherwise. He sits slumped against the boxes and scrambles for answers in the miasma of despair. Where to go from here? She won't tell the truth, and it's doubtful that anyone else would know the facts, either. There is nobody to turn to and nowhere to seek answers regarding this identity crisis aside from the ethereal Eleanor, but can she truly be trusted? Glen has never had anything to fight for, nor much to live for, and it is now causing him to search for meaning in the strangest of places ... or so he hopes.

"Tell me, Brock. Any regrets?"

He stared directly into the camera, into Glen, with a twisted and undeniably charming glint in his eyes. "Getting caught."

"You murdered at least dozens of innocent young women, girls with families, friends, and futures to look forward to, and your only regret is getting caught?"

"Let me ask *you* something, Jim. Why would I have killed that many so-called innocents if I felt bad about it?"

"Why do you use the phrase 'so-called'? Did they deserve it?" the interviewer posed.

"Why do you automatically assume they were innocent and therefore imply my guilt? I thought better of you, Jim."

The interview replays over and over in Glen's mind without restriction. He had heard plenty about Brock Blackwood back in the eighties, as did most of the country, though he never made a habit of watching the videos. Admittedly,

Glen would have only been an infant when Brock was finally incarcerated for good, though his execution was expedited due to the severity of his crimes and occurred only ten years later. In Glen's short-lived community college career, he took a criminology class for shits and giggles, and they studied Blackwood's methodology closely, including his infamous last words in the electric chair; *see you all soon.*

One of Glen's classmates had been personally affected by Brock's killing spree, losing an aunt when the girl was an infant. A few others seemed to be entirely obsessed by the stories, and they knew everything about his victims, modus operandi, and obscure facts related to his childhood. One of those girls even had *see you all soon* tattooed very visibly on her forearm, which upset the niece of the victim. It made for an interesting class but could not have possibly prepared Glen for this bombshell of information hitting him now.

Glen remembers watching the news in their living room and seeing reports that Blackwood had been executed and his reign of terror was finally over for good. His mother bawled and acted awfully strange for a period of time before he was sent off to live with his grandmother in another state. She would tell Glen that Mom was 'sick', and he could go home as soon as she began to feel better. The nine-year-old boy prayed nightly for his mother's well-being and wanted nothing more than life to go back to what he thought of as normal, which it eventually did. Maybe, hopefully, she was only a super fan like that girl in his criminology class, although that only brings up further emotions to sort through. Why would she be obsessed with a serial killer?

Glen never knew anything about his father, never even saw as much as a photo or heard anything about the hypothetical man. Whenever he attempted to pose the question in the past, she would say such things as, "He is dead so what does it matter?", and "You have never met him and never will".

He squats to push the heavy pile away but slips his footing and knocks into the top boxes with his shoulder. Anticipating a loud crash that might wake his mother, God forbid, Glen winces and waits for the noise that never happens.

Soft and muffled thuds litter the basement as he scoffs and continues to scour the shelves behind the wall of boxes. The flashlight reveals nothing but an old bowling ball, a few scattered gardening tools, and a rather nice wooden box that seems out of place. Glen turns awkwardly from a kneeling position and places his hand on one of the fallen boxes to help himself stand. He notices the black writing of permanent marker on the lid beneath his fingers that he hadn't seen before.

"BB …" Glen whispers in the dank basement. "Brock Blackwood …"

He takes a deep breath to regain his composure and inspects the other three cardboard boxes to find "BB" on two more of them and "PO+BB" on the last one. *Penny Overton*, he thinks with a shudder. She has saved four container's worth of boxes for decades devoted solely to his murderous father.

What sort of horrific things might he find inside? How will he be able to keep this a secret? Should the boxes be destroyed? So many questions flood his already overflowing mind as he struggles to move in any direction, surrounded by what is likely to be his father's last remaining memorabilia.

Glen grabs a rusty hand shovel from the pile of gardening tools and slices the packing tape along the closest box. He grabs both sides of the top and pauses to take a final deep breath, hardly unable to contain himself yet not quite ready to find out the contents either. Peeling the two halves open and feeling nauseated by relating the action to Brock separating a ribcage, he closes his eyes and yanks outward.

Clothes. Old stained and tattered shirts and worn denim jeans on top. He tosses it to the side and digs into the next box marked "BB". All black leather boots, only about half full.

He is not entirely sure at this point what he was hoping to find, although it was only the abstract dream about Tiffany that drove him down here at all. So far, all Glen has found is boxes of clothes to suggest his mother was storing them secretly for … Brock's improbable escape? Early release? Both were equally unlikely and repulsive. He eyes the last two boxes, one marked "BB" and the other "PO+BB". The former is likely only useless personal effects, but the latter ... he will not be able to pack up and exit without at least opening that one. Reaching for the garden tool once more, he carefully slices the tape in anticipation of a novelty snake popping out to scare him.

Separating the two sides just as before, Glen is greeted with stacks of paper, envelopes, photos, and other handwritten notes. The motherload of information, as it were, leaving him feeling simultaneously revolted and engrossed. The top piece of paper is a letter, dated May 1st, 1980.

*My sincerest apologies for being gone so long, darling. Work has taken longer than expected to complete, and I should be heading home soon to see you again. Wait for me. Just wait a little bit longer and then nothing will get in our way again. Promise.*

Glen stares at the piece of paper for a full minute after reading the final word. *Promise.* What was it that she said on her birthday? *I was promised the world.* It feels like a punch to the gut—or maybe more like a stab. Reading Brock's own handwritten words gives him the chills in the worst way while now knowing firsthand what he was guilty of doing. Learning of his human side, or his human facade, is like peeling back the devil's face to see what makes him tick beneath. This is information that the average person shouldn't be made to shoulder.

Morbid curiosity overtakes morality as he digs into the center of the stack, pulling out another letter from what seems to be a different time period than the first judging by the jagged and stressed writing. This one is dated December 11th, 1980.

*You're pregnant and waited this long to tell me? I should have killed you when I had the chance ... Hell, I still might. I only brought you with me because I wanted to bash your pretty face through the dash into the engine block. I can't wait to have your memory tattooed on me, bitch.*

Glen places the angry letter to the side and rubs his eyes in exasperation. She had every opportunity to turn Brock in to the police yet did not do so even after having her life threatened. What did he see in Penny that made him hesitant to kill her? God, what did *she* see in *him*?

Feeling a knock in his chest, Glen finally connects the dots and realizes he almost never made it to birth. She probably would have preferred that outcome, to maintain freedom and the ability to follow Brock around the country without the responsibilities or weight of tending to a newborn as a young, single mother. Even more questions arise, such as wondering how she managed to survive the threat? He might have been caught before coming back, or distracted, or maybe she was not nearly as important to Brock as he was to her.

He shakes his head, preparing to stand and exit when the wooden crate catches his eye again. There would be no reason to hide a container like that while Brock's clothes wait in the open, even if they took a bit of effort and digging to find. Lowering himself back down on one knee, Glen pulls the surprisingly heavy crate out as metal objects rock inside and clink together.

He pulls the lid off carefully to reveal a row of film reels inside their pewter-colored canisters on one half, all in nearly perfect condition, while stacks of VHS tapes sit on the other side. Glen's heart skips several beats as he imagines what kind of horrific treasures might be hidden within those recordings. He removes the first and squints in the dim light to see a piece of tape across the can that reads 'Penny'. She is obviously still alive now, so it can't be that bad, he decides.

Inside is an eight-millimeter reel. Beside his mother's video lies Betty, Rhonda, Tara, Courtney, and *Tiffany.*

*It really happened.*

He rises and places both hands on his head to pause and take a deep breath. These reels, the photos, memorabilia, and letters ... *Brock's knife* ... have all been resting two floors beneath his bedroom for decades.

Glen places the video artifacts on the coffee table and prepares to pop the first tape into the VCR.

Feeling that he already knows how his mother's video ends, he instead chooses the 'Tiffany' tape, hoping to silence the visions of her erupted skull altogether. Glen slides the cardboard jacket off of the VHS inside and loads it into the tray before sitting back uncomfortably in preparation for the worst.

The video shows a young woman in her early twenties pulling into her driveway and bringing what appears to be groceries inside the house. It cuts to the next scene, a brief clip of arriving home again, followed by half a dozen more where Tiffany pulls up to her house within a five-minute window all six times. Each day, she exits her vehicle with a backpack like a college student, generally looking down at the ground and aloof with her surroundings.

The next scene shifts to the same house in darkness with a timestamp of eleven at night. The camera peers through a window to show Tiffany asleep in bed for the first clip followed by others where she is brushing her hair or finishing a phone call, all marked anywhere from ten o'clock to midnight.

"Good morning, Glenny. I helped Brock film this, you know," his mother whispers from behind the armchair.

# CHAPTER TWELVE

A jolt of electricity shoots through Glen as he continues staring at the screen, feeling as if he had been the one caught committing the murder. "Good morning," he replies coldly with a thousand-yard stare and flickers of the television set flashing in his eyes.

"I see you found my video collection. Go on and watch them, as you deserve to know. I have to admit, I had hoped you would never stumble upon any of those boxes down there, which now feels like a foolish and naive wish. Of course, you would find them eventually, they weren't exactly buried underground, although the basement seemed like the next best thing. Maybe I subconsciously hoped you would find them one day to free me of my secrets, I don't know." Alcoholic mist envelopes Glen as he sits in her chair, and she speaks from behind it. Whether she has been drinking or still radiating the scent of vodka from the night before has never been something Glen could determine on his own.

"What do you mean you *helped* with this video? This is Tiffany—"

"Schwartz, yes, and she was found dead in her home after supposedly committing suicide. Go on and keep watching if you really want answers."

"I just don't understand ... Why would you help him hurt people?"

Penny sighs and taps the top of the chair a few times. "I didn't do so willingly or at least not with the intent to bring harm to anyone. He was naturally good at everything, your father. Anything he set his mind to he was better at than just about anyone out there, including things I wasn't aware of at first ... Manipulation, evasion ... He was a ghost, although many called him demon. Inhuman willpower and the ability to both disappear in a flash and also appear to be everywhere at once. I had begun to have my suspicions about what he was doing off on his own, but Tiffany was the first time I couldn't pretend anymore."

"And you're still defending him to this day! Still making excuses for why you were both only victims of circumstance!"

"Glenny ... you have been asking me questions about your father since you could talk, but now that I am finally feeling able to speak about it, you don't want to know what happened?" They sit in tense silence for a moment as Glen grits his teeth. "He lied to me, manipulated me, and promised we were working on something special, constantly told me *I* was special ... Although I was young and put my blinders on most of the time because I thought it would make him love me more. It felt like I always needed to earn his approval, even though he never asked. So, when he gave me a job to do and handed me the camera equipment, I didn't think twice about it or ask why at first ... I only knew I wanted to make him proud. This was the beginning of the end for him, when he began to feel the walls closing in, although what you are seeing here is Brock gathering information on Tiffany so he could study her routine." Light flickers in the dark living room as the television reveals the young woman's morning rituals. "He learned everything about the victims, from their habits and schedules to what they liked and disliked ... The clothes they wore, their favorite foods, and so on. Your father was both a chaotic force of nature and a meticulous control freak at the same time. It defies logic, which is one of the many reasons he still has so many devoted fans today. For all his faults, he was unlike anything else this world has ever seen."

A bell rings within Glen's head. The devoted fans, *Brock's Babies*, Eleanor ... It all rushes his mind as the fog clears from the night before. "Can you tell me why you have a video too if you weren't a victim?" he asks, trying his best to only deal with one catastrophe at a time.

"Oh, but I was. I was the first girl he followed with the camera because the pressure was building from law enforcement agencies tracking him in other states. He was trying to be more careful and not ever be seen publicly in the presence of the victims. The night we met, I was meant to become one of the scores of young women whose lives were halted in place by Brock Blackwood, a faceless and nameless corpse who would get far less attention than the infamous serial killer himself, but I survived, and he took a special liking to me. I swear I'll never understand it, maybe he didn't either, but the best I could tell myself was that it was fate aligning to make you, Glenny. I don't have any other answers. That's why I *had* to keep so many secrets all these years, not only to protect us both, but also to hide my own shame. Most of us don't realize when we're young that our actions will echo throughout the rest of our lives, which is especially unfortunate for those of us who do incredibly stupid things during those years. When I met Brock, I couldn't have even imagined ever living to be fifty, yet here I am, still paying for the whims of an eighteen-year-old girl who just wanted to be loved by the wrong man. We don't know what we don't know, Glenny, that's all."

He clears his throat and tries to carefully think of an appropriate response to the stampede of thoughts and emotions hitting him all at once. "The damage has already been done, which means they know who you are too. We have been exposed."

"It was only a matter of time, I suppose. If anything, I'm somewhat surprised it stayed a secret this long." She chuckles weakly. "How did they find out?"

"The EMT from the other night was no friend. She apparently lost a family member to Brock and used my saliva sample to run a private paternity test ... Seems she has been telling everyone in town."

Penny scoffs and shakes her head. "Only a matter of time. It's a blessing that the truth stayed hidden for so long. They would've taken you away from me. I imagine the police will be coming any day now?"

Glen swallows hard to stifle words that can't be unsaid. They seem to have very different opinions on the time they've spent together. "No. Not yet. At-home paternity tests are considered circumstantial evidence and not legally binding, although I don't think they will wait around forever. God knows you have plenty of hard evidence hidden. What about Abby then?"

"What about her?"

"You tell me."

Penny sighs with an underlying sense of deep sorrow. "Brock killed her. The circumstances were murky, and the evidence was thrown out in court, so the house fell in my lap for almost nothing. He told me what he was going to do, but I ignored the warnings and stayed silent. Youthful stupidity, closing my ears to what was right in order to get what I *needed*. In some ways, I'm not sorry because it gave you a home to grow up in … But her death happened exactly as you saw."

They both watch Tiffany arrive at her college campus on a beautiful autumn day, filmed at a slightly slower than normal speed. Hues of bright orange and brown throughout the trees complement the young woman walking gleefully amongst leaves falling upon her. She is hugging textbooks to her chest with both arms wrapped around them as her long, straight hair flows gently in the wind in conjunction with her carefree attitude as she saunters onward gleefully unaware of the world around her. Both Glen and Penny stay silent as their attention falls into the screen.

"Ironic, don't you think?" he asks at last without moving his eyes away. "How something so beautiful could be made from such a repugnant situation?"

"That's life, though, isn't it?"

Glen pauses for several more minutes and remains focused on the screen. "Is this the whole video?"

"That's almost the end," she says, trying to discreetly lean over the edge of her armchair and pour a drink as he rolls his eyes.

Tiffany is arriving home across the street, now late at night. She seems to have had a long day at school and has lost some of the energetic luster from before. Unlocking the front door, she walks inside and flicks the living room light on, followed by several minutes of nothing.

"This is what you wanted me to see? A house?" Glen complains, feeling as if he needs to pour a drink of his own to stave off the hangover.

"Shh ... Just watch. Brock never did anything by accident. Young Tiffany's parents went on vacation for the weekend earlier that evening, as they often did. It was a Friday night and the neighborhood was always quiet, which made it really easy for him to hide with a running film camera. We later converted them all to VHS tapes for ease of access when the technology became more readily available."

He glares at his mother, who forgot to prepare for more than a couple Christmas mornings and probably doesn't remember his birthday now, yet she can recall every minor detail of a horrid night over thirty years ago.

"You know something, Glenny," she continues, "I used to blame myself an awful lot for the people that he killed during our time together, like I was responsible for not speaking up or turning him in, but it took me years to realize he would have done the same thing even if angels were waiting there to save those poor girls. They could have been dragging him backward and clawing at his shoulders to stop him, yet he still would have killed them all. That's how strong his willpower was. He created the world around him to fit his own needs, or so it seemed through an idealistic young woman's eyes. I truly believe that no god or devil could have kept him from doing what he wanted, and he was the only entity capable of stopping himself."

Cope, denial, justification, and delusion are all words that run through Glen's mind, although she might be right. Brock more than likely preyed on girls with a weak foundation to make himself seem even more powerful by comparison.

The living room light finally clicks off in the video. A heavily tattooed arm reaches in front of the lens to grab the camera and lift it just enough to reveal the lower half of Brock's face. He grabs the complete setup and walks across the street slowly as the recording sways side to side with each step. Black asphalt fills the screen, followed by hazy green grass under minimal moonlight. He circles around the house through the side gate and approaches the back door which has never been locked in any of the videos. The camera, and Brock behind it, slips inside as everything goes black.

"What happened then? Why did it end?" Glen asks.

"It didn't. Haven't you been listening? Everything, even the unnoticeable details, are exactly as they should be. That's one of the things he always used to tell me."

The film remains black with barely visible movement around the fringes and only slightly audible knocks. Brock appears to be walking for a moment longer before the tape seems to jam. Glen leaps up to fix it so they can get to the ending.

"It isn't broken. Just watch," she says.

He sits down to see the last few seconds of darkness before Tiffany reappears on screen, now sitting unconscious in a chair. The video is blindingly bright as the oversaturated white walls cause Glen's living room to glow. Brock approaches her and snaps a small capsule under her nose, causing the woman to jerk awake and scream.

Glen's mouth drops open as he turns to look at his mother, then back to the video. The audio is muffled and sounds distant, but Brock is speaking to Tiffany as he hands her the chrome revolver with a slight glint from the overhead light. She is distressed and crying.

"That was her family's home office which is why the walls were painted white. Brock specifically wanted white for the ending."

Glen stares at her in disbelief while knowing she isn't aware that he has already seen the ending in his dream. Tiffany sticks the barrel in her mouth for only a second and pulls it out, pleading and sobbing as Brock's back gives off treacherous body energy toward the camera. *Here it comes.*

"This was something he tried out for a while, a different version of Russian roulette. The only difference is Brock used—"

*Five bullets, yes.*

Just like in Glen's dream, Tiffany takes the gun with a one in six chance to walk away safely and pulls the trigger. The tape presents a straight on view as the bullet blows out the back of her skull in a red shower of blood spatter and brain matter against the blank white wall behind her.

"Ha! You got the hollow point!" Brock mocks through murky audio, though Glen clearly remembers his expression without seeing it again. Tiffany remains facing the camera as Brock leans in closer ... until his wide, toothy grin shines through her perpetually yawning mouth.

Glen leaps from his chair and knocks it over, covering his face and chest as he paces back and forth while the image burns like razorblade slashes across his eyeballs.

"There you have it. Now you see why the vast majority of Brock's crimes were never found out. No formal investigation, no hard evidence. He was a ghost, even to me, forever finding new ways to coax people into their own graves like a demonic magician."

Glen continues to pace the room, overwhelmed, dizzy, disoriented, and sick in no particular order. He glances over at his mother who looks back at him with glazed eyes as she speaks, though her gaze seems to be peering through him and focused on a faraway, ethereal place.

"He was there and then he was gone. I never knew for how long or where he went, but I waited patiently because who could compare to him? That type of magnetic personality is a hard drug to kick, let me tell ya ... Course, I didn't know right away he was hurting that many women, or maybe I just feigned ignorance for my own selfish reasons. Although times were different back then, we didn't have the internet or cellular phones to pay attention to left and right. We went out there and *lived* every chance we got, and I'll tell ya what ... I never felt more alive than when I was Brock's girl."

Tiffany sits on the screen with her lower jaw dangling and an abstract velvet mess painted behind her. Brock walks away and allows the camera to continue recording as his unfortunate victim observes the Overton living room judgingly with both eyes trapped at half-mast.

"Hard to feel alive with the number of substances you abuse," Glen mutters.

"There were times I became jealous as I learned of the others," she continues, ignoring his quip. "I don't know, maybe that's partially why I helped him out and stayed as long as I did. I wanted to feel *special* ... Or at least more important than the rest. Even when he was eventually caught and thrown in prison, there were lines of those stupid little *whores* outside waiting to see him and I would become furious ... Suddenly, I felt the type of hatred that would make me fantasize about killing them all myself ... Until he saw me in the group and beckoned for the guards to bring me to the front. Then all those girls boiled with envy as I felt on top of the world. As I said, a drug like no other, something I have longed to feel just one last time for thirty years now."

On the screen, Brock re-enters the room with his tattooed arm reaching across the lens first. He grabs the camera to walk it toward Tiffany's lifeless face and pauses there as the video cuts off with a click and the television goes blank.

# CHAPTER THIRTEEN

*Can I stop by?* The message vibrates Glen's phone to disrupt an unexpected daydream. He's been through so much this week already, and his brain has sought shelter more and more often.

*Sure thing. I'll be here.*

*Okay, on my way from work.*

The drive from the office is only a few short miles and is one of the reasons he has stayed there for so long. The location is convenient, the coffee is free, and the coworkers are great if one were to exclude everyone aside from Dana.

*Here.*

Glen opens the door, looking somewhat gaunt in his appearance, though everything else seems to be fine. Dana scoffs at how drunk he got last night. "Hi! I didn't want to knock and wake her," she greets while walking up the driveway.

"She's been upstairs since early this morning. Haven't heard any more from her."

Dana takes Glen by surprise as she approaches with a big hug, knowing he would be uncomfortable with the embrace. "How are you? I was worried all day."

"I'm fine ... Nothing to worry about. Come in and we can talk there."

She shuffles inside as he closes the door behind. "You seem ... better today. Still a bit pale," she chuckles, trying to break the ice.

"I might have taken things a bit too far yesterday. Lesson learned. I won't do that again. Coffee?"

"Of course. How is everything else?"

Glen walks toward the coffee pot and stands silently for a moment with his back to her. "I'm not ... I don't quite know how to answer that one yet."

"Why not?"

Glen thinks of all the things he needs to keep hidden from her. Eleanor and Brock's Babies, all the items he found in the basement, Tiffany, his mother's admissions, his father's identity ... There is only one thing he could share that wouldn't immediately open a larger can of worms. "I've been having these dreams about Brock, but it seems they are memories of things that really happened."

"More than just Abby? How do you know the rest were real?"

He sighs, feeling as if he backed himself into a corner already. "My mom told me; we finally talked this morning."

"Maybe you're having memories from childhood or something like that? Did you overhear a conversation when you were little or watch something that you shouldn't have seen?"

"I'm not positive, but come to think of it, that would make sense. I found out my mom has a ton of videos taped from whenever Brock was on TV." Glen bites his tongue to stop himself there, not wanting to dig any deeper than that.

"That's it, then. Makes perfect sense." She nods, playing psychologist again. "You were exposed to something as a kid that's popping back up now for whatever reason."

"But Dana, I've never had a dream about Brock before. Now I am seeing him ... do what he did to people in my dreams." Then the corpses continue to mock and chastise afterwards. *Bite your damn tongue.* "She also ... The rumors are true."

"Which rumors?"

"You know which ones ... Brock is my father."

Dana's eyes widen across her face as she opens her mouth but stops just short and sneers with a pause. "It figures the plainest guy in the office would be unknowingly hiding a horrible secret."

"That's all you have to say?"

"What else is there? You're still my best friend, and the past doesn't change who we are now."

"But Dana ... How do you explain these dreams? Or visions?"

"You've never been under this much stress before, Glen. Strange things happen inside the brain when it is forced to endure such strain. But remember, extreme pressure produces diamonds." She winks.

"I don't think I'm following."

"It means that you will push through this and become stronger than ever. One day soon, you will go back to simply being boring old Glen Overton and the rest will have fallen by the wayside. This too shall pass, right? Have you heard that one?"

"Yes, I have." He cracks a smile at last and sits next to her with both cups of coffee. "I hope you're right, and it would be nice if it happened sooner than later. I'm not doing well right now, Dana."

"I can see that. Well, I'm here with you, if that helps any. I also gave it to Monica pretty good this morning on your behalf, so that should give you some breathing room when you come back to work."

"Really? What did you say?"

"She was being herself, and I used my lawyer magic again. I may have quasi-threatened her life on your behalf, even without knowing what I know now." Dana laughs.

"You told her that I'm going to kill her?"

"Not directly. I told her that *if* you were going to go on a killing spree, hypothetically of course, that she would most likely be your first victim.

"That's hilarious. She definitely had it coming. I would've loved to see it."

"Definitely. I'm sure she won't even come near you at all on Monday, if you feel up to going, that is."

"I'm going to try." Glen trails off as he attempts to hold himself together and push his feelings down but fails. "I'm just so tired of never *winning*, Dana."

"I don't mean to come off as callous, but I think a lot ... Shit, *most* people feel that way."

"Did you just curse?"

"I did. It needed to be said." She nods with confidence.

"It's just funny hearing it from you. I'm sure you're right. I don't know how much it makes me feel better right this second, but logically, I bet you're right."

"Of course, I am. When have I ever steered you wrong? Trust me, life will begin to feel more normal before too long. I can't even imagine what you're going through right now, but there's no way you could have this kind of week and walk out of it unscathed. If anything, I would be a bit worried if you *didn't* feel like you hit rock bottom."

"Meaning what?" he asks, looking up from his coffee.

"Meaning you're human, Glen. Monsters don't get stressed, they don't feel bad for other people, or even consider their feelings. You're struggling right now because you caught a peak behind the scenes and don't want to be like Brock, and that alone makes you better than him."

"I appreciate it. I just can't wait for the day when normalcy actually feels *normal* again."

"I'm sure. Unfortunately, it doesn't quite work that way, but that's exactly why I wanted to come by today. Remember, you aren't alone, and we're going to get through this together. I'm in way too deep to quit now." Dana grins warmly at him as he finally relinquishes a smile in return. They share a nice, peaceful moment until Glen slams his eyes shut and grabs his temples.

"What is it? What's wrong?"

The image of Tiffany drills its way into the forefront of his vision. "It's nothing, just the nightmares again." He shakes it off and straightens up to face Dana once more, his light at the end of the tunnel if only he can remember to keep driving toward it.

"I mentioned this last night, but you probably don't remember … Have you considered speaking with a mental health professional?"

"Like a shrink?"

"Sure, or a therapist. Whatever you want to call them." She shrugs. "You know I'll stay here and talk about whatever you want until we both turn blue in the face, but I also can't really *help* you, Glen. Not in that way, at least."

"I would've already gone crazy without you, but I know what you mean. I'm not so sure they can change my DNA, but I am open to just about anything else at this point."

"My sister is a social worker. I'll see if she knows anybody, and we'll have you fixed right up. Everything is going to be okay. You believe me, right?"

"I think I do … Maybe it's only wishful thinking. At any rate, thank you for trying so hard, Dana. That is more than anyone else has done for me, and I appreciate it more than you know." Glen bites his bottom lip hard.

"Of course, and I know you would do the same for me if in some strange alternate universe, I was the daughter of an infamous female serial killer. Why are there so few of them?"

"I don't know … I thought you were the expert."

"I know a lot about Brock, not necessarily all serial killers. Hey, maybe that's a question you can ask your new shrink."

# CHAPTER FOURTEEN

**Seattle Metro PD**
**Tape Recorded Interview:**
**Brock Blackwood**
**Detectives Alan Schaeffer, Robin Kerkhoff**
**8.19.81**


**AS**: This is detective Alan Schaeffer, Seattle Metro Police Department. Today's date is Wednesday, August 19, 1981. The time is 3:36 P.M. This will be a taped conversation with Brock, spelled B-R-O-C-K, Blackwood, spelled B-L-A-C-K-W-O-O-D. Date of birth 06-03-1946.

**RK**: This is detective Robin Kerkhoff, Seattle Metro Police Department.

**AS**: Today we will be conducting the introductory

interview with suspected murderer Brock Blackwood. Audio recording is live. Brock, can you hear me? Nod twice for yes.

RK: Let the record state that he does not nod.

BB: Yes, I can fucking hear you. Jesus, did any of your intel state that I was deaf?

AS: Brock, today you are accused of murdering Officer Peter Baker in the first degree. You are entitled to legal counsel if you choose.

BB: That would be pointless. I did it.

AS: You admit to killing Officer Baker?

BB: Well, no shit? You found me standing next to his body. Covered in his blood. But yes, I confess. I'm a guilty sinner.

AS: Okay. Can you tell us why you removed his jawbone? Killing him wasn't enough?

BB: You wouldn't understand even if I told you.

AS: Humor me.

BB: I just—I knew you guys were closing in and I wanted to taste pig one last time. I love pork, you see.

**AS:** You son of a bitch—

**RK:** Alan! Don't do anything stupid!

**BB:** Yeah, Alan. Listen to your lackey.

[Tape stops]

**AS:** So, you came across Officer Baker and decided to murder him. Do you care to tell us why?

**BB:** No.

**AS:** Okay.

**RK:** You are suspected of killing a great many people, Brock. Would you like to tell us any more about them?

**BB:** No.

**RK:** Alright.

**BB:** Not yet.

**RK:** When would you like to tell us?

**BB:** When the time is right. But not now.

**AS:** Regardless, I'm sure you realize that you're in a world of trouble.

**BB:** No. You only know what I want you to know. All you have are theories and blind guesses.

**AS:** [Clears throat] For now, Blackwood. For now. We know you killed Abby Hawthorne.

**BB:** No, you don't.

**AS:** Excuse me?

**BB:** You heard me.

**AS:** You seem awfully sure of yourself for someone who has just confessed to a murder. We have you dead to rights.

**BB:** As I said. You only know what I have willingly given. The rest is a matter of speculation.

**AS:** But you are aware of the consequences of even a single murder confession?

**BB:** Yes.

**AS:** Okay.

**RK:** Do you feel any remorse for your actions?

**BB:** No.

**RK:** Do you remember all of the murders?

**BB:** Yes.

**RK:** Can you tell us anything else about them?

**BB:** No.

**AS:** It's going to be a long and boring day if you don't want to talk to us. But suit yourself.

**BB:** I have nothing but time now. My work is done.

**AS:** What does that mean?

**BB:** Doesn't concern you.

**AS:** You already know how this is going to play out.

**BB:** Yes.

**AS:** We recommend you for an expedited visit to the electric chair based on killing an officer of the law in cold blood. Combining that with the reputation you've built for yourself, we don't need any more evidence.

**BB:** I said I understand. I'm aware.

**AS:** Good, because you're going to rot in a cell until then. It might take ten years.

**BB:** Looking forward to it. I'm still going to kill anyone I see any chance I get. Might even be you. Nothing happens by accident.

**AS:** You seem excited to die. Is that it? Suicide by cop?

**BB:** No. You can't see the vision.

**AS:** Then explain it to me.

**BB:** I don't feel like talking any more today. We have years together.

[Silence]

[Tape stops]

# CHAPTER FIFTEEN

G len pulls into his typical parking spot about thirty minutes earlier than usual, even more peculiar on a Monday. There are at least a dozen people parked already, and he spots Dana's white sedan in the rear-view mirror. Climbing out of the car, he hears footsteps pounding toward him from behind, causing him to stand on edge.

"Be wary of dissidents, sir," a man whispers as he walks by quickly.

"We have your back, sir," a woman follows, though Glen stares long enough to recognize her as Kathleen once she reaches a certain distance and disappears from view. Both comforted and chilled, he floats toward the glass doors in a surreal haze while thinking about the realities of his new life. Today begins week two.

"Good morning," the building security guard wishes as Glen waves dismissively and rushes into the stairwell where he surely won't run into anybody.

*This was a mistake. You should not have come today.* He clears his throat forcefully to brush off unwanted thoughts and stomps each concrete step with firing pistons for legs. *They don't want you here.*

"Shut up!" he screams with a cavernous echo in the stairwell as he bursts through the door.

"Good ... morning. Did you take the stairs?" Dana questions from the other side.

"What are you doing in the hallway? Yeah, I mean ... sometimes I do."

"Okay, goofball. I forgot something in my car, but I took the elevator back up like a normal person. We must have just missed each other down in the lobby."

"We probably did, although to be honest, I was spacing out hard. I'm a little nervous coming back after what happened the last time I was here," he grimaces.

"You're fine, I doubt anyone remembers. Steer clear of Monica, though, especially after what I said to her Friday. You know the routine; she scurries away in embarrassment and comes back more aggressive than ever to try and save face."

"Yes, I've been on the other side of it more than once. Hey, I do have good news, though. Your sister got me an appointment with a co-worker of hers tomorrow night. She said she doesn't know the doctor personally, but they work in the same office."

"That's fantastic!" Dana beams. "We are starting the week off on the right foot, I see. This is going to help tremendously, Glen, and I know it isn't easy to accept assistance sometimes. Just think of it like you aren't going in because there's a flaw within yourself, but you've just had to face so much alone."

"I am. At the very least, we get a funny story out of it to laugh at and move on to better things."

"Of course, we can only hope that happens. All kidding aside, though, I am happy you are being proactive. You're too good of a person to be suffering this much, Glen."

"Good morning, murderer," Peter mutters as he pushes between them.

"Murderer?! Then that makes you a dead man walking, loser!" Dana screams after him.

"Did you just threaten Peter's life under my name?"

"Yes, I suppose I did. Don't worry, I'm an amateur lawyer, and it wouldn't hold up in any court."

Glen snorts as he laughs and wipes his face for any embarrassing evidence left behind. "Sorry, I just didn't expect that from you."

"Yes, well, it seems some people don't take too kindly to *me* being here either, simply because I'm friends with you. That's bullshit, you didn't do anything wrong, and neither did I for defending you."

"Wow, you cursed again?"

"You better get used to it if people are going to keep being so dense," she groans. "Come on, let's go get our last coffee before work starts. Everything will be fine."

"So far, so good, right?"

"Peter's a prick, what can I say? Most people barely have the energy to handle themselves, let alone worry about what you're doing."

"Just like a bandage, right? Rip it off quickly and move on from there." Glen nods and walks through the threshold of the working world, voluntarily relinquishing control of himself to become another cog in the corporate machine.

"Right behind you. We would both do well to lay low today and stay within our cubicles as much as possible."

"Agreed. See you in my emails later."

Dana snickers and ducks into her workstation as Glen surveys the office quickly to realize there was nothing to fear. Peter's teasing words are empty and meaningless, although he has weathered chastising before as a child walking home from school. No big deal ... although one of those children pushed the issue too far and nearly ended up stuffed inside a hollow tree trunk. The bully and his friends found Glen out in the woods one day after school, where he was sitting peacefully on a fallen log and stacking rocks. The boys rushed him from behind and forced his face down in the mud for dangerously long periods simply because they could. Nobody else was around to stop them, and he was outnumbered five to one. By all rights, Glen should have been at their mercy and felt powerless beneath the freezing muck until his scrambling hands managed to find a jagged rock and smashed it against the boy's arm to break free with a gasp of air. There was a brief window of opportunity when the attacker laid vulnerable on his back, and Glen leapt on top of him to bash in his eye sockets and cheekbones with that rock as the four friends stood by and watched in equal parts horror and fear that they would be next. Finally, after half a dozen hits, they jumped in to pull their bloodied buddy free and scatter in all directions as Glen fell to the ground in a whirlwind of cackles and euphoria. He sat up at last with the mud rapidly drying on his face and grabbed that red rock to stuff deep within his pocket and took it home, for it held the magic to protect him from feeling powerless, or so he thought at the time. The rock still sits in his closet, wrapped in the remnants of an old shirt, although it does not seem to be nearly as effective these days.

Wherever Peter went off to, he deserves the same fate as that boy, later found out to be named David, who went back to school with a horribly disfigured face and was then bullied himself for looking strange. He would stare across the lunchroom at Glen, who glared back calmly between bites of his peanut butter and jelly sandwich without expression. David developed a reputation as the kid who would frequently wet himself in class for a period of time before disappearing altogether. Glen sits back in his office chair to wonder where the boy ended up and if he still has those horrible scars from the rock. *Serves him right.*

"Psst ... Glen, did you check your email?"

Dana startles him from atop the dividing wall and disappears, though the message is received regardless. *Monica on the prowl* is typed into the subject line, though the body is empty. He blinks away the final fragments of the daydream and tries to make sense of the warning as it becomes abundantly clear.

"Wow, Glen, you actually made it in today," she snarks behind him before he is able to prepare.

He spins around in his chair to see Monica staring at him as she bites her bottom lip nearly hard enough to draw blood. Her arms are folded as if she is about to burst under the pressure of not being incredibly critical instead of only mildly bitchy.

"Good morning, Monica. You look nice today." Glen nods. He can practically feel Dana cackling in the cubicle next door. "Did you get a haircut?"

Her jaw muscles visibly tighten in knots as her eyes widen. "What did you say to me?"

"Nothing, I only complimented your appearance today. I am not used to you looking nice. Now, if you will excuse me, I have plenty of work to complete after taking several personal days recently. You understand."

The veins in her temples pulsate as she lowers herself into the cubicle and gets within inches of Glen's face. "You are on practically non-existent ice, you pathetic little *fuck*. Too bad your daddy didn't leave you any of his riches, so you're stuck working a dead-end job like the rest of the derelicts. I'll make sure of it."

He scoffs and stares directly into her eyes with renewed vigor. "Bite me, or better yet, kiss me. God knows you're close enough."

Tiny eruptions take place behind the facade of her facial expression. She leans even closer and whispers into his ear. "You would be so lucky. Perhaps if you had even a shred of Brock's charm." She pats him on the head like a child and walks toward the cubicle opening, turning back to blow him a sarcastic kiss and raise a sharp middle finger below the sightline.

Several seconds of silence follow the interaction before Glen bursts into laughter. If the last week has taught him anything, it is how small most problems truly are. People are boring, and they repeatedly seek validation by their very nature, either positive or negative. This job doesn't matter nor do Monica's opinions. It's utterly hilarious.

Dana scurries around the divider and keeps low to avoid attention. "What happened over here? I heard whispering, but most of it was pretty murky. Did you just tell her to kiss you?"

"She got in my face, so I only suggested it as an option."

"Vile."

"Yes, well, it was meant more to embarrass her for being that close. I even told her she looks nice today to disarm her." He snickers.

"That's a tough lie to tell for any reason, but I'm glad you did. She probably has no idea what to think right now."

A heavy thud against one of their office windows causes them all to freeze in position and wait for answers as another knock hits.

"Everybody get down! We're being attacked!" someone unknown shouts as flurries of panic begin to spread. Several people hit the deck and crawl under their desks.

"Don't be ridiculous! We're on the third floor!" someone else responds.

Dana and Glen rush toward one of the windows as a large rock hits it in front of them. The sound of chanting from the parking lot below grabs their attention while they increase in volume with each recitation. *Kill the killer! Kill the killer!*

Glen looks up at Dana in a panic as he realizes the mob is there for him. "I … I have to go down there."

"That would be really stupid, Glen. No offense. Why not just stay in here and we can call the police?"

"I agree, that would make a lot more sense. I will explain later, okay? Wish me luck."

# CHAPTER SIXTEEN

"What the *fuck* were you thinking, Glen?" he mutters to himself while staring down the monolithic glass doors to the outside world. The small group of protesters have gathered with signs and a megaphone in front of the office to declare their dissent regarding his presence.

*Kill the killer! Kill the killer!*

Glen blinks hard to push away his own negative thoughts and steps forward. If he doesn't act quickly, Kathleen and the rest will make short work of these clowns and allowing a bloodbath on company time will only exacerbate everything wrong with his life at the moment. And it's just Monday morning.

He finds himself standing outside atop the steps, staring down at the five picketers who quickly stop shouting and lower their heads with blind hatred. Glen's heartbeat intensifies rapidly until it nearly punches a hole through his throat.

Four figures in hooded trench coats step out from different rows of cars across the parking lot as the morning sunlight shimmers across their steel blades. They converge in the center aisle and glare with shadowed faces that will leave no survivors if given the opportunity to act. That is why Glen forced himself in harm's way, to protect his attackers, and therefore save himself from further trouble by extension.

The four of them take a step forward without sound, followed by another as they quickly progress into a full sprint. Glen throws his hands up to stop them, causing the protesters to wince and gasp in shock.

"He has something to say!" one of them shouts.

"He's going to attack!" another screams.

He waves the members of Brock's Babies off, and they flee into the cars once again as the protesters turn and run with Glen following closely behind.

"We'll be back and ready to fight tomorrow!" the first turns and yells.

A sense of power floods his chest as he realizes the five of them were clearly there because they're scared of his existence, yet they ran away when given an opportunity to act because they are terrified of his presence. And it feels *good*.

Kathleen steps out after a moment and pulls the hood back to rest just past her hairline. "You should have let us deal with it. They will be back with even more people, you know. They will only grow more bold."

"Unfortunately, I do ... Although you have to realize seeing 'Monday Morning Office Massacre' plastered across every regional newspaper would only make my life even worse."

"We need to respond with strength. Your father—"

"But I'm NOT my father. This is Glen you're talking to, not Brock," he slashes back.

Kathleen scoffs. "Who are you trying to convince? Me or yourself?"

"Kathleen! We need to move!" Thompson calls.

"Anything you need, sir, we will never be far away from The Only Son." She nods and disappears between the cars to leave only the lingering echoes of averted chaos within the parking lot.

Glen stands quietly for another moment as the sounds of cars driving in the distance fill his ears. He turns to walk back without even looking up at the building, not wanting to see their reactions.

The security guard only stares with wide eyes and does not greet Glen again. No matter, he doesn't have anything to say in return anyway. True hell awaits him upstairs as further sneers and whispers will fill the air. He should have run away with Kathleen. The elevator door opens to reveal his exit floor, and he regretfully steps forward. The only silver lining here is that he is growing unnaturally accustomed to being the center of negative attention. Here it comes again.

Glen walks into the office as the workers scramble to get back to their desks without creating a scene. Some of them appear genuinely fearful, while others look lost. Nobody in the city, including Glen, knows how to appropriately navigate their transition toward living amongst one another; the potential predator coexisting peacefully with pallid prey.

*Think of how fearful they were as they scurried away.* He clears his throat to shush the inner voice and steps forward once more.

"What happened out there?!" Dana asks as their co-workers continue to rush around. "Who were you talking to?"

"What?"

"Who was that person?"

"I scared them all off, the protesters," Glen lies as tunnel vision closes in. He continues to walk forward with outward confidence but feeling shaken to his core within.

"Yeah, but you seemed to know her, and she wasn't scared. If anything, she looked rather ... comfortable approaching you."

How to answer that one? How much does Dana need to know? Radiating rings of light close in on her face as his own cheeks begin to tingle. "Oh, really? I don't know," he answers weakly, not sounding much like himself. *Just get back to the cubicle and hide for the rest of the day.* Maybe everything will be fine tomorrow, he continues to lie to himself, though the fibs fall flat at his feet every time he tries.

"Glen! What the hell do you think you're doing interrupting the entire office like that?! Is this what I get for trying to be nice to you?! Handle your personal business on your own time!"

"Leave me alone, Monica. I'm not in the mood right now." Those rings of light increase in speed and intensity to continue forcing away any outside thought.

"Leave you alone?! Oh, wouldn't that be convenient?!"

"I said fuck off, Monica!"

The office freezes as someone drops a single object, sounding like a boulder crashing through the floor. Three words that have been in the fantasies of every employee but never before mentioned. Nobody dared but Glen.

"EXCUSE me?!" she asks with teeth chattering from anger.

"You heard me. Move." He pushes past her and heads for his own desk, where he can pretend to work and hide from his life's problems as he has done since the day he started working there.

Monica scoops her jaw off the floor and retreats to her own office to regroup. Glen sinks back into his comfortable ergonomically designed chair with reinforced forearm padding and additional lumbar support. He closes his eyes and takes a superfluous nasal inhalation to the heart, feeling the rare sensation of comfort in an even stranger place; work.

The office is metaphorically on fire, the outside world is less safe for him than ever, and even more militants will revolt against him by the day ... Yet the present moment in time within his cubicle feels rather nice. The better aspects of his drunken escapades last week float back comfortingly into his mind.

"Glen," Dana nudges from over the divider. "Glen, are you asleep again?"

"No," he answers with his eyes still closed. "And so what if I was? What does it matter now?"

"I don't even know where to begin with that one. Aren't you scared, Glen?"

"Scared of what? I've already been through the worst of it."

"Have you, though? Well, I think I'm scared for you. I've been trying to stay positive and believe everything will work out in your favor, but ... things are different now, don't you think?"

Glen opens one eye and glances at her. "Different how? I don't mean to sound rude, but this is *exactly* what I've been expecting would happen. If anything, there is a small amount of relief to not be dreading the moment anymore. People always need to feel afraid of something, Dana, and apparently right now it is *Glen Blackwood*."

"Well, you know me ... Always trying to see the best in people, even to my own detriment." She smiles without confidence. "I'm glad you're so sure of yourself, at least."

"Oh, I'm a mess. If anything, this morning was a wakeup call to embrace the chaos around me because I can't control any of it. Or some shit like that, I don't know anymore."

"Okay." Dana goes quiet for a moment as Glen closes his eye again. She remains standing over him from the edge of her cubicle, quivering from the knees up. The light has fallen dim. "Glen? You don't think you're in danger, do you?"

He sits upright with both eyes open and turns toward her. "Real danger? Probably not, but there will be more protestors, that much is certain."

"But how can you be so comfortable knowing that?"

"Dana, I've only felt comfortable maybe five times in my entire life," he cackles. "That might be the answer; I've grown rather comfortable feeling constantly uncomfortable. Some people say that can happen once you reach your thirties. I wouldn't necessarily call it comfort, but I am distinctly choosing to reject stress today."

She smiles softly in return and visibly struggles to sort through her own thoughts. "Well, I hope you're right, that's all. It is terrifying to think there are people like that out there."

"I don't know anything, none of us do, and that's exactly it; we're just guessing all the time and hoping for the best in return. I might throw myself through those windows if I continue to believe I'm in control of anything because apparently that is false. I would've never willingly chosen any of this."

# CHAPTER SEVENTEEN

"Have a good night, Dana," Glen whispers from his cubicle before exiting for the evening. With so many new changes over the last week or so, even the smallest semblances of normalcy feel like a welcome commodity. No answer.

He grabs his bag and heads for the door, overjoyed that Monday is done at the very least. There is a sense of déjà vu within that circulated office air as Glen senses his presence leaves them breathless. No response from Dana, and that is okay. She is scared, and reasonably so, although he has spent the last several days not entirely certain that continuing to live would be worth the strife. There is a sort of inherent comfort that comes with accepting that level of internal peril. He is the son of Brock Blackwood and no amount of worry will change it. Dana will have to adjust. They all will.

It's a strange sensation to have gone from a relative ghost within the company to a virtual villain overnight. He was a faceless corporate robot amongst a sea of them, now turned public enemy number one for nothing but the contents of his blood. Brock was imprisoned right around the time Glen was born and they never met, but the shadow of his scores of sins hangs heavily still.

He takes a final glance back at the office to look for Dana, but the place cleared out quicker than normal this evening, and she is nowhere to be seen as expected. They will be able to speak tomorrow when she is hopefully feeling better, though Glen acknowledges regretfully that it will never be safe near him or at least not until the majority of the public forgets about this story.

Walking out into the early evening air, he is immediately relieved to not see any protesters or trench coats either, though he is positive they are watching from afar. The skyline is rather beautiful, all things considered, and he takes a moment to appreciate the jagged mountainscape before finally walking to his car with just a bit of tension relieved from that knot in his chest. Maybe, just maybe, the worst has passed and what felt like a catastrophe all weekend will now become the new normal. That is the adjusted reality he will settle for. Not every question needs an answer, and not every issue needs a solution. So be it.

Glen turns the key quietly to unlock the front door in what has become a nuclear habit. He hasn't seen her since Friday morning when they watched Tiffany's video together, though it's not entirely uncommon for her to spend days or weeks entrenched in bed and unable to crawl out. It wasn't until high school when Glen finally had a friend close enough to visit his house, where it was made painfully apparent to him that most mothers don't disappear for long-term pharmaceutically induced comas.

He steps inside and immediately sees the TV glowing, as well as her arm resting on the side of the chair. *At least she finally got out of bed again,* he thinks, tiptoeing closer toward the stairs and hoping she is still asleep. They will need to speak again eventually, but now doesn't seem like the right time to force the issue. Following the morning assault on the office building, he has been mostly at peace and had a surprisingly good afternoon, if boring means good.

Glen continues by her armchair and hangs a right in the hallway toward the stairs, deciding to come back down later for dinner after a few more hours of solitude. A piece of paper catches his eye on her end table, where there would typically only be two different bottles and a glass. Two halves of him shout opposing directions to either investigate or continue upstairs, but in the end, per usual, curiosity triumphs over logic.

He slides gracefully toward the table as a part of the television show flickers back and forth between light and dark. She must be in a deep sleep to not be flinching after the flashes. Glen lunges forward silently, with years of training in the art of stealth, and pulls the paper toward him.

*I'm so sorry for everything, Glenny. I have wished every day of your life for eighteen-year-old me to know what her actions would do to you. Please forgive her.*

He stares at the paper in bewilderment and reads it again. *What the hell does that mean?* He can't remember a single instance when she showed remorse for anything, much less with a direct apology. She must've dug deep into the pill cabinet and found the strong stuff today.

Leaning forward again to place the note back on the nightstand, he notices three empty pill bottles and a plastic handle of vodka on the floor, a bit much even for her. She rests unnaturally still in her armchair, pale and pallid with her mouth hanging open as the classic sitcom on TV plays a laugh track over a joke. She slightly resembles an older version of Abby.

Glen walks toward their fireplace and leans against it rigidly before sliding down to the ground, knowing all too well what has happened. His pounding heart comes to an abrupt halt as a sense of weightlessness overtakes him followed by numbness. This day has been something he knew would come eventually, walking into their dusty old home from work to find that she had left the mortal world, though he never guessed it would come so soon and by her own hand. He stares at her blankly as she returns the expression, a lifetime's worth of missed conversations spoken between them without words. *I'm so sorry*, she wrote.

Words Glen had never heard her physically say under any capacity, typically too numb to feel contrition.

He rises after a moment and walks into the kitchen to dig through her "secret" hiding spot for vodka and pulls out a sealed bottle. Glen had watched her store it there for years even after he was old enough to start buying it for her, though she never knew he knew, and he would sneak sips of it as a child from time to time. Returning to her armchair, he slumps beside it cross legged and sits unmoving on the worn shag carpet and watches the sitcom with her for the remainder of the episode, something he was never allowed to do when he was younger. Her rules were always strict for him to be downstairs when she was up there and upstairs when she was in the living room. Secretly, he had wished to watch a television show with her since the first time his high school friend's family sat down as a unit and enjoyed each other's company while they laughed heartily to primetime silver screen entertainment. Now seems like as good an opportunity as he will ever get.

There isn't a light on in the house aside from the tube flashing and not a sound outside of their manufactured happy family dynamics. Glenn and Penny sit in silence enjoying the show, as he cracks the seal of the plastic bottle and takes a few sips, not wanting to get as drunk as he did last time but wanting to enjoy a bit of his mother's self-described favorite thing in the world. *How ironic*, to feel closer to her now than at any time when she was alive. Hopefully the vodka offers some helpful assistance in facilitating a spiritual embrace.

The internal voice whispers for him to turn off the sitcom and look back toward the fireplace. The wooden box of film reels and video tapes still sits unmoved and beckons for him to open it once again. He rises and floats to the crate, removing the second VHS labeled 'Penny' and stares at it for another moment. This is all that is left of her now, the finale of her story filmed more than thirty years in advance. Glen prepares the VCR again and loads his mother's tape into it, sitting back down by her side to watch it unfold with another swig of booze.

She appears in the first frame, walking toward her house much like Tiffany did before. This video is much shorter judging by the tape in the cassette, which makes perfect sense as she was not yet helping with production, he thinks as it begins. The morning routine consisting mostly of sleeping in, the evening routine of getting dolled up and hitching rides to bars then working deep into the night, and eventually, a close up of her sitting in a chair. His mother, Penny... she was beautiful ... a side of her he had never seen, for as far back as his memories stretch, she already appeared to be a worn out and pill-filled copy of the fiery young woman adorning the screen.

For a brief moment, Glen stares into her youthful eyes, more than ten years his junior now, and he feels bad for her. Up until the present moment, where she has recently departed, her life had been an internal hurricane of mostly self-inflicted pain, yet he feels sorrow, nonetheless. She abused pills and liquor to *cope*, not for fun, which is something he subconsciously knew within, though it was difficult to see through the smoke of his own emotions.

Brock enters view to ceremoniously pass her the same silver revolver, explaining the game exactly as he did with Tiffany. Five bullets and one empty cell, though Penny does not break her determined demeanor and pulls the trigger as soon as she takes the gun. An empty click rings out and she stares at Brock as if she knew the outcome all along.

*Well done, you were destined to be the survivor. I had high hopes for you, and I am glad you were chosen,* he speaks to her from the tape.

*But I didn't do anything other than pull a trigger.*

*Yet here you are now, while others before failed miserably. How else would you explain that?*

*Luck?* She shrugs her shoulders, entirely unfazed by the game.

*There is no such thing. Everything ends exactly as it should, and you are the only person to pass the test. You are special, Penny—*

The screen goes blank as the tape hits its end with a click. Glen stares vacantly at the television set where the bright white light continues to shine. *She was one of his victims.*

Once again compelled by deeper desires, he stands up and rewinds the tape to watch it from the beginning and see her again. She is, of course, in an eternal sleep beside him now, though it's invigorating to see her so young and full of life on screen. The person she was *meant* to be, unfortunately derailed by a masochistic demonic humanoid named Brock before she ever had the opportunity to flourish. Life is unequivocally cruel for all inhabitants.

Glen pauses the video on a frame where she appears to be smiling and leaves it there for a moment longer. Something he rarely saw, if ever. The face he would prefer to bury in his memories, as opposed to the broken vestibule that raised him and rests in the armchair now. He takes a hearty chug of vodka and walks toward the screen, placing his hand on his mother's in a brief moment of understanding as a single tear runs down his face for the life that could have been.

"She was the lucky one," another young woman nods next to him. "The rest of us ... not so much."

Glen turns to look at her, peering through the bloody hole between her eyes that nearly connects them. "Haven't you heard? There's no such thing as luck."

"Easy for the lucky to say. I didn't deserve to die, yet it happened anyway. Penny was always his favorite, and he probably cheated to make sure she would win."

"How could *he* cheat when it was his game?"

"Russian Roulette is a game of chance! He must've rigged the cylinder to stop on the only cell that wouldn't hurt her! How convenient that his favorite girl just so happened to evade all five rounds?" She rolls her eyes hard and spreads blood from the bullet wound into them.

"What if she was truly chosen by spiritual forces? How do you know Penny … my mom … wasn't meant to be with Brock? I don't know why I'm asking you. What's your name anyway?"

"It's Myrtle. Oh, how I wish it was me to survive and not Penny. I was so jealous of her, we all were, but Brock obviously wanted nothing more than a dull moment with the rest of us. We were only pieces of meat for him to slaughter, but Penny … Well, he never killed her for a reason, the lucky bitch."

"She actually just passed away today," Glen sighs.

"Oh, really? I'm sorry to hear about that. Nobody told me. I'll tell you what, though, it was an honor to take that pistol from Brock and pull the trigger. Even a one in six chance to be his girl was worth all the blood in my body and then some. The ironic part is I lost on both accounts, as he never cared about me *and* my blood was splattered across those walls for nothing. See?" She pokes her index finger in the hole between her eyes and turns it back and forth with several squeaks.

"Yes, I see, now please stop that." Glen winces as he turns back toward the video of his mother. "She might have been special to Brock, but … Can I be honest with you, Myrtle?"

"Who else can you speak freely with if not me? I know every deliciously dark detail about you."

"Well, my mom never felt special to me. She was an alcoholic, pill-abusing burden whose depressive black cloud sucked the life out of this house from the day I was born. My earliest memories are all of her passing out on the floor, asking me to fetch her pills and vodka bottles, or crying … Oh yes, she cried frequently during my childhood and slept the rest of the time, and all that began nearly thirty years ago. It only got worse since, to the point I … secretly hoped this day would have come sooner for both our sakes, but you know what?"

"What is it, Glen?" she asks with a comforting touch.

"Now that she's gone, and knowing what I have recently learned, I kind of miss her. I wish we could have spent more time together speaking openly, like we did the last time I saw her. It was freeing, like a huge weight had been lifted that I never realized was crushing me. Is your mother still alive, Myrtle?"

"No. She suffered a similar fate as Penny a few years after I lost at Brock's game. She couldn't bear the grief any longer and blamed herself."

"Oh. I'm sorry to hear that." He places his hand on her knee while he clicks the television off to avoid any further suffering.

"That's okay, Glen. It was just collateral damage in the pursuit of Brock's plan."

"Brock's plan ... What did he aim to accomplish?"

"You are going to figure that out for yourself, Glen. You are his son, after all, and it will hopefully grow more intuitive to you over time." She reaches over and twirls his hair with the bloody finger.

"Thanks, Myrtle." He wraps around her shoulder and smiles before looking into the black television reflection and seeing himself sitting alone with his arm outstretched over open air. He recoils and tightens.

"What's wrong? You don't like me anymore?"

"Sure, I do, it's just ... I have a lot going on in my mind right now that I'm not entirely ready to process yet."

"I understand. Grief is a hell of a hurdle to overcome. I'm here for you in your time of need, Glen ... We all are." Myrtle leans in for a heartfelt embrace as a dozen more women with bloody holes in their foreheads and temples trudge into the room and wrap their arms around him.

# CHAPTER EIGHTEEN

Questions abound. Should he do the moral thing and call an ambulance knowing she has certainly been gone for hours at the very least? Or should he do right by her and bury her body himself? That is what she obviously wanted, to fade away without any extra attention surrounding the ordeal.

And what of the ambulances outside lighting up the block? Every house in the neighborhood will pour out onto their lawns to stare with nosy and judgmental ignorance. The spectacle alone will only attract more hatred, yet … she clearly wanted to go on her own terms.

"Myrtle? Are you still there? What should I do?"

No answer, as expected. What would a dead girl know about how to handle life's problems anyway? She has been deceased now far longer than she lived.

Glen rises to his feet at last, albeit a bit woozy and reaches for the telephone.

"911, what's your emergency?"

"It's my mother. She's … I came home and found her. She's gone."

"What is your address?"

"Zero eight zero six … Gateway." He fades from the conversation and doesn't hear another word the woman says, eventually hanging up the phone and sitting back down on the floor. Déjà vu strikes him as he stares at her, vividly remembering nights when he would sit in this exact spot and stare at her as she looked eerily similar to how she appears now. Preparation from birth to accept feeling utterly alone in the world, suffering through endless nights when he wasn't entirely sure the sun would rise again in the morning. How could he know? There were no parents around to explain.

Glen remains still on the living room floor, unsure of what to do next, just like when he was a child. His mother is gone, buried under the weight of her own bad decisions. Dana is shaken to her core, shocked by reality crashing down around them. Even Myrtle, who is probably nothing more than a confusing vision, has abandoned him in the dark as he waits for help to arrive. The bar has been lowered to nearly zero.

A forceful knock breaks up his depressive daydreams with several reverberating thuds. Glen opens the door and only points a finger toward the old armchair as first responders pile in. Their heavy footsteps ring through the house as he stares forward blankly. "What?"

"I asked what happened here?" an EMT questions.

"Nothing happened. I walked in to find everything exactly as you see it."

"And where were you before?"

"Work. Do you want to call them?" Glen snaps back.

"What is your name?"

"Glen Overton. Her name is Penelope Overton."

"Ah ... Glen Blackwood, is it?" someone else interjects as he steps forward. "This is the Blackwood residence, yes?"

"*Overton*. This is the Overton residence, and that is my mother. She needs your help. Or rather, she needed it several hours ago. Now it's too late."

The man turns and walks toward Glen, taking offense to the insinuation. "And tell me why we shouldn't suspect *you* as a potential suspect? Mr. *Overton*?"

"Because even an over-the-counter drug test would tell you she overdosed on her own medication, prescribed by her own doctors. You may call them, if you wish."

The EMT scoffs as they load Penny onto a stretcher. "You understand, what with the family history and all."

They take his mother outside without another word as someone else leaves a piece of paper on the table by the front door, though Glen is too far gone to hear what they said. Within a matter of seconds, the house is cleared out and silent once again, as he prefers. There's nothing else to say, about his mother or otherwise, and a toxicology report will quickly reveal everything the medical examiners need to know.

Glen glances at the off-white bedsheet draped over her armchair as his ears seem to ring. His legs carry him to the blank space of wall next to their fireplace where he slumps in a heap and continues to stare across the living room at his mother's chair until his eyes fail him.

Glen's prescheduled phone alarm goes off to wake him up for work. His subconscious mind finally relinquished the struggles he'd been resisting against and allowed him to fall into a deep sleep throughout the night. Today is Tuesday. Therapy day.

He rises and yawns with a deep stretch before walking toward the coffee pot and dumping fresh grounds into it. The house is eerily quiet and lifeless, even compared to its usual mausoleum like state. A beam of light pokes through the window to reveal a collection of cobwebs in the corner of it, which Glen uses as the perfect place to lose his focus and stare blankly until the coffee is ready. The previous day's events are now cloudy. and he sips on the black elixir to simultaneously attain the peace of balance and uncertainty of a chaotic mind. Oh, of course ... How could he forget? His mother died yesterday.

No use staying inside to rot all day, and it's difficult to mourn someone who was already dead inside for thirty years. Off to work he goes, already deciding not to tell Dana about what happened quite yet as he continues to fight for a normal, boring existence. They didn't talk about his mother much in the first place, mainly due to her knowing Glen would groan whenever she brought it up. There isn't much new ground to cover anyway; an unavailable alcoholic mother tends to continue course and remain absent.

He locks the front door and turns toward his car as a tall, black passenger van pulls up to his curb. The back door slides open and a familiar face pokes out. "Get in," Kathleen commands with Thompson and Reginald close behind.

Glen's heart drops as he stares out at them, his *servants*, who have burrowed themselves so deeply into his new daily life without being invited. These people claim to have his best interest in mind but have given him next to no reason to trust them. Then again, who else does he have to trust?

"Glen! We don't need to draw any more attention!" she shouts as he snaps to attention and leaps inside the van. The driver pulls away in a hurry, traveling in the opposite direction of the office.

"Glen, darling, we have problems," Eleanor speaks in a soothing tone from the back of the van. "Rather large problems, I'm afraid."

"What is it? What now? I'm already dealing with lunatics attacking me at work and on top of it, yesterday my mother—"

"Died, yes. That is why we're here. Rest in peace to Brock's Best Girl."

"Rest in peace," everyone else inside the van whispers in eerie unison.

"Glen, dear, you should have called me," she continues. "We would have taken care of her, but now ... Sensitive information has spread among the public rather quickly, and it is always dangerous to give any more ammunition to the masses, dense as they are."

"What are you talking about?" he stammers.

"Your mother ... It is now public knowledge that she has passed on, and there are those among us that believe it is *you*, Son of Blackwood, who is to blame."

"Me?! She killed herself!"

"Yes, of course. We know that, but do you realize the amount of negative attention that you brought upon yourself at the worst possible time? Bright lights, sirens, pictures taken of your mother being loaded into the back of an ambulance ... You cannot control what people think, Glen, but you must at least try to be in control of what they perceive. Protesters are on their way to your house as we speak, and you are no longer safe there."

He swallows hard and looks around at the concerned faces of Thompson, Reginald, and Kathleen, who appears most pained of all. "What am I supposed to do now?"

"Keep out of sight, stay away from work or anywhere else you might be easily recognized. Take your father's house, and you will never want for anything again. I will personally make sure of it." Eleanor takes his hands and smiles as they lock eyes. An unusual warmth rises in his core, and he can't help but feel a sense of attachment to her somewhat ... motherly presence.

"But what about my job? My old house?" *Dana* ... "I can't just toss my entire life aside and walk away."

"Sure, you can. People spend forty or more hours a week doing something they hate for piss-poor money because they were never shown something they *love*. What *do* you love, Glen? Because we are all here to love you, same as we adored your father, and whether you like it or not, his blood courses within you. They will judge you unfairly regardless, so why not embrace your identity? Own it! Or do you prefer to be Glen Overton, the data technician? We can offer you the world."

He stares into each of their faces, beginning with Eleanor's elegant yet powerful features. Looking at Thompson and Reginald, both slightly older than he is, though they show extreme resolve and nod back at him in agreement. Glen realizes quickly that they would kill, and probably die, for him without question.

Then there is Kathleen, seemingly younger but even more determined than the other two. He notices for the first time that she is disarmingly pretty, particularly for someone dressed in militant clothing. Her eyes glisten as she stares back at him with extreme focus. Even the driver gives a nod in the rear-view mirror.

"How about this, Glen?" Eleanor continues. "Come back to Brock's house and camp out until the storm blows over, because there *are* people out for your head now, thinking that you murdered your own mother on top of the other ridiculous accusations. Consider my offer and enjoy the amenities. I know you are going to be reluctant about accepting our help, but we are here for you, to protect and follow you."

"Yes," he speaks instinctively without thinking. "I will spend the day there, but I do have an appointment tonight that I need to attend."

"Don't you worry about a thing, Glen. We have a new car for you to take. Anything you need is yours."

# CHAPTER NINETEEN

"Do you need anything, sir?" an unknown man asks from the kitchen doorway.

"I would like some coffee, but I can get it myself."

"With all due respect, sir, Eleanor strongly advised me to serve you today. It would be my utmost pleasure to make you as much coffee as you require."

Glen scoffs quietly and looks up at the man again. "Very well. Can I have a glass of water too?"

"Sparkling or still?"

"Uh ... still is fine, please, and the coffee black."

"Coming right up, sir. Anything you need, sir."

Glen purses his lips as the man walks away, still having a long way to go before getting used to this sort of treatment. He opens his phone to send Dana a text message but freezes before he begins, not knowing entirely what to tell her. *Hey,* he types before staring at the tiny screen blankly. She is no doubt getting sick of his shit since he has already had enough of it himself.

"Here you are, sir, a bottle of spring water and cup of black coffee as requested. The pot is still hot and waiting for you. I will be here the moment you need anything else."

"Thank you … What was your name?"

"Patrick, sir, and it is entirely my pleasure." He nods.

"Well, Patrick, I am curious if you know anything about my car? I was supposed to be given one for an appointment this evening."

"Yes, sir, I will look into the matter right away." Patrick bows and disappears from the room to leave Glen in silence.

The team, Brock's Babies, has cleared the house for the day to allow Glen the relaxation time he needs. The opportunity to mourn properly, as Eleanor phrased it before telling him they would be scouring the city for further protests and so-called resistance fighters. Accepting the position of a quasi-prophesied figure has been difficult at the very least and absolutely absurd in reality. At least the coffee is damn good, though Eleanor doesn't seem the type to buy her soldiers instant mix.

Opening his phone once more, he stares at the initial *Hey* and decides that it is unfair to leave Dana in the dark like a distant acquaintance. She has been by his side through so much without complaint, and it feels selfish to hide now.

*Everything is fine, sorry if I made you worry … again.* Send.

He places the phone down on his knee and takes another sip of delicious coffee, at peace for the first time in what feels like ages. Possibly truly the first time.

*Thank you. So, you are safe?*

*Yes, totally safe,* Glen types, biting his bottom lip to not slip and reveal something he shouldn't, though that list of information has continued to grow rapidly. "Don't do it, Glen," he whispers low enough so Patrick doesn't hear, wherever he ran off to.

*My mother passed away, so I am sorting out her affairs today.* Send.

Glen sighs and slaps his thigh, not wanting to divulge that information just yet. Dana brings out the human side of him, for better or worse, weaknesses and all.

*Oh, Glen, I'm so sorry … please let me know how I can help.*

*Thank you ... she killed herself while I was at work,* he types before reading it over and quickly erasing the bulk of it. That is enough sharing for one day. *Thank you.* Send.

At least now she isn't left wondering throughout the workday, which Glen knows firsthand to be a nightmare of its own. Besides, Eleanor pulled all the strings for him to be at ease today and it would be a great shame to waste the rare opportunity.

Upon finishing the magnificent coffee and not seeing Patrick nearby, Glen decides to snoop around and immediately feels silly for being bashful. This is apparently his house, after all, and he doesn't need to ask permission. The home has been cleaned recently, but the decor and design are entirely vintage; outdated wallpaper in shades of mustard yellow and olive green, strange furniture and flooring, and the old family television set sits large and encased in wood. Brock would have been born back in the forties or fifties and this was likely all commonplace at the time, although it is no more strange than his childhood home of dark and pale grays. Plain walls, dirty floors, and dim rooms are all he has ever known.

A narrow door in the hallway catches Glen's attention due to the damage it has sustained over the years. The wood is bowed, scratched, chipped, and appears to have been hit and kicked many times over based on the shape of it. He turns the handle and pulls it open with great anticipation of what might be hidden inside. At first, it appears to be an ordinary hallway coat closet until Glen finds a dangling lightbulb and pulls the chain.

Faded, brownish blood stains line the walls and inner half of the door. Deep scratches in the wood shake him with the desperation that must've been felt by someone locked in this tiny room, left so helplessly alone to suffer in confinement. Every shelf is broken, as is the coat rack, snapped in half down the middle with small piles of sawdust on the floor beneath. Distant memories of a vivid nightmare cause Glen to feel an indistinct chill across the back of his neck, although he is unsure of the associated emotions brought along with it.

"That was Brock's doing, you know," a woman whispers in Glen's ear, causing him to leap into the heights of the closet from fright. Her eyes are bulging and bloodshot while deep, nearly black bruises line her neck. They appear to be in the shape of handprints. Her flowing top, headband, and bell bottoms feel as out of place as the home's wallpaper.

"You scared the hell out of me."

"There is still much hell left in you. I can feel it." She giggles. "This was Brock's room, or at least, where he spent most of his time as a child. That blood is his and those scratches are from him trying to escape like a naughty boy."

"Brock? Who hurt him?"

"His parents, of course! What else is family good for?" The girl smirks a bit too widely and chokes unexpectedly, popping her left eyeball from its socket to leave it dangling on her cheek by the optic nerve. She scrambles to push it back inside while hiding her face. "Gosh, I'm so embarrassed!"

"Don't be, it's not a big deal. I hardly saw anything."

"Thank you for being so sweet. Anyway, they locked poor Brock in the closet, and the rest of us neighborhood kids were always worried about him. He would show up at school every morning in such bad shape, sickly, exhausted, and pained in raggedy clothes and no lunch to eat ... Though we were only children and didn't realize what was happening to him at the time. Our teacher knew."

"I hate to ask questions with obvious answers, um, miss ..."

"Nancy."

"Thank you. I hate to ask, Nancy, but what exactly happened to Brock? Why would his own parents hurt him?" Glen asks, gulping down the reminder that those were his *grandparents*.

"Little Brock was not allowed to talk or speak, and if he did, they made him drink. If he drank and made a peep, they beat him till he fell asleep. Do you like my rhyme? I thought of it myself."

"It's good, yes. You said they made him *drink*? Like alcohol?"

"See with your own eyes." Nancy points to the corner beneath a dusty coat where an old-timey looking whiskey bottle lies uncorked and empty on its side. He spots another before blinking hard and trying to push away thoughts of a child being forced to suffer this punishment, then feels conflicted about thinking of Brock as a victim in any capacity. "His father came back from the war a completely different man and demanded absolute solitude inside the house. The Blackwood boy was obstinate, however, and refused to follow commands, so they locked him in this closet to teach compliance. When he would complain, they gave him whiskey to quiet down and finished with relentless beatings when all else failed. Most nights saw a combination of both until he physically couldn't fight anymore."

"That's horrible, Nancy, but how did you find out?"

"He told me so himself. Brock and I knew each other from the second grade onward. I always thought he was pretty groovy, you know, but finally in high school, he invited me here to his house. Every girl loved his quiet, shut off, bad boy, totally cool type of attitude so I was super thrilled he liked me. We were supposed to play seven minutes in heaven in this very closet or so he tricked me into thinking. The next thing I knew, we ended up in the darkness when these bruises appeared around my throat, and I never saw light again. Such a bummer ... No seven minutes in heaven ... Brock didn't actually like me."

"Hold that thought, Nancy," Glen interrupts. "Brock killed his first victim when he was in *high school*?"

"We were still in high school, yes, though I was hardly his first."

"Then who was it? Who did he kill before you?"

"He was plenty experienced by the time he murdered me," she continues. "Feel my bruises, they're indented from him squeezing so hard. Feel them, the divots are throbbing."

"No ... thank you." The closet falls silent. "Nancy, are you still with me?"

She looks up at him in a daze and pushes both eyes in slightly before they escape again. "I'm right here, why?"

"Do you know how many other women he killed in this closet?"

"Oh, I don't know for sure … Why don't you step all the way inside and find out?"

"Inside there? Like Brock?" he asks incredulously.

"Of course, that is where the Blackwood we adore was made. Step inside so you may see from his perspective and answer your own questions."

Glen clears his throat and stares at Nancy's varicose, blue-gray cheeks. An inkling of fear, the choking sensation he has been fighting for the past week, returns as he prepares to enter the closet, yet he falsely attributes it to sympathy pains for Nancy's crushed windpipe. "Here I go."

"Go on. I'll be right outside here waiting."

He nods and steps inside the closet as Nancy slams the door shut behind him. "Make sure you turn off the light so you can truly see!"

He takes a quick deep breath and yanks the chain too hard, pulling the lightbulb down to smash on the floor and shroud him in irreversible darkness. All is quiet as expected, until another young woman steps closer and stops only a few inches from Glen's face. He can see her clear as daylight despite being surrounded by blackness. She raises her index finger before her mouth and shushes him, though neither of them has said a word. "Do not speak. Do not move. We must remain still."

A sharp shiver crawls up his spine before he begins to feel more brazen than ever. "And if I don't? This is my house by birthright. Who's going to tell me no?"

The girl cackles as she fades away, though the sound of her echoing voice remains. "Stupid boy, you couldn't shut the fuck up if your life depended on it! You deserve every bit of pain and more for disturbing your father!"

The sound of a separate girl gurgling for air fills his right ear, while juicy, meaty stabbing overwhelms the left. A distant, yet piercing shriek enters his mind from a faraway location, though it increases rapidly in volume and crescendos between his ears. Glen digs his heels into the carpet with a willful resolve to not let their tactics bother him. Conversing with corpses has become commonplace, and he would rather not relinquish his strength to give them an inch of advantage.

"Please don't hurt me anymore, Brock!" an unseen voice shouts desperately before several blunt force blows shower him with still-warm blood spatter. A slow, demonic rumbling laugh fills the closet as Glen forces his eyes shut again to drown out the overwhelming noise, reaching his breaking point. The other girls begin to scream in a type of pain that he has never experienced before, which only multiplies several times over by the second. All he can see in his future is anguish.

"Okay, Nancy! I think I've had enough now!" he shouts, kicking the closet door behind him in a panic.

"But you've only just begun the journey! There is so much more to see!"

Glen turns the doorknob and tries to push through, but she is holding it shut with her entire bodyweight from the other side. "Save me ..." a feminine voice pleads in his ear. "Please ... I'm too scared to die ..."

"Where are you? How can I help you?"

"Just reach out your hand to grab mine. Pull me back to safety."

Glen lunges forward in desperation, swatting through the air to feel for her hand before meeting resistance. She grabs the base of his wrist with a clammy grip that struggles to hold tight and continues to slip. He grasps her forearm with his other hand and attempts another pull but the feeling of sinewy muscle and slick tendons forces Glen to realize he is tugging on her skinned arm. The girl is torn away screaming into the shadows like the rest as their pain travels through sounds and compounds upon Glen in the corner. Every frightful thought he has fought off the past week returns in full strength all at once.

"Nancy! You let me out of here right now, God damn it!" He kicks and pounds on the door as the corpses pull at his shoulders. "I said RIGHT NOW! I need out of here, Nancy, let me out!" The cadavers lean closer and place their cold lips on his cheeks for a final kiss as the door opens and he spills out in a pathetic, shivering heap.

"Sir? What on earth were you doing in there?" Patrick asks in a panic himself.

"I thought ... I thought I heard something in the closet and went in to help. Where is Nancy?"

"There is no Nancy here today, sir, or any other day for that matter. It's only you and me now. Are you alright? Do you need anything?"

"No, I'm fine," Glen pants, trying to ground himself again as he continues to glance back at the now empty closet.

"It's interesting, though ..."

"What is? What's interesting?"

"That you would be immediately drawn to this closet, just as Eleanor suspected. Come now, allow me to fix you right up. Your car is ready for your appointment later." Patrick grins.

# CHAPTER TWENTY

"Tell me, Glen, what brings you in today? I mean, obviously I watch the news and am aware of your situation, but what is it you are struggling with exactly?"

He scoffs and rubs his burning eyes. "Is 'everything' an acceptable answer?"

"Sure, it is, if that's how you truthfully feel. The biggest thing to remember is that I'm here to listen and advise, Glen. Right and wrong don't apply in the safety of this office."

"Okay, Doctor Hawthorne. Well, those are my honest feelings right now. Every single aspect of my life is a trainwreck and I only wish I was exaggerating ... I wish I could do a better job of putting it into words, but I'm drowning."

"That's quite alright, Glen. Aside from your ... rather unique circumstances, what you're suffering through internally is quite normal, especially for adults around your age. It's common to feel entirely overwhelmed as you enter your thirties, when most people report feeling like they are suddenly *old* and have wasted their lives away," he chuckles.

"Right, it feels somewhat like that ..." Glen pauses and bites his tongue, thinking back to childhood visits with social workers when his mother told him to answer the exact opposite of how he really felt. Although she's gone now and can't control him anymore. "But the difference is I didn't do any of this to myself. I didn't cause my mother to love a serial killer and become an alcoholic. I didn't make her kill herself."

"As I said, Glen, *unique circumstances*. Gosh, I wish all my patients were as easy to work with as you! We are making great progress, believe me, and I have great hope for a full recovery. So, you say your mother killed herself? I saw on the news that she died, but they didn't say how or why."

"Yes. It has been a tumultuous twenty-four hours, to say the least."

"I could only imagine. You mentioned she was an alcoholic; would you care to expand upon that a bit more for me?" Dr. Hawthorne folds his hands on his knee, which is crossed over the other leg. He has a notepad sitting on the arm rest but hasn't written a thing yet.

Glen's throat tightens with an inherent sensation of filth after feeling like he has shared too much personal information. *What's next? Dana? Eleanor?* He shakes off his doubt and prepares an answer, reminding himself he is here precisely to share. To get help. "She was a drunk my entire life, among other things. Our relationship had been strained since I was a kid."

"I'm very sorry to hear that, Glen. Surely you can see how that sort of instability might affect a young, impressionable child. Even today, growing up in that environment has left a lasting imprint upon you, as it would for us all."

"I honestly never thought about it. She was my mom, and that was my life. There was nothing I could do."

"Correct, but that doesn't mean you deserved the hand you were dealt, either. Now, I have alluded to this already before, but allow me to squarely address the elephant in the room that you also recently found out that you are the son of a serial killer ... and not just any nitwit criminal but the biggest and baddest of them all," he says.

"I suppose, although I didn't choose that either. To my knowledge, every one of Brock's kills happened before I was even born, yet people around town have been giving me trouble for it."

"Trouble in what way?"

"A group of rebellious types attacked me at work yesterday," Glen grumbles. "Or rather, they attacked the office itself and I ran them off, although I suspect more will follow."

"I see. And today? Any incidents?"

"I didn't go. I thought it would be safer to stay home."

"Hmm." Dr. Hawthorne finally picks up his notepad and begins to scribble. "We call that avoidance behavior, Glen, and avoiding the places or activities that stress us out actually creates a cycle that can quickly snowball out of control if not addressed quickly and appropriately."

"Okay, and what should I do instead? Go to work and potentially be attacked? Put everyone else in the building at risk?"

"You are deflecting. Not surprising, given the sudden spotlight you have been forced into. I have cared for actors, musicians, and business executives that feel similarly after having been thrust into a position of extreme power and influence before they were ready to handle the load. To answer your question though, you should not *avoid* going to work and what other people do is out of your control. By that logic, you are probably not safe at home either. Do you feel safe at home, Glen?"

"Not particularly ... although I have never felt safe anywhere I go, including home," he relents.

"The addict mother and absent father, of course. I know you aren't living a life of luxury and glory, Glen, but I must ask you the same question I posed to the aforementioned clients; what is it that you want? This is your life now, whether you like it or not, so what do you feel would make it more comfortable for you?"

"I ... honestly don't know. What do you think I need? How can I be happy?"

"That isn't really my job, Glen. Happiness is as fleeting as a rainbow, and just when you think you've found the pot of gold, it tends to disappear again. I'm not here to tell you how to be happy but rather to help you find it yourself. Does that make sense?" the doctor asks.

"Mostly. Can I just ask what you recommend? I accept that I'm living a life I wasn't prepared to handle, and I'm aware of my sudden public profile. How do I adjust? How do I cope without chugging vodka every night? Because that is starting to sound better and better."

"Well, as a therapist, I can't recommend drinking alcohol, though off the record you might want to use it at your discretion if it helps. Professionally speaking ... that is rather complicated, Glen, as your particular situation is one that has never been seen by any mental health professional, guaranteed. Just as Brock himself was one-of-a-kind."

"I'm ready to hear anything you've got because I'm feeling near the end of my wits," Glen pleads.

"Well, let us relate life to the ocean for a second because it most closely resembles the ebbs and flows of a rising tide. Imagine you are the captain of a ship out at sea ... you have to expect to be hit with a few waves. The trick is not to try to hide from them but to prepare yourself by bracing for impact instead. We call that exposure therapy. Luckily, I planned ahead and prepared an exercise for you." He rises from the armchair and walks back to his wooden desk, pressing a button on the telephone. "We are ready for Cassandra now."

"Who the hell is Cassandra and why is she here?"

"Please hold your questions for a moment, Glen. The special guest will be joining us in just a second." A brief period of silence follows before a woman enters the room. She appears to be slightly older than Glen, maybe mid-thirties, and her gaunt cheeks and twitchy facial expressions suggest a hard life of extreme trauma. "Cassandra, please tell Glen why you're here."

The woman shakes like a leaf as she stares at him, struggling to force out words. "My ... My name is Cassandra ... and ..."

"He already knows your name, but tell him *why* I invited you here today," Doctor Hawthorne urges.

"I ... your father, Brock Blackwood ... He killed my mother when I was very young." She stands in place appearing as if she is going to either pass out or become violently ill.

"Cassandra, I'm so sorry. I don't know what to say." Glen sighs as the knot in his upper chest feels like it will be expelled in the worst way. The room starts to spin slowly.

"Don't you see now, Glen?" the doctor nudges. "How can you continue to drown in self-pity when there are so many people that have been impacted for life by your father's actions? Your problems suddenly seem rather inconsequential, don't they? What do you have to say for yourself?"

"I'm sorry ... I didn't do anything wrong ..."

Cassandra opens her mouth to speak before the doctor interrupts. "She is speechless, Glen, absolutely destroyed forever because of what Brock did. You say you're concerned about people seeking vengeance upon you ... Well, I say they absolutely deserve every bit of payback they aim to achieve and more."

Glen remains silent and stares at the two of them, unsure of how to proceed. The whole world seems to be against him.

"It's okay, Glen," Cassandra says. "I know—"

"Shut up, Cassandra. Glen needs to answer for all of Brock's sins because God knows Brock isn't here to speak for himself." Doctor Hawthorne smirks and stares directly at him, folding his hands on his knee once again. "So, Glen ... How do you choose to answer? You owe Cassandra your life, but how would you decide to move forward? Brock's heinous actions affected thousands in this city alone."

He looks back and forth between the doctor and Cassandra, feeling utterly lost for words. Brock's transgressions aren't his fault, nor is her life an issue for him to be concerned with. Glen looks into the woman's dark pools for eyes, knowing he will never know how to answer to the impossibly complex sequence of events that made up her story ... Yes, Brock was the catalyst, but how many decisions have been made since then? And how is he supposed to resolve them on her behalf on the spot? He stands quickly and sprints from the room, knowing there is nobody to explicitly trust anymore except for Brock's Babies and Eleanor.

He skips the crowded elevator and runs down the stairs, exiting from the back side of the building into an abandoned area of the parking lot and sprints toward his car. Once behind the safety of the steering wheel, he begins to ponder the value of his own life versus theirs. Would people feel better if he was gone? Many of them, yes, although something in his brain perks up to remind that dying is simply not an option.

Glen drives down his street slowly, looking back and forth for attackers or protesters that might be waiting for him. All is quiet, though he parks the car a few houses down to keep up the appearance that nobody is home. Even though three decades of misery were spent here, it is the closest semblance of comfort he has ever known, or perhaps the feelings of positivity are simply familiarity in disguise.

He walks through the back gate to avoid any potentially watchful eyes and heads straight for the kitchen window which his mother never locked. Whether it was due to superstition or wanting to leave a secret entrance for Glen, he will never know for sure, but it comes in handy now. Not daring to turn on any lights in the house, he walks quietly to avoid suspicion and only uses the backlit display of his phone to lead the way.

The box of film reels still sits in the living room, serving as a reminder that there are several more containers in the basement that will need to be relocated. Kathleen and her team might be able to assist with that task to get it done more quickly and therefore safer. They are of no matter tonight, the boxes or Brock's Babies, as Glen marches up the dark stairs and enters his old room.

So many endless nights spent here, suffering through uncertainty, discomfort, anxiousness, or often all of the above. On this night, there is a touch of despair thrown in the mix as he climbs into bed, seeking comfort in the worst way when the world would seem to be devoid of it.

Glen reaches over his shoulder and opens the nightstand drawer. Even in the darkness, he knows exactly where the desired object is located; Brock's bloody dagger, tucked in the back underneath old collectibles and junk papers. He grasps it firmly and pulls the blade into bed with him like a safety blanket and falls asleep for the night with it tucked against his chest in his now forbidden home.

# CHAPTER TWENTY-ONE

The moonlight is sickening as it pours into the bedroom between the two curtains that aren't quite closed. Glen has been staring at it for far too long, having woken up in the dead of night in a panic and lying still for hours, wishing desperately for the salvation of morning light.

He is alone in the house for just the second night in his thirty years, and even though his mother could have often been declared clinically deceased during that time, her presence was still felt. She had very little to offer in any capacity, but it was still enough to have another human life force present under the same roof.

Glen lies in bed and stares at the ceiling, hoping for her drunken, pharmaceutically preserved corpse to appear in the darkness and spill every daunting detail he will never know. *That* little voice resurfaces to whisper that only those who Brock killed are able to speak with him now, though she was just as much a victim of his than any of the others. The suicide was only a prolonged fate that was set in motion the moment she shoved that revolver in her mouth.

He leaps up and dresses himself, unable to lay down quietly any longer. An eternity could be spent wondering about what-ifs and the things that could or should've gone differently, but this pitch-black corner he finds himself shoved into has been incredibly insightful if nothing else. The ancient winds of change have arrived after many years of lingering dread. Nobody could have predicted they would have taken this shape, however.

Nothing in the bedroom is worth saving aside from the dagger, which he stuffs into his back pocket with the blade sticking upward precariously for safekeeping. They can buy more clothes, Eleanor said so. He doesn't own any pleasantries or keepsakes to take with him, a humbling reminder of a life spent in the shadows.

There are only a couple boxes worth saving in the entire house, those being the collection of tapes in the living room and the rest of Brock's belongings in the basement. The wooden box whispers to be taken first, though his mother's tape still sits in the VCR deck and needs to be retrieved. Glen presses the power button to eject it, but his fingers stretch and push play of their own power to see her another time.

The screen is black with white tracking lines running, left at the end of the tape where he turned it off without rewinding after her death. One more glimpse of her lively face should be enough closure. He reaches out again to press rewind when the room lights up from another video clip playing at the end. The recording begins with the camera lens struggling to focus. The operator moves it gently from side to side to reveal Brock lighting a cigar. He walks effortlessly, yet with purpose, seeming to be at peace with his surroundings as he surveys the area.

He appears normal and alarmingly human while staring forward with all the evils of the underworld buried behind his infernal eyes. Brock blows out a billow of tobacco smoke as Penny approaches, and he smiles at her. This is not the twisted grin of a serial killer that Glen has seen seared into his dreams and other videos, not the maniacal cackle shining through Tiffany's excavated skull cavity. It is a simple happy smile. Joy.

Penny places her hand on Brock's shoulder, and they speak inaudibly. She appears to be happy too, listening intently to his every word as he vividly details actions with his hand motions, leaving behind a smoky trail with the cigar. They must be planning a kill, yet the tone of the video would suggest anything but, with a beautiful backdrop of green trees and forest landscape around them.

The screen cuts to the river as Brock kneels to cup the flowing water, drinking the first handful and splashing his face and hair with the second. A leather sheath is attached to the back of his belt holding the same bone white dagger handle that Glen has come to know all too well. He turns toward the camera and points at the water with garbled speech while a gentle breeze blows through the foliage along the riverbank.

The implied threats of violence loom heavily in the video yet never come as Brock continues to wander the river with boyish wonder. Penny steps in front of the camera wearing a flowing summer dress that blows in the breeze. For the briefest of seconds lasting only a few frames, she appears to be pregnant before the fabric shifts in the wind again and she walks out of the shot.

The third scene transitions to the inside of a dark house and is noticeably more blurry. Brock is stuffing trash into black plastic bags with the infamous silver revolver sitting on an end table. No blood or gore in sight, yet his entire facial structure looks different from the man that Glen has been watching in the previous few clips. His eyes appear enflamed, or rather, engulfed in flames above a venomous snarl and protruding fangs. Glen blinks and thinks he sees the echoes of black leather wings stretching wide behind Brock's shoulders before blinking several more times and is left only with eye floaters and a lingering twitch.

Brock's demeanor changes rapidly as if he has been sedated. The sharpness to his features softens, the fire in his eyes has been extinguished, and though the sadism no doubt never left him, it appears to have fallen dormant on screen. The thorn was removed. "You can come back now, Pretty Penny. Time to go," he says through muddied audio, though his voice is also calm.

She walks into the room and stares at the vacant chair with hesitation. "Just the camera?"

"Yes. I already took care of everything else." He stares blankly at her for ten long seconds before his lip curls into a smile.

"What?"

"You truly are special, you know that? It's proven often but rarely do I get to *see* it. I can't wait for all that we accomplish together." The video pauses on that frame of him smiling at her for several minutes. She was the camera operator, and suddenly, it all seems too obvious.

*Penny cut this video of Brock's human side to convince herself that it really existed.* Perhaps she felt guilty and wanted to absolve herself of any responsibility or maybe to convince herself that he really did love her. Glen imagines her watching this video repeatedly to relive the tiny pockets of time when he might've been considered normal, though it likely took many hours of filming to compile even that short of a montage. That was her delusion, her illusion to cope, as the unbearable weight of guilt would have begun to wear down. To hell with it all.

Glen ejects the tape and moves swiftly in what little remains of the morning darkness to load the box of videos in his new car without being detected. He returns and enters the basement one final time and quickly carries the rest of the crates upstairs to stuff them into the increasingly crowded trunk.

Giving the house one last look over, he knows he won't shed a single tear for all his years spent living there nor for any of the useless objects left behind by his pack rat mother. Stacks of newspapers instead of family photos, piled up envelopes and past-due bills in place of meaningful heirlooms that could feasibly be left over from Abby's family before. Sickening. He feels the tug to leave it all behind so he may begin anew, free to live the next thirty years differently and under his own control.

Glen scoffs as he surveys the house one final time in a state of numbness. The voice reminds him to follow his impulses, and he walks to the not-so-secret kitchen cabinet where she hid her vodka. Half a dozen half gallon bottles remain, and he cracks the seal on the closest one to take a few quick swigs. Glen ignites all four stove burners and spits vodka over them on a whim, then grabs a handful of newspapers and tosses them nonchalantly onto the range.

Bright orange flames begin to lap at the walls as black and gray ash sprinkles the kitchen. Glen tosses more mail, bills, and papers on top to grow the fire out of control. He takes a few more swigs and grabs the other five bottles of vodka before walking into the living room and heaving one onto the stovetop. A small explosion rocks the house as he throws two more for fun and spreads the third across the room. The final two, following a massive chug in his mother's honor, are poured over her vacant armchair where she spent the majority of her adult life.

Glen backs up to the front door which he opens and steps outside as the unleashed flames follow the path laid out for them and frolic amongst the great many useless belongings left behind. "Burn, motherfucker," he whispers from the yard, knowing the job is done and that the house, and every memory within it, are to be dissolved into soot before the hour is up. It feels good.

He circles to the back and leaves his old car where it was, hoping people believe him to be dead for a while, at least. It might only buy him a day or two to move freely and fully disappear from sight, which would be the best gift he could ask for at this point. The house erupts in radiant flames as he watches for a final second from behind and drives away in the car to leave his previous life's messes for somebody else to handle. The Overton bloodline is gone; he is now effectively Glen Blackwood.

Glen pulls into his typical parking space with just enough time to spare before clocking in. He wrestled mightily with how to proceed, where to go, which path to follow, yet decision fatigue fought against logic and backed his brain into a corner where muscle memory eventually won out. Now he finds himself at the building he hates most, which is ironically the only place left he feels an inkling of familiarity. Instinct has resorted to autopilot.

Voices whisper as Glen enters the office and walks through the row of cubicles toward his own. He should not be here, words he has repeated to himself on countless mornings, although it has never been explicitly for reasons related to safety. They continue their outrage and whisper in fear and confusion as if a demon has walked inside a church.

"Glen?" Dana asks as she steps into the hallway. An angelic figure in a sea of darkness, the one person left who sees him without prejudice.

Her voice acts as an unfortunate call to the mob of hapless co-workers who didn't know his name a week ago. Dozens more heads pop up until the office is filled with their inquisitive, fearful, simple faces.

Glen freezes, only twenty feet from Dana and the safety of his workstation, yet the chatter lingers still. Their peering eyes, gossipy whispers, and nosy expressions; Glen absorbs their hatred and magnifies it within himself tenfold.

*How dare they ...* He trembles, feeling betrayed by the universe from the inside out. The whispers ... They began as indiscreet chittering but now sound like constant scratching of nails down a chalkboard, growing more aggressive by the second. *They all hate you,* a voice whispers. *They would rather you be dead so they can return to living under a false sense of security.*

Glen takes a daring step forward, and then another. Their responses grow more energetic as the whispers turn to vengeful scheming. A burning itch forms at his core that struggles to break free against his every impulse. *Stay quiet, step forward.* The apex predator cannot concern himself with the opinions of ... what, cockroaches? Maggots? Boring, burnt-out, corporate slaves like himself? The office fax machine beeps and begins to print several pages to pile on his inner noise level. The discomfort is all-consuming, causing him to feel utterly exposed as he takes another step to intensifying horror.

"What the fuck are you all looking at?!" Glen charges a cubicle and boots the portable wall onto its inhabitant. "You wanted a monster?! Well, here I am! Is everyone going to whisper in silence all day, or does anyone here have anything to say to the son of Brock fucking Blackwood?! I'm asking every one of you pieces of shit here a fucking question!" Glen kicks another cubicle wall over before smashing the copy printer with both fists.

"Glen?! What the hell do you think you're doing?!" Monica exits her office and stands before him, glaring down from atop her mountain of pent-up rage.

"Great, just what I needed today ... the office bitch! You're done giving me orders, Monica!" Glen eyes her devilishly and heads for the exit, seeming to shake the ground beneath each step as the onlookers cower in their corners and the affected employees crawl from the rubble.

Monica convulses, watching the pathetic pissant storm out of the room, challenging her authority publicly and winning.

Glen hangs a quick left for the stairs instead of the elevator to avoid seeing the security guard, receptionist, or any other humans in the building. He is done here, and his time as a data clerk could not be more forgetful except the moments spent with Dana. She will unfortunately be left alone to answer for his supposed sins, but that can't be helped now. Glen must leave the job and never come back if he has any hopes of self-preservation.

The stairwell leads through a steel security door behind the building where the morning sun hasn't yet reached and into a gloomy alley where he can pause for a second to plan an escape without event. A moment in time to reflect on all that has happened so he may plan accordingly for what is to come ... Something peaceful would be nice, but experience would suggest that won't be the case.

"The office bitch?! You're the only bitch I know!" Monica shouts as she kicks the door open and stomps toward him in her high heels with her finger pointing accusingly. "Whaaa, poor me, I can't ever go to work because my life sucks! Sounds like a little bitch to me! You think you're special now, don't you? Fame-seeking attention whore!" She moves closer and pokes him hard in the chest several times. "You always were a quitter ... weren't you, little *bitch*!"

Monica steps forward and shoves him as he digs his back foot into the ground and moves very little.

The rope tied around his chest is pulled tighter until the knot nearly snaps within. *Kill her ... Nobody would ever know.*

"Lazy shit-for-brains slacker!" she shouts, shoving him again.

"I'm warning you, Monica," he growls through gritted teeth. *Don't warn her ... Smash her smug face on the brick wall.*

"And what're you going to do? The rest of them inside might be fooled by the media, but I know the truth. You won't ever stand up for yourself because you're a little ... fucking ... bitch ..." she mocks with another shove between each word.

A shot echoes throughout the back alley like a volcano erupting as Monica's head explodes in a shower of raining liquid and skull matter. Glen stands frozen, staring at the remnants of eviscerated flesh before her headless body crumples.

"We have to get out of here, sir!"

# CHAPTER TWENTY-TWO

"Sir! With all due respect, we have to move right now!" Thompson shouts as he grabs Glen's shoulder with a strong shake. Glen continues to stare at Monica's body as his ears ring and pulsate. He looks over at the pistol grip shotgun hanging from the lanky Thompson's hand. "Sir!"

Glen shakes his head to clear the fog.

"We have people to take care of the mess, but you aren't safe here!"

"What about the building cameras? Haven't they already seen everything?"

"Eleanor had those shut off a while ago," Thompson mutters as he motions toward the end of the alley. "You don't have to worry about anything ever again, sir. We will clean this up, but you have to get to safety right away."

Two black vans speed behind the building with the first pulling beside them as the side door rolls open. Eleanor sits inside with a calming presence and pats the seat beside her. Glen takes the cue and jumps in, unknowingly sitting between her and Kathleen, who was hidden from sight before. He looks out the window as they round a corner to see the second van stop in the alley behind them while a team rushes the crime scene.

"What are they going to do with Monica's body?" he asks at last.

"She will be disposed of." Eleanor smiles coldly. "They will flood the area with enough chemical solvents to render any leftover drop of blood useless. We have been anticipating an event like this."

"Won't everyone I work with, or used to work with, suspect me? She followed me outside and will never be seen again. Isn't that suspicious?"

"As we learned from Brock, all that matters is what can, or cannot, be scientifically proven beyond a shadow of a doubt in court. That is why he was so efficient. Besides the point, dear, you have done nothing wrong. There is nothing to worry about."

"Nothing to worry about at all," Kathleen follows. "You're just not used to having people stand behind you."

"Congratulations, Glen. You are finally a free man and nobody can tell you what to do now. How does it feel?"

The gunshot sound followed by Monica's skull exploding like a bludgeoned watermelon echoes in his mind. "I'm not sure how to feel about it yet. I suppose I should be happier."

"In due time. This is a lot of information to process in a week, isn't it? New identity, becoming a public villain, losing your mother, killing the boss, burning your house down ... Nice touch on that one, by the way. Now your enemies will be sent into a tailspin for a while."

"Yes, well ..." He blushes. "Wait a minute, I didn't kill Monica."

"You've certainly thought about it, though, yes? Do you mean to tell me you didn't wish to murder her after she chased and chastised you in a dark, abandoned alley?"

"I ... was thinking about a lot of different things. That's why I didn't do anything, because I was trying to think through my options."

Eleanor scoffs. "You're a good guy, Glen, but that's also your biggest problem. You spend a lot of time making sure people think you're a good guy instead of acting how you want to, how you *should*. You don't know how to feel inside because you're so used to feeling like shit. So, I'll ask again ... How did it feel to see your boss be eradicated?"

"It felt ... good, like a wave of relief knowing I would never have to hear her shrill voice again. My hands have been tied for so long as she took advantage of being the manager, but I was forced to endure so much *bullshit* for a pathetic paycheck. I felt great knowing that even if I got caught, I would never have to answer to her again."

"Very good, now we are getting somewhere. The upsides to your new life will be vast; you are going to be financially independent and report to nobody. You already have access to your new home, and I can promise we have set aside a substantial amount of money for upgrades and modernization, anything you want. People work for you now, and unlike your recently deceased boss, they love to do it. They *worship* you."

"Can I ask about that part? I am still having a difficult time understanding why I deserve all of this," he laments.

"Why are the children of kings and queens special? You can't buy yourself into carrying sacred blood, Glen, no matter how much money you have. Do you know how many people would kill to be you? Yet, it is impossible. I came from nothing and made my own way through immense sacrifice and hard work that would have broken someone who didn't already grow up poor. Kathleen is the same she has earned her position by being the most dependable person working for me. But there is a dirty secret to the world, being that the wealthiest and most successful people are often simply born into it. You are a member of the latter group."

Glen thinks back to childhood nights without dinner, cooking himself barely edible meals, risking eating old and moldy food and hoping for the best. Wearing clothes that were too small, not washed, purchased secondhand, or full of holes. He remembers going days without speaking to another human and wishing for a friend, praying for things that never happened, and spending harrowing nights alone with nobody to lean on. The notion of royalty seems farfetched at best, although he keeps the opinion to himself this time. "I think my mind is having a hard time processing everything, that's all. Like you said, a lot of change at once."

"Indeed, and I will leave it alone for now after I remind you that a normal person would not have adapted quite so well or, more likely crumbled under the pressure. Once we get back to the house, you can have a drink, rest, read ... whatever you like, really. Kathleen will stay with you today. She is much more personable than Patrick."

Kathleen grins and grabs Glen's hand. "We are going to take care of you. *I* am going to take care of you. Everything will be fantastic soon enough."

"We are here to support you, Glen. All of us. You have not met all of Brock's Babies yet, but we are a family of sorts, the family you never had. You will learn to allow yourself to feel comfortable, no matter how long it takes."

"Thank you," he concedes. "I wouldn't have anything without you, Eleanor ... Kathleen. I aim to be the best leader I can be."

"That's the best part of your new life, Glen. We don't need you to do anything else but be there. You have already won. Like those kings and queens, you are an idol while those beneath you perform the hard work."

He nods, hearing the words without yet absorbing their meaning. His face flushes with the tingling sensation of an unfortunate epiphany.

"What is it? What's wrong?" Kathleen asks.

"My car, *your* car, back at the office, it's full of boxes from my old house. All of Brock's belongings and keepsakes." Though there is plenty of important and damning evidence to be found, he immediately thinks of the dagger first and video tapes second.

"It has already been moved. We could never allow such sensitive information to fall into the wrong hands nor would we risk it being destroyed. Much like Thompson had to make a judgment call to protect you, Glen."

"I will need to thank him for that as well."

"You do not need to thank us for anything; your presence is enough. Remember that the will to power is what drives all life. You are fortunate to have been born with it."

"Do you need anything, Glen?" Kathleen asks from the doorway.

"No, I'm doing fine, thank you."

"I can get your coffee, you know. You don't have to do it yourself."

He takes another sip and sets the mug down. "I'm not sure how to feel about this yet. I never even had a parent do anything for me, let alone people I just met."

Kathleen scoffs as she walks into the living room. "And? Did that make you happy?"

"Not particularly, although I never knew anything else to use for comparison. It just feels somewhat strange to ask you to serve me, that's all."

"That's why we're here, Glen, to serve you. That is our collective life's purpose."

"I thought you were a part of *Brock's* Babies, not Glen's Babies," he chides. "It doesn't even sound good."

"You go ahead and make your jokes, as is your right, but our reach is vast and it's all for your benefit. We've been searching for you since Brock was murdered, even if we didn't know for sure if you existed, and it sounds like you were subconsciously looking for us too."

"I hate to be rude, but—"

"Do not fear judgment here," she interrupts. "You could never hurt our feelings, so speak freely. You are, after all, The Only Son."

"Yes ... Well, you seem to be even younger than I am. How long have you been one of Brock's followers?"

"Most of my life. Eleanor adopted me at a young age after my mother suffered a similar fate to your own. Years of alcoholism led to an early, intentional ending."

Glen shifts uncomfortably, uncertain of how to respond to Kathleen, and still unsure of how to feel about his own mother's demise. "I'm sorry to hear about that."

"Don't be. Everything happens for a reason, and Eleanor gave my life purpose. *You* have given my life purpose, even if it was unintentional. Thousands of people, or more, have lived to serve the memory of a lost prophet who has delivered us another in his stead. We are elated."

"That is humbling, Kathleen, although I don't feel like I deserve it. I'm no idol."

She walks toward the couch and sits, then takes his hand in hers and smiles at him. "There will be an adjustment period, and that's why I'm with you today. Nobody knows or understands Eleanor like I do, and she has repeated stories to me as long as I have been able to listen to them. I'm here to support your needs as your transformation continues." Kathleen moves her hand toward his cheek slowly, pausing before touching the skin to await his response. "Glen, you said it yourself, you are not accustomed to being happy ... but you will get used to being important."

"I certainly don't feel important yet. People are dying ... Monica died because of me."

"And? Do you feel bad about it?"

Glen stares into her shimmering eyes. "No, I don't."

"Are you sad when you think about Monica?"

"No. I hated her."

"And she learned the hard way that there are consequences for provoking a beast. That's the natural order," she soothes, grabbing his hand again. "Besides the point, you didn't kill her; she did it to herself, essentially."

"I have a question, Kathleen, and I need an honest answer."

"Anything."

"Why Brock? I get he wasn't a normal person, but why is there a cult still dedicated to him twenty years later?" he asks, exasperated.

"That all depends on who you're having conversations with, doesn't it? Monica thought you were quite the prick, yet we adore you."

Glen smirks, trying to hold back a laugh. "Yes, that's correct. She held a special type of hatred for me."

"And? What did you ever do to her?"

"Nothing. Perception, maybe rumors spread by other people, or it might have been because I never kissed her ass, but nothing in particular sticks out."

"So, she was determined to not like you and went out of her way to do so? She was biased and would've hated you no matter what you did, is that what you're saying?" Kathleen lifts her leg onto the couch to get comfortable and turns to face Glen fully.

"Yes, although not in that exact wording. What does that have to do with Brock?"

"I am only making the comparison that people often judge others harshly with little to no information of how they arrived at that opinion. Most of the world only heard of him because the news plastered his face on their screens and called him a murderer, but he was so much more than that."

"But he *was* a murderer," Glen rebukes. "Brock killed a *lot* of people."

"So does cancer. So does heart disease, suicide, car accidents ... Need I continue? In Brock's Babies, we do not argue morality because it is as subjective as debating the best flavor of ice cream. All we know is something led him to do what he did and it's not for us to decide why. Brock represents ultimate freedom to do as one will, unbound by worry, emotion, or any of the other drawbacks associated with humanity. The chaotic nature of his actions might seem to make little sense from the outside looking in, though we wholeheartedly believe everything happened exactly as it should have. He saw something in your mother that other women didn't possess; he knew exactly what he was doing to have brought you here. Tell me, Glen, do you think a man who lived his lifestyle for as long as he did without capture would do *anything* without intention, including choosing who would birth his offspring? There are even those that believe he was only caught because his work was finished. You've been programmed your entire life to be repulsed by his name and image, but we are free to use our own minds here."

"Are you suggesting the people he killed weren't innocent? That they deserved to die?"

"No, I am only stating the fact that most people who die don't *deserve* it. Do you believe a young woman who dies in a car crash was a bad person and deserved that fate?"

"Not necessarily, no. That's why it's called an accident," he sneers.

"Right, and regardless of whether you call that bad luck, or some sort of elemental force that chose it was her time to die, does it make a difference? The outcome is the same."

The urge to argue rises inside his mind, along with a dozen other voices with conflicting opinions, mostly all spouting the propaganda he had been force fed since birth. *There is no such thing as luck.* "Yes, you're right," he concedes.

"I'm glad you understand now." Kathleen rests a hand on Glen's shoulder and leans in to kiss his cheek. "You will only begin to accept your new life, your heritage, as time progresses. I have a question for you now, if that is alright."

"Yes. You can't upset me."

"You have already told me bits about your mom, but have you always been alone? Or has anyone ever been by your side?"

*Dana.* "No, nobody," he fibs.

"You poor thing. We will be there from now on; you will never have to face the world alone again."

# CHAPTER TWENTY-THREE

*S*orry everything turned out the way it did. *Coffee tomorrow?* Send.

Glen sits on the edge of his bed and tosses the phone to his side, feeling just a touch foolish about destroying the office in front of Dana. It's late and she might already be asleep, but the offer is worth extending anyway, if only to reaffirm that no malice was directed at her.

This is his first night in a new house since the day he was brought home from the hospital, and it is as strange as expected. The floor is different, as are the noises, air, and wallpaper. More than anything else, this bed is uncomfortably comfortable. Eleanor wasn't lying when she said plenty of money was invested to modernize the house; his last bed was decades old and hard, while this one probably feels how a good mattress should.

Glen opted out of taking Brock's childhood room and chose the master upstairs instead. Eleanor proposed that Kathleen would also stay in the house during his adjustment period because he feels most comfortable with her. Patrick, Thompson, Reginald, and Carol take alternate shifts patrolling the perimeter.

His phone lights up the dark room after a slight vibration to the bed. He reads the text from Dana: *No need to explain. You know what time we're off.*

At least one thing is similar to his old house, that being the solitude inside. His mother would usually have been passed out long before this hour, and the most noise she would make was from the TV set downstairs. Brock's home feels similar in some respects, sort of like a big, brooding, haunted house.

Kathleen also turned in early, though Glen suspects she will remain on high alert until the dead of night in case of an event, though he is skeptical anything would happen. This place is as safe as any, though he admits part of that comfort comes from knowing they are just downstairs. She is certainly Eleanor's daughter, even if not by blood, though the intense presence and demeanor have imparted well.

Glen rises and walks around the master bedroom, feeling tension fade away with so much space to spare. His old room could barely fit a bed and the cramped layout often reflected upon feelings of being trapped in his own life. This is a small throne room for a king, or at the very least, a place to escape reality's many burdens. A place to hide, some may say.

"Psst, Glen ... Over here."

"I'm doing fine, Kathleen. I don't need anything else. You should get some sleep too."

"Not Kathleen—Louise. Please, help me down from here."

Glen turns to see a young woman dangling from a noose and recoils. Her legs kick several feet off the ground and a bone sticks out sharply beneath her jaw where the neck snapped. The skin is stretched as if her entire body weight hangs by the flesh that is at risk of tearing.

"Get me down ... I can't breathe," she continues.

"You seem awfully calm for someone who can't breathe."

"Yes, well, I have been stuck here for quite some time. That box in the corner, just put it under my feet so I can stand for a moment."

Glen eyes the crate of Brock's keepsakes and slides it over. "There. Now you can be comfortable until I find my knife."

"Don't worry about that. You shouldn't have come here, Glen, it isn't safe."

"The protesters, I know, but they won't find me. Not yet."

"It's not the living that worry me," she broods. "Not all of us have accepted our fate in equal favor, and there are those who still seek vengeance on Brock. Tell me, who is the only Blackwood left standing now?"

His face tingles. "Me ..."

"They will be coming. You should not be here. So blinded by hatred, they will gladly attack you in your father's place. Go now, seek shelter."

"Go where? How do I defend myself against the dead?" he asks with desperation dripping from every word.

"You don't fight. You can only endure."

Glen turns quickly in all directions searching for Louise, but she has disappeared. "Where are you?"

She drops from high in the sky as the rope catches her weight and snaps her neck. Louise sways gently with bulging eyes staring at him and blood running down her chin. Glen looks down to see a loose shoe and the tip of her tongue on the floor, bitten off during impact.

A lifelong phobia of entrapment begins to smother him again. The house is not safe, outside is not safe ... His mother's house wasn't safe even when it was still standing. He remains frozen, unable to flee for fear of what might await outside his bedroom door.

"Louise? Are you still here?" Glen calls out.

She doesn't answer.

Taking a shaky step forward, the floorboard creaks to send a rippling shiver throughout his body. He glances at his phone with half a mind to call Kathleen upstairs yet feels even more ashamed to have entertained the idea. She is in the house to protect him from real threats, not console him like a mother comforting her son after a nightmare.

"Louise is dead. You can't speak to her now," a voice calls out from the shadows.

"She was dead when I spoke to her ... What would have changed?"

"Yes, she was dead ... and it's *your fault*!" a woman screams as she dashes toward Glen and violently slashes at his chest with a rusty blade. Her hand passes through without injuring him, though the pain of icy despair lingers in his lungs. "No violent person ever feels guilt for their aggression, otherwise they wouldn't have committed such heinous acts! How convenient of you to feign innocence once we have cornered you!"

"I've never hurt anyone before. You're looking for my father, Brock!"

"You've never hurt anyone? Don't make me laugh," a teenage boy scoffs from behind him as the walls dissolve into a suburban backdrop.

"Ronald?"

"Yes, it's Ronald. Don't you remember nearly beating me to death? I finished the job on your behalf after high school because I felt so ashamed!"

A shadowy vision of Glen walks home from school alone and cuts through the woods. Two boys follow him from a distance, breaking into a jog to catch up before he disappears in the trees. Ronald sneaks behind and yanks the loop at the top of Glen's backpack to throw him to the ground. The boys laugh and high five with an overabundance of arrogance, having conquered the younger and smaller Glen yet again. He grasps a fallen branch quietly and snaps to his feet, swinging the thin end across Ronald's face to open a pulsing laceration from ear to cheek and drops him helplessly to the ground. The other boy flees, crunching small sticks and pinecones on his way back to town, leaving his shrieking friend behind to writhe in pain helplessly on the forest floor. The young Glen turns the branch over in his hands, grasping the thinner side as he swings the thick end into Ronald's ribs with a crunch and a thud.

"Don't you see? You have been predisposed to violence since day one, almost as if you were *born* to do it," Ronald sneers as the vision of the woods fades away and the room returns to black.

"You attacked me! YOU bullied ME! I felt dread walking home from school every day because of you, never knowing when I would be senselessly beaten!"

"And yet ... Which one of us never reached adulthood, Glen? Which one of us killed himself because of the shame that came with being seen as a weak school bully who couldn't even beat up a younger kid? You made me feel powerless and inadequate which were the reasons I picked on other kids in the first place! You killed me, Glen ... just like your *father* killed my *mother*."

"No! You don't know that for sure! You can't blame me!" He thrashes through the air to push Ronald away. Glen runs toward his new nightstand and grabs Brock's still bloody dagger for protection before fleeing through the bedroom doorway.

He dashes down the stairs and finds himself in utter darkness again. Gravestones shoot up two at a time from the suddenly grassy ground all around him, each with a dim candle beneath to illuminate the names and dates of death.

"Look around you," a woman hisses. "Look at their names, burn them into your memory, and don't you goddamn dare say it's not your fault!"

A hand grasps the back of Glen's neck firmly and forces him to stare at each stone. *Olga Orloff, September 21, 1972.*

"I wasn't even born yet! How could I have done this?!"

Olga bursts through the ground and climbs out with nearly forty years of dirt covering her body and dropping from her dehydrated lips as she speaks. "Who else is there to castigate? Lucky Brock rests in hell while we are stranded here with *you!*"

Glen panics and rushes Olga, stabbing Brock's dagger into her phantasmic cheek. She dissolves in a pile of dust as her gravestone rumbles and sinks back into the earth.

"You killed her and we saw it!" two more feminine voices shout from opposite corners of the cemetery and charge toward him.

*Maria Gonzales, April 18th, 1978*, and *Patricia Andersson, May 1st, 1980*.

"She was already dead! I didn't hurt her!" he shouts, slashing through the throats of Maria and Patricia as they lunge at him, reopening decades old gashes coated with scar tissue. Patricia falls to the ground face first and the back of her head erupts as if a bullet blows through it.

Rows of graves stretching to the horizon burst open as dozens of women climb from their tombs and glare at him with an assortment of mortal wounds. Some with gouged eye sockets, others holding their own severed heads by the loose neck flesh. They all scowl hatefully at Glen. His knees begin to clatter as he clings to the dagger.

"And what of me?" another voice asks from beyond the circle of corpses. The rows of bodies slowly back away to create a path for the new arrival to approach. Her face remains mostly obscured behind a wedding veil as she lumbers forward.

"Mother?" Glen calls out. "What are you doing here?"

Young Penny looks up at him at last with the same fresh and vibrant face from the videos. The twinkle in her eye fades to gray as her features begin to darken and pulsating lesions open on her decrepit face. Hints of crimson bleed through the abdomen portion of her pearly white wedding dress and increase in volume as her midsection throbs. "Did you not cause me immense anguish? Brock would have continued to love me if it wasn't for *you*! The sniveling, needy toddler that became a parasite of an adult! We would've gotten married and lived happily ever after, but you ruined my life!"

Glen drops his head to look at the dagger for strength before responding. "Brock ruined your life, Mother ... Then you allowed your addictions to finish the job ..."

She walks closer toward him and rips the veil open, then takes his face in her hands and speaks with rank breath of alcohol and musty earth. "I only drank because of *you*, Glenny. You have to know that. You did this to me."

His cheeks grow unbearably cold beneath her touch as the surrounding victims step closer.

"You always were a whiny little shit," she seethes.

He struggles to break free while more and more hands grasp at his clothes and grip his skin with their clammy palms. "You must join us ... Atone for his sins," they chant in unison. "Brock's Only Son must face his punishment!"

"Stay with me, Glen." Kathleen pats his cheek while holding a wet washcloth to his forehead as his body twitches across the couch. "Wake up."

He finally opens his eyes and leaps up, tossing the much smaller Kathleen to the floor as he pants like a caged beast. "Where am I?!"

"You are safe and at home," she replies, rising to a knee.

"I'm sorry; let me help you up."

"That's alright, it wasn't your fault."

"I'm still plenty embarrassed." He blushes, kneeling to lift Kathleen and help her back to the couch. "What happened to me? Why am I downstairs?"

"You were having fever dreams, I'm afraid. It didn't seem like a whole lot of fun."

"Fever dreams? Am I sick?"

"Spiritually sick, yes." She stares with comforting eyes. "You're struggling to accept who you are deep within instead of the false illusion you have been led to believe."

"I don't know what else to do."

"You are doing an exceptional job. It will only take time. Your sense of routine will fight with your instinct as they both battle for dominance. Overton versus Blackwood, if you would rather think of it that way. There is a folding cot in your room that we placed there in preparation for this happening. I will sleep there for the next few nights, if you don't mind, of course."

"No, I don't mind," he pauses, thinking of how trapped he felt in the room. "Although I would like to rest down here for a little longer."

"Whatever you need."

Glen lies still as she continues to dab the wet cloth on his forehead, periodically giving it a snap in the air to make it cold again. The comfort and care he never received his entire life, and didn't realize he was subconsciously craving, now have him lying paralyzed on his back as Kathleen takes complete control over him. He stares at the ceiling mindlessly, feeling himself melt into the couch without the will to move again.

"Is there anything I can get you, Glen?" she asks after a long silence.

"No," he answers truthfully, though his voice sounds to have come from a faraway place. "I feel ... comfortable."

"As you should." Kathleen dabs his forehead again and runs the droplets of water through his hair. "That's a sign that you are getting better."

"Good."

"Yes, it is good. It won't be long now until you are feeling like yourself for the first time in your life."

"I do feel different, like ... I'm home. This is where I belong, next to all of you."

"No, Glen, we belong *behind* you. But for tonight, just rest." She continues to run the water from the washcloth through his hair, decreasing in pace with each subsequent pass.

His breathing begins to slow as he stares at the ceiling in contentment, realizing even getting drunk to drown his sorrows didn't feel so secure. This is something worth fighting to hold onto at all costs.

# CHAPTER TWENTY-FOUR

Glen returns downstairs for coffee to see that Kathleen too has disappeared and likely gone back to her bedroom. He did disturb her sleep after all, and she deserves to rest as long as needed.

The one thing he will never get used to is having others serve him his coffee. The ritual of grinding the beans and watching boiling water turn into his morning beverage is too soothing to pass off to someone else who probably wouldn't make it right anyway.

"Good morning," Kathleen startles him from behind.

"Good morning. I thought you were still sleeping after the night we had."

"Funny, I thought the same. Besides, I've been in this house cleaning and preparing for the past week as we waited for you. There's no way I'm going to sleep my days away now."

Glen looks back to check the coffee pot and has an odd feeling come over him to think that they have been waiting and planning ever since they heard about him. Something between pride and uneasiness. *What made them so sure you would come here?*

"I'm making myself some coffee. Would you like some?"

"How dare you, Mr. Blackwood. You know it's my duty to make *your* coffee."

"What does a man have left if he can't make a cup for himself?"

"You will have *everything*." Kathleen lights up. "Anything in the world within our grasp will be yours, and I can assure that Eleanor's reach is vast. You'll like her. She's the single most determined person I have ever met."

"I already like her."

"Then you will love her as your own mother. She will—please forgive me, I did not mean to be insensitive. We hold great respect for Penny, as any woman who was special to Brock must be truly important."

"You don't need to apologize. I know what you meant," he dismisses. "But yes, she was certainly a complicated woman. As is Eleanor, I suppose, though they are polar opposites in nearly every sense aside from their connection to Brock—I mean, my father."

"Don't worry, it will feel more natural in time. You're lucky; not many people get to find out their father was someone famous."

"I'm still working on that part."

"You met me because of it, didn't you?" She blushes. "You're still adjusting. Keep an open mind and be cognizant of all the good things coming your way. Anyway, what do you plan to do with the first full day of your new life?"

"I have a few more loose ends to tie up before I can disappear from all my old circles."

"Is that wise with all that's happened?"

"I'll be fine. This is something that has to be done to collect everything I left behind and tie up my loose ends. My ... co-worker will bring the items, and I trust her with my life." Glen nods.

"Very well. I hope she's able to come through for you. We'll send a caravan behind for your safety, although they will stay far enough away to allow you plenty of privacy."

"That's fine. What about the car? Has it been emptied of Brock's belongings?"

"Yes, I believe they've been stored in the basement."

*How fitting.* "Then tonight I will be able to close the book on my old life and focus my attention here. She won't be a factor moving forward," he fibs.

Dana takes a step closer than usual and embraces Glen in a big bear hug, having suffered through two days of work mostly alone for the opportunity to do so. "I'm so sorry to hear about your mom. Please tell me you're doing alright?"

"Yes, I'm fine, try not to worry."

"How can I not? You just lost your mother, and the last time I saw you, someone pushed you far enough to kick our cubicles over and storm out of the building," she snickers.

"Yes, well ... I'm not totally proud of that. I shouldn't have lost my cool at work in front of all those judgmental eyes. God only knows what they're thinking now."

Dana stares at him for a moment as a twinkle swells in the corner of her eyes. "Fuck 'em."

"What?! Did you just drop an F-bomb?"

"Yes. Fuck 'em," she cackles. "They don't need to know anything about what you're going through nor do they have the right to ask questions about it."

"I can't say I disagree, although I didn't expect you to take that sort of stance."

"Why not? The company is falling apart, and the workers are more focused on spreading gossip every day than working, not that any of us ever did much to begin with. Monica didn't even show up this morning."

"Oh ... she didn't?" he asks in a discordant whisper, sounding like a stranger to his own ears. "That isn't like her."

"Yeah, and nobody heard from her either. It's weird. Maybe she finally got tired of being reviled by so many people."

"You know she loves being awful."

"Yes, she does." Dana chuckles before clearing her throat. "So ... that's it, then? You're done there?"

"I can't go back. It's not safe for me or anyone else if people know where I work, and things will only get worse with Monica moving forward. You know she won't let this go," Glen says so convincingly, he momentarily believes she's still alive.

"Let you get away with something? Never. What will you do for work? How are you going to afford your bills?"

"I will ... I'll be staying with a friend of mine."

"Oh ... *a friend*? Can't say I've ever heard you speak of them before," she chides. "You do realize that houses still cost money even if you aren't actively staying there, right?"

"It won't be a problem. I'm going to go grab my coffee now, would you like one?"

"Glen."

"What, Dana? It isn't going to be a problem anymore." He clears his throat before leaning in close to her and whispering, "The house burned down, alright? My old home is gone."

"Burned down?!"

"Keep it quiet, would you? We don't know who is waiting around, but yes, there was an accident and it's gone."

"You haven't been attacked again, have you?" she asks with concern. "Were they the ones that lit it on fire?"

"No, it was just a freak occurrence, although the thought has definitely been on my mind since Monday. I'm sure they've been waiting by the office for me."

"I haven't seen anything, but yes, you're probably right. I don't blame you for not going back; you would be a sitting duck up there."

"I already was once. Thank you for understanding, I didn't know how you would take it." He sighs.

"It's your life, dork. I just want you to be safe until everything returns to normal. We're going to get you through this."

"Thanks, Dana. If I'm being honest too, it's only you that I want to protect at work; I don't care about anyone else."

"I knew what you meant," she says while blushing. "But fuck 'em, right?"

"Yes, exactly." They share a cackle just a shade too loud, but Glen doesn't care. An attack here would be unfortunate, but Thompson has already proven himself a maestro with a shotgun, and he is undoubtedly close by.

"Do you ever get dark thoughts that appear out of nowhere? Like things you can't control thinking about?"

*Yes, all the time.* "No," Glen says. "Why do you ask?"

"I was just wondering because of everything you've been through ... strangers attacking you ... don't you think about hurting them, even if it's only hypothetical? Don't you want to make them pay for it all?"

"I did when we were standing face to face, yes, although I suppose I felt more calm than anything else. I felt at ease."

"I guess that makes sense too. I don't know; I get these thoughts sometimes, and they pop up out of nowhere. Sometimes it's horrible," she grimaces. "Like I'll be driving and my brain tells me to run my car into a crowd of children."

"Jesus, Dana."

"Okay, I was only kidding to see if you were really paying attention. Your eyes were beginning to look rather glazed over, but seriously ... I do get dark thoughts at times, like the urge to jump when standing at a ledge or feeling like I might accidentally drift into oncoming traffic. I have felt that way since I was a kid, right around the time my mom died. Anyway, my dad said it stems from feeling a lack of control, or something like that, so that's why I asked. I imagine you might be feeling similarly. Actually, I can't even fathom what you must be going through."

*Control*, something Glen has never experienced until it began to manifest in the past few days by Kathleen's doing. "It's difficult to describe in only a few words."

"You don't owe me any answers. I just hope you never feel alone, that's all. At the very least, I'll be here for you."

"You always have been before. Likewise, although I could never repay all that you've given me."

"No need." She smiles. "It's unfortunate that someone so kindhearted has been thrown into this mess. Though I also find it ironic how many people would love to be in your shoes and experience a type of fame, even if it's the wrong kind."

"I don't want it ... All I ever wanted was a normal life, to feel content with being boring."

"I know, but it seems that is the reason you were chosen. The universe has a way of force feeding us what we don't want and withholding what we do."

"Life sounds awfully cruel when you put it that way." He smirks.

"I was going to suggest it is a way of keeping balance, but malevolence shouldn't be ruled out either."

"Like the supposed grass always being greener on the other side to keep us from ever reaching it?"

"Something like that. Or maybe we're at our best when we're uncomfortable and off-guard. What if everything happens for a reason and you were born the son of Brock simply because you would hate it? Sort of like a test," she muses.

"I hate tests."

"I do too, but like my dad always used to say, it's hard to see the world clearly through amber colored eyes."

Glen stares at her before releasing a genuine guffaw. "I'm sorry, but I don't have even the slightest idea what that's supposed to mean, Dana."

"It means you can't see life for what it is if you are constantly under the influence of alcohol; being drunk becomes the new normal. A drink or two is nice, but too much will kill you."

"Too much of a good thing, yes, I understand. Everybody wants to be famous until they realize it's a death sentence one way or another."

"Exactly," she says with a smile. "It was a long day at work today, since some of us still go, but that's what I'm trying to say. The way you reject the spotlight only bodes well for you in the long run. The people who crave fame all eventually become consumed by desire."

"First of all, nice burn. Second, I hope you're right. I would give anything to go back to being a simple office worker, entering data and sending you email forwards all day."

"Fingers crossed. I also had a thought, and it might just be the fake lawyer side of me talking, but have you considered filing an insurance claim on your old house? You might make enough money to buy yourself a new home and live comfortably until this mess is over. Just a thought."

"No, I hadn't thought of it yet, but I feel like I will need a bit of coffee first before we dive into that topic. I'll go get us some and then we can continue." Glen gives her a nod and rises from the tall table to walk toward the register. The two of them have been visiting this coffee shop after work for years, and the sense of routine is comforting.

A young couple at the front of the line take their time to order. Glen looks around the shop, having already been here what seems to be a million times before, but there is something new to see each time. A large television screen hangs on the wall displaying a news channel, though he has only ever seen sitcoms or game shows playing on it before. The reporter speaks to an older man on the wrong side of middle aged.

*And who do I have the pleasure of speaking with today?* the perky female reporter asks before shoving the microphone into the man's face.

*My name is Liam Moore, and I am the president and organizer of a community group called The Defenders of Virtue.*

Glen takes a step forward as the couple finally walks away to sit at a table and wait for their drinks.

*And why are you here, Liam? What are The Defenders of Virtue hoping to accomplish with this showing?*

*We are gathering in the streets to drive away the filth! Blackwood's blood has returned to the Pacific Northwest, and he will terrorize another generation if we allow him to walk freely among us! Our numbers are now in the hundreds, and we are growing every day!* Cheers wash through the city so loudly, Glen almost believes he can hear them outside.

*But isn't he due a fair trial like any other American citizen? Shouldn't he be given the opportunity to speak his side? What happened to innocent until proven guilty?* The reporter appears almost alarmed on-screen.

*What about our daughters, sisters, and mothers that were never given a fair chance? What about the innocent young women that were given an unearned death sentence because of that sick son of a -BLEEP-?!* The mob behind Liam bursts into a roar as police officers stand by with their hands at ease. *We will never have peace until the cancer is rooted out for good!*

"How can I help you, sir?" the barista asks from behind. Glen turns around quickly as he feels the blood drain from his face, having momentarily forgotten where he was. "Sir?"

"Oh, I'll have the umm ..." he stumbles while searching for the words, anything at all, though the television set calls for his attention once more.

*All of you out there need to be aware, THIS is your enemy; Glen Blackwood, formerly known as Glen Overton.* Liam holds up a photo that Glen doesn't recognize, though it is clearly him. *If you have any information, please call The Defenders of Virtue at-*

The news broadcast cuts off, leaving only static behind. Glen turns around in horror with his eyes bulging and beads of sweat forming on his forehead. The young barista holds a similar expression to his as he turns and quickly walks toward the back.

# CHAPTER TWENTY-FIVE

"I have to go, Dana. I'm sorry," Glen announces as the crowded coffee shop sits up and takes notice. She only nods fretfully as he dashes through the doors but leaps up and follows closely behind.

He spots the black van of Blackwood's Babies parked down the street, choosing instead to duck down a side street and avoid attracting attention. *Headed back home. Situation turned ugly.* Send.

Ugly indeed, as the militia could have popped up anywhere nearby the coffee shop, or possibly even inside it. He didn't recognize the street on the news right away, but that doesn't mean it was safe to be alone that far into the city. Someone might have seen him and made a phone call to set up an ambush as soon as he walked out.

*We noticed. Heading back now.* Kathleen's text comes through as Glen reaches his car and surveys the area for attackers. He parked in an isolated area to begin with, and the coast seems to be clear. A second vibration comes through his phone. *Do you need us to escort you?*

*No, I'm safe. Don't want a scene.* Glen pulls out of the parking lot quickly and quietly with his eyes ritualistically checking the three mirrors in succession for followers yet sees nothing out of the ordinary. A distant car finally appears in the rear-view, although it's several blocks back and by itself. Clearly not an ambush.

Glen takes several odd turns to avoid the main streets and notices the same gray sedan behind him that resembles Dana's. His eyes glance back and forth between the road and mirror as the car speeds up to keep just close enough. Is it truly her? Or another attacker? A bead of sweat rolls down his temple as he considers stopping and allowing the situation to play out until the person disappears after another turn. Of course, there must be tens of thousands of gray cars in the Seattle metro area.

Glen pulls safely into his new garage tucked away in the backyard and breathes a sigh of relief to have made it back to home base. He slips in through the back door as the front door opens to reveal Eleanor walking in first, followed by Kathleen, Thompson, and the others.

"Glen ... I'm glad you are safe," Eleanor greets with her voice of worldly wisdom.

"I was never in danger, but I fled the city before anything could happen."

"As you should have. I was watching the news broadcast myself, and this is no threat to be taken lightly. You see, Glen, for every one of us who celebrate your return, there are even more who oppose it, and they have begun to grow violent. That is of no concern to you; we have both the numbers and financial muscle to counter their every move. However, I have dealt with Liam Moore personally, and he was a young police officer while Brock was at large in the early eighties. He is expressly motivated to hunt you down and will not stop fighting until that happens. It seems your father murdered his young wife while Liam was working an overnight shift. Unfortunate, really, as that was one of the driving factors that led to Brock's capture, if you believe he truly was caught. At any rate, I feel you should not be alone at any point until this civil war of sorts has ended. I will triple your security here at the house and ensure that you are never out of sight once you leave, which should only be sparingly, though I do not want you to feel like a prisoner. It is quite the opposite."

"Thank you, Eleanor, and everyone else here. I agree; we must proceed cautiously and move in the shadows until peace has been made."

"I'm glad you are in agreement, Glen." She smiles. "Though there is another matter that must be discussed and perhaps even more urgently given the circumstances."

"Of course, what is it?"

"One of your father's ulterior motives was to leave an heir to carry on the Blackwood bloodline before an unknown enemy might imprison or kill him. He understood the importance of leaving another behind and very intentionally sought your mother for reasons only he understood."

"Are you saying that you want me to find a spouse and have a child?"

"We already have your willing partner, Glen. My only daughter, Kathleen, would be honored to carry your child, and she also holds a special connection to Brock as well."

His expression softens as he watches the young woman step forward and bow her head. They lock eyes as she allows herself to grin ever so slightly. "I am the granddaughter of Virginia Harrington ... Brock's very first victim."

"And my birth name is Eleanor Harrington, Virginia's daughter. It is so nice to finally meet you as my true self, Glen."

"Wait, the two of you are related by blood?! Kathleen told me you adopted her and that her mother was an alcoholic?"

"Not a far stretch by any means," Eleanor scoffs. "I was an alcoholic, Glen, not unlike the late Penelope. I was only a young girl when Brock killed my mother, and it sent me into a tailspin for decades, until I was nearly your age. Virginia visited this very house to check on one of her students, who had been displaying sudden signs of alarming behavior in the classroom. Times were different back then, as teachers were more involved in their students' wellbeing, although this particular time ended up spelling the end of her. She knocked on the front door, but Brock's parents were out on a bender of their own, and he invited her inside before butchering her in the hallway closet you have already come to know well. Thus began the Blackwood Legacy."

Glen places his hands on the back of his head and tucks his elbows to his ears. "I'm so sorry that happened to you, Eleanor ... Kathleen ..."

"Are you truly sorry, or is that simply the further regurgitation of societal programming? Do NOT be sorry; Brock made me who I am, who we *all are*. After decades in the gutter, drowning in self-pity and having my own daughter taken away from me, I finally broke for good and was reborn like a phoenix in the ashes. I could never have been as successful as I am today on my own, not without Brock initiating the everlasting butterfly effect that continues its influence even still today. Do not dare feel sad for me, Glen, because your father forced me to become superhuman, the likes of which your corporate zombie co-workers could not even fathom reaching. Brock was my idol, because I learned of the utter hell he was born into that would have broken the gods themselves ... Not him, though. No amount of suffering he endured could break his otherworldly willpower, and much like myself a generation later, he learned to ignore the pain and used it as fuel to transcend. I am thankful for him every day and would gladly give my own life if my daughter might reap the same benefits."

Kathleen notices Glen's bewildered expression and sits next to him just as she did after his supposed nightmare. "I know this is a lot to handle, and that's why we didn't want to overwhelm you at first. But you see ... you are The Last Blackwood. The line of succession simply cannot end so soon."

He turns to gaze into her eyes, feeling utterly lost within his own existence in what has become a shockingly common occurrence recently. "Brock's Babies ... That's what this is all about? To force me to give you a child?"

"To preserve your lineage, yes, in one way or another," Eleanor cuts in. "And you are not being forced to do anything, although I hope you come to understand how crucial it is that you father at least one child so your bloodline can live another generation. Kathleen will take great care of you and your baby, should the day come, and my resources are of course at your disposal."

Glen nods at her with shellshock as Kathleen squeezes his hand. "It's alright. You don't have to make any decisions right now. We will still remain by your side."

"Yes, we will. Our loyalty runs much deeper than your need to produce an heir, Glen, and Brock's Babies are at your service indefinitely." Eleanor stares at him with her regal blue eyes and begins to speak but pauses for another second instead. "Let me tell you a little story, though. Once I pulled myself from the depths of hell to create EcoHarbor Solutions, I drew direct inspiration from the pain I felt my entire life up until that point, how helpless and weak I had become through my multiple tragedies. You see, Brock was directly responsible for forcing me to reach my full potential and become something I never knew was waiting within; a transcended human. All it took was a push in the right direction for me to evolve beyond emotions and simple desires. I created an empire, and EcoHarbor currently employs over fifty thousand who are all paid competitive wages. I donate millions to philanthropic causes, environmental initiatives, children's hospitals, medical research, and more, while I myself live a lavish life beyond belief and fully fund Brock's Babies through my own profit. All of this ... *because of Brock* ... Now tell me, who are we to judge his actions if they have led to such prosperity? What was my mother's tragic death compared to infinitely positive outcomes in return?"

Glen and Kathleen listen intently as Eleanor tells her story with more passion than he has seen her express thus far. She's now running her fingers through his hair while they listen for more.

"As my company continued to grow, I began to think about all the others that were affected by Brock's whimsical killings. Were they thriving as I was or still stuck in the thralls of addiction and suffering? And thus, Brock's Babies was born as a way to help others dig deep inside themselves and find their true purpose as an alternative to tragedy. I searched far and wide to gather the broken orphans, siblings, and parents to offer them a way to break free from his transgressions, how to rephrase what they were feeling as a bottomless well of inspiration, rather than a death sentence of their own. Once there was a sizable group gathered, we began to administer DNA tests to each of our members, hoping someone might be the lucky winner to match with Brock. Surely, *someone* must have been fortunate enough to be his child, right? Yet none of them were, and we continued our search for years to come. Believe me when I say, Glen, that we have been hoping to find you for well over a decade now and your sudden appearance did not disappoint. Everything happens for a reason, no matter what else you believe in, and I am certain this is my purpose; Brock's grandchild will be the same as my own, finally uniting us under one purpose only he understood. That is the only way to make sense of all I have been through."

"I will need some time to myself to think this over," he speaks finally. "That was quite a story, and I am thankful for all of Brock's Babies keeping a close watch on me now, though I need a bit more time before making a decision."

"Take as much as you need. We are united under his vision, yet you are the only remaining living carrier of Blackwood blood, Glen. You must be protected, even if all of us need to die in the process. All of my money and successes mean nothing if I don't allocate my efforts toward preserving that which gave me power. Our families were destined to be joined ... Brock may have made you, but my mother made Brock by visiting this house on that fateful day. You may take your time in deciding, but I am positive you will lean in Kathleen's favor." Eleanor smirks as she rises and places a hand on his shoulder. "I must be going now, but there will be plenty of security posted up and down this street. If you have any unfinished business out there, I would make arrangements to resolve it tonight and make sure you take more than enough bodies with you. See you soon, Glen."

Everyone in the house exits through the front door to leave the two of them sitting side by side on the couch in a brief and awkward silence.

"I don't want this to be weird now," she laments.

"Kathleen, I don't think my life could get any more strange at this point than it has over the past week."

"Are you saying ... Do you not want me?"

Glen turns his head to stare at her for several seconds. "I do. Nothing seems real at the moment, that's all. I feel like I'm watching everything happen to me from a distance."

"We can fix that with rest and time. You've got nothing else to do now but enjoy yourself, possibly for the first time ever." She leans in and kisses his cheek then lays her head on his shoulder. "Our child would be something this world has never seen. Even though it would be technically born from a long line of tragedy, I believe it's still possible for us to raise it with love, as originally intended. Imagine the power that Brock and Eleanor's grandchild might possess if given a proper chance at life?"

"Yes, that would be great. To be honest, I wouldn't even know where to begin as a father. Mine was obviously absent."

"That's okay, so was mine. What's inside is what truly counts though, don't you think? Do you believe we are born to be the way we become, or are we made through life experiences and teaching?"

Glen blinks rapidly and allows his own head to lean against hers, feeling closer to another human than he ever has before. "I don't know. I don't really think about things like that."

"Well? What do you think now?"

"If I had to choose, then it would be the first option; I believe we are born to be who we are and can't really change. Some people start off rich, or poor, and that sets them down a path that guides them their entire lives."

"Then you agree our baby would be born into power?" she says as her face lights up.

"Yes. It will have money, caring parents, and the blood of royalty. I grew up with only one of those, although I wasn't able to reap the benefits of it at the time. At the risk of asking a ridiculous question, do you happen to have any names in mind already?"

"Of course, I do. My mother has been reminding me of my destiny for most of my life. I like Melinda Blackwood for a girl and Brent Blackwood for a boy."

"Brent?!" he exclaims.

"Yes, Brent. It's the closest thing I could think of that is a cross between Brock and Glen. You should be thankful I considered you."

"I am, but who would be terrified of someone named Brent?"

"Probably the same people that are afraid of a Glen," she snorts.

"Fair enough."

"And what would you name your baby boy?"

"Colin. Colin Blackwood," Glen states proudly.

"I would love to make fun of you the same way you did me, but I actually kind of like that. Colin Blackwood."

"I do like Melinda, though."

"Thank you. I have been dreaming about having a daughter named Melinda since I was five years old. I even wanted it to be my own name for a while, because I hated being named Kathleen at the time," she admits, sinking into his arm even further.

"Really? I like it. That's a classic name but still undoubtedly feminine. My name is *Glen*, remember?"

"Yes, how could I forget? Although ... I like your name too. Or maybe I like it more because it's attached to you. I can't even explain how much of my life has been devoted to searching for you, Brock's son, or just hoping you even existed. My mother and I spoke about it every chance we got, wishing he left an heir behind and musing over the potential opportunities. Do you want to take a guess at what I wished for after blowing out my birthday candles or whenever I saw a shooting star?"

"For me?" he shrugs.

"For you. For Brock to have a son out there somewhere, because he and I barely shared a world together. The wildest part is that it took us another twenty years to find you."

"Well, if it makes you feel any better, I didn't know I existed until just last week, or at least not the real me. I had been living a lie with a mother too drunk and drugged to remember who she used to be."

"Don't worry about a thing, Glen. You're home now," Kathleen soothes as she nuzzles next to him. They sit in peaceful silence for several minutes before a burst of agitation causes him to jerk away. "What is it? What's wrong?"

"I was thinking about my mom, and there's one more thing I need to do. We need to go back to my old house and make sure there is nothing left, nothing that could give anyone more ammo against me."

"But you burned it to the ground."

"Exactly. I burnt the walls down to expose our secrets to the world."

# CHAPTER TWENTY-SIX

"Why are we parking this far away? The house is at least a few more blocks up the road," Kathleen comments, slightly annoyed.

"Eleanor's orders," Thompson replies as he begins to exit the van. "She wants us to do this quietly and leave as quickly as possible. 'Without fanfare', in her words."

"Although if there *is* fanfare, we are at a huge disadvantage being this far away from our vehicle, don't you think?"

"Sorry, Kathleen. Our sole job is to protect The Only Son while he accomplishes his goal here."

"Thank you, Thompson. I'm sure everything will be just fine," Glen reassures Kathleen, though she's not convinced.

"Patrick, stay with the van and we'll call for help if needed. We will look less conspicuous with fewer people anyway and there are still five of us."

Patrick freezes, presumably unable to make the decision for himself. Glen nods his approval for Kathleen's plan, and they exit the van with Thompson, Vince, and Carol rushing to form a loose semi-circle around The Only Son.

"I don't want to stay long, just enough to scan the remains of the house for any undamaged evidence," Glen affirms.

"Are we looking for anything in particular?" Thompson asks.

"Anything related to Brock. My mother hid his old photos, clothes, and memorabilia." *And murder weapons*, the voice adds, though that is the one secret he hasn't allowed himself to relinquish just yet. "Boxes and boxes of incriminating evidence."

"Sounds *amazing*," Carol adds.

"It was, although any piece of it could give the police the ammo they want and make life even more of a living hell alongside our new friends, The Defenders. I have nothing else to tend to once we handle this errand, and then we can hide out in the house until the storm is over."

"And what a storm it's been," Kathleen chides. "You've made quite a few people very unhappy simply by existing, Glen."

"Yeah ... no shit," he mutters under his breath.

"We have someone approaching, sir," Thompson whispers as the four of them take a step closer and hover their hands above the pistols on their hips. "Hold here until he passes."

"We're going to just sit and wait? What if he attacks?" Vince frets.

"It's five on one, and we're *armed*. What damage could he do?"

Glen stares at the young man, who is no older than about twenty, and feels a sense of familiarity deep down. He approaches quickly through the street light shadows and sidesteps closely around the group as he passes, staring directly into Glen's eyes. "Good evening, sir."

"Do we know him?" Kathleen asks in a hurry. "Is he one of Brock's Babies?"

"He's my old neighbor," Glen responds. "Benny. I haven't seen much of him since he was a kid, but his house is a few doors down from mine ... my old home."

"We need to be even more swift now. No matter who he is, you have been recognized, and we can't afford much more risk."

Glen nods and continues walking the short distance to the burnt and decrepit lot that used to be his own. Charred wood beams jet out in jagged patterns that now seem like an even more fitting home for the son of a serial killer than his current, borderline lavish, living arrangement. The scorched, black construction echoes memories best left forgotten of tumultuous days and harrowing, sleepless nights. Of the greatest ironies, he spots his mother's recliner in the center of the foundation, mostly untouched by fire, though a wooden plank has fallen from the upstairs and now rests across it. Glen exhales sharply and steps past the 'condemned' sign and over caution tape.

"Be careful, sir. Nothing about these remains inspires a sense of stability," Vince warns.

"No, it's not stable ... it never was." Glen steps forward gingerly into the old living room and looks up toward the bare night sky. "Most of our belongings were upstairs and that is obviously gone now. The only other place to check would be the basement, and then we can go."

"Sir, do you believe it's safe to be down there? What if the roof collapses around you? Allow me to go instead."

"We are standing on it now, and I have not felt as much as a creek in the wood. It should be fine, and regardless, you wouldn't know where to look in the dark."

"Very well, sir, although might I go down with you just in case? I will provide cover if we are suddenly in danger," Vince vows.

"Of course. There is only one area to check. My mother was something of a packrat, but she kept all of Brock's belongings and keepsakes in one specific corner. Kathleen, Thompson, Carol, the three of you wait here and scan for anything else that appears out of place."

They nod solemnly and watch Glen and Vince climb down the stairs into the abyss. Kathleen's face sours.

"When we reach the floor below, we'll go to the direct opposite corner of the basement and search there. Do you have your flashlight, Vince?"

"Of course, sir." He removes it from his pocket and shines the thin, bright beam of light into the specified corner. Thoughts of ghouls and evil eyed creatures scurrying into hiding seem appropriate in the dark, yet there are only towers of wavering cardboard boxes waiting. Most of them have been left undamaged, though a few show signs of being kissed by flames from above. "If you don't mind me asking, what is all this stuff, sir?"

Glen scoffs. "My mother's every belonging, old dishes, clothes, you name it. I hardly ever ventured down here because she said it was unsafe, probably to protect her secrets. Nearly all of it's junk. This is the area, right here."

An open space with a square of dirt between two stacks on either side reassures Glen that he grabbed everything in the pile at the very least. He *knew* he did, but the itch to return, whether psychosomatic or not, needed to be satisfied while in a clearer state of mind. Closure, maybe.

"The empty space is good, right? That's where the artifacts were?" Vince shines the flashlight in the hole and waves it around.

"Yes. I did grab the bulk of it the last time I was here, but I also don't know if there is anything else hidden. My mother was incredibly secretive, and there's no telling what else she had tucked away down here. That's what worried me more."

"We could burn it on our way out and leave nothing to be found."

"I have considered that as well, although I wouldn't want to raise any more red flags while the community is so agitated, or at least, not while we're still here. Eleanor is going to send another team tomorrow to destroy whatever is left, but we didn't want to risk losing anything of Brock's," Glen trails off as he scans through the dozens of cardboard boxes, reading each label, and moving on rapidly. There is no guarantee that any of the labels are accurate or truthful, but they don't have the time to empty each one and separate every item.

"Yes, that makes sense. It would be a great shame to leave something irreplaceable behind."

*Or something I might need*, the voice reminds selfishly. Glen put them all at risk to come back in hopes of finding something else of Brock's that provides the type of value given by the dagger, something else that will help teach him *how* to be a Blackwood. This is his last-ditch effort to grasp a buried secret from the past and use its influence to guide his future. "Although the problem with irreplaceable objects is they are also often easy to trace. That should be it. I checked all the boxes."

"Nothing?"

"Nothing." Glen takes the flashlight from Vince and scans the open floor space one last time, catching the lid of the shoebox that says 'Brock' across it. He placed it on the shelf when moving the videos and left it behind. "Or maybe not."

"What is it?"

"Just what I needed. We got it; let's get back to the house." Glen smirks as he turns off the light and stealthily digs out the photograph of his parents before placing it in his shirt pocket. He cradles the box in his arms like a baby and returns upstairs with Vince closely behind. "I knew there was something I left behind, the most important piece of all." He holds out the shoebox to show Kathleen, Thompson, Carol, and Vince the collection of items they couldn't do without.

"Well, what is it?" Kathleen asks.

"Let's get back to safety and we can go through it then." A piercing burst interrupts their conversation and drops Vince to the ground with a veil of red mist left behind where his head was. Glen stares as his sworn ally crumples and tumbles back down the basement stairs seemingly in slow motion with much the same sensation stirring in his mind as when Monica was dispatched.

They all turn quickly to look across the street and see a gray-haired man leaning out his upstairs window, pulling back the bolt of a hunting rifle. A streetlight catches the brass sheen of the spent shell as it is discarded and spins through the air, bouncing multiple times on the window sill before falling to the ground beneath.

"Glen! Get to cover!" Kathleen screams. "He's going to fire again!" Thompson leaps into action and wraps an arm around him as another bullet whizzes by and blows a hole in the armchair. He shoves Kathleen and Glen behind the still-standing fireplace while Carol unholsters her pistol and returns fire from the old living room. "Let me help you!"

"Not a chance. We can't risk anything happening to either of you."

"It's a little late for that, don't you think?"

Thompson only stares at her stoically and removes his pistol before turning to take his place by Carol, firing as quickly as his index finger will allow.

"Patrick, we need you the fuck over here right now! Call everyone within shouting distance for backup! I repeat, get down here right away and call for backup!" Kathleen screams into the radio.

"Yes, ma'am, right away."

"He shouldn't drive in front of the house. He will only get shot. There is a road behind the backyard where we can meet him," Glen adds.

"Scratch that, Patrick, Glen says you can get us from behind the house. DO NOT pull up in front or you will be taking fire. Copy?"

"Copy that, be right there. Cavalry on the way."

"Who is that? The cavalry?" Glen asks.

Kathleen stares at him with a blank expression that turns to a shimmer in her eye. "We did tell you there are many more members of Brock's Babies you haven't met yet; well, here they come."Another shot fires in the night air from a separate house and drops Carol to the ground in a lifeless heap. Thompson dives behind the armchair and shoots the first attacker once through the forehead, causing him to drop out of the window and fall to the yard below, landing headfirst in a scorpion shape and snapping his already dead neck. The second shooter rings a siren from his house and continues to fire before he too is dispatched by the militant Thompson.

"We need to go!" Kathleen shouts to him, gesturing toward the backyard.

"What about Vince and Carol?" Glen asks.

"They are long past saving and would've gladly traded their lives for ours. Our safety is more important than anything else."

He nods before noticing Thompson's condition and pauses. "You've been shot."

"No worries, sir, it's only my shoulder, and I have another. I will serve until I die." The lanky, yet strong Thompson winces as he places a hand on each of their arms and pushes them toward the exit in the backyard. The van approaches with Patrick in the driver's seat, his headlights serving as a homing beacon for escape.

Thompson grabs both Carol and Vince's guns before leading Glen and Kathleen to safety, driving them forward through his own visible agony. With only ten feet to go until they reach the van, another man steps into view with a rifle of his own pointed directly at them and quivers as he reaches to yank the bolt. Thompson leaps in front of Glen and blocks him with his body while bracing for another projectile to pierce him.

A sickening crack fills the alley as the three of them flinch to see which one wears the bullet. A body collapses on the floor in a pile, yet Thompson, Kathleen, and Glen all remain standing unscathed.

"Benny?" Glen asks.

"At your service, sir." The young man bows as he holds a baseball bat over the armed man, who lies on the ground with the side of his head caved into a crescent shape.

"We owe you a great debt, Benny." Kathleen nods in return. "You can come with us once Thompson searches you first. No offense."

"Of course."

"Hop in the van, Glen. We don't need any more stray bullets finding their way toward you."

He climbs inside as Patrick rejoices. Thompson gives her a nod and shuffles Benny in the back, followed by Kathleen, and then himself.

"Get us home, Patrick, and please do it quickly."

"Yes, ma'am."

"What the *fuck* was that all about?!" Kathleen exclaims as she rubs her eyes in exasperation.

"The neighborhood watch, um ... ma'am," Benny answers. "The Defenders have been organizing factions throughout the suburbs, although they've been on high alert here because they assumed you would return eventually. I have been attending their meetings to learn more about you, sir."

"Thank you, Benny. I shouldn't have come here, but we can't repay you enough for saving us," Glen commends him.

"It's my pleasure to serve, sir. I always wanted to be like you when I was a kid, and it was unbelievable to learn that you, my old neighbor, had been Brock's son all this time."

"How many more militants are out there?" Kathleen interrupts.

"The Defenders? There must be thousands of them now throughout the city and more are joining across the state every day. Retired law enforcement, pissed off housewives, bored dads, they're all joining in droves."

"It might be time to get you into deeper hiding, Glen. This is bigger than we expected, and my mother owns properties across the country. We could disappear for a while and let people forget."

"That's the problem, Kathleen, nobody seems to be forgetting about Brock." Glen bites his bottom lip and furrows his brow. "He's been dead for twenty years, and the very mention of his name has stirred up this much trouble."

"With all due respect, Glen, it's you they are worried about now, not Brock. They aren't concerned about the memory of him; they're worried you are the reincarnated version of him returned from the dead. Metaphorically, of course. Jesus, we expected a bit of pushback, but this—"

"This is only the beginning," Benny cuts her off. "Liam plans to increase pressure throughout the city and kill him whenever they get a clean shot, as you just saw. At the very least, they want to scare him away, but it won't stop there."

"And that's the problem; who should be afraid of whom here?" Kathleen seethes and smacks the seat beside her. "They have taken the offensive based on whispers of fearmongering within the community. They have become embold-ened without reason, and we need to put them back in their place." The van screeches to a halt as the three passengers slam into one another. "Jesus, Patrick, be careful! Thompson is dealing with a gunshot wound already!"

They idle in position while the sound of the engine humming smoothly rings through the cab. The headlights illuminate the suburban road to reveal a mob lined from one curb to the other carrying torches, hammers, pipes, and other blunt weapons. Several of them part in the center to allow their leader, Liam Moore, to stand at the front with a megaphone in hand.

"Patrick, we need to get out of here right now," Kathleen urges as Thompson primes a rifle for safekeeping.

"I can't make a clean U-turn on this street. It will take too long and they might catch up to the van."

"Then put us in reverse and gun it until we can turn!"

"Glen Blackwood, I hope you can hear me in there! My name is Liam Moore and we are The Defenders of Virtue!" His voice is muddled through the mega-phone, yet the message is clear as Patrick speeds backward as quickly as the van will travel. "We will not allow the filth of your family to infect our community as it once did! Kill the killer!"

The mob erupts in rowdy cheers and hollers as they repeat the chant with increasing vitriol. "Kill the killer! Kill the killer!"

Kathleen pulls out her radio and raises it to her mouth. "Are you getting close, Oliver? We desperately need that cavalry!"

"Yes, ma'am", an older sounding, gruff male voice speaks from the other side. "Closing in now, just need an exact location."

She smirks and stares at Glen as his eyes widen. "Didn't I say you were a powerful man? Now you will see the full extent of it." Kathleen raises the radio once more with the faintest shimmer of Eleanor's ethereal ego. "Yes, Oliver, we are staring down a mob on the corner of Cedar Drive and Birchwood. Keep it non-lethal unless it is absolutely necessary otherwise."

"Copy. Be right there."

"Wait here, Patrick. Let Glen see what happens to those who stand against us."

Another black panel van, identical to theirs, rounds the corner ahead of them and skids to a halt diagonally across the street. The back door slides open and ten soldier-like figures file out with large guns in their hands and masks on their faces. They begin to fire grenades into the encroaching crowd as smoke fills the neighborhood and shockwaves cascade toward Glen's van down the road.

"They're only non-lethal rounds … for now." Kathleen smirks. "We wouldn't want to make a bigger scene than necessary."

The Defenders attempt to scatter, coughing violently with tear-stained cheeks, and falling to the ground after the attack of smoke and percussion grenades. Glen watches through the windshield with wonder as dozens of his enemies begin to panic and struggle to breathe.

"Oliver, do you hear me?" she continues.

"Loud and clear, ma'am."

"Make it hurt, if even just a little."

"Yes, ma'am. With pleasure."

A few of Oliver's soldiers don gas masks and reload their grenade launchers before marching directly into the crowd and firing large projectiles into the chests of the protesters as they continue to choke on the smoke from the initial assault. Another man steps forward and shoots three more percussion grenades into the chests of The Defenders. They bounce off and ignite only a few feet away, knocking their limp bodies back in a type of ragdoll shock. One soldier inadvertently launches a projectile into a protester's mouth which erupts to blow open the unhinged jaw like a toothy Venus flytrap.

"The Defenders should feel lucky. We have plenty of firepower ready to go, but hopefully this will make enough of a statement to deter them. No sign of Liam, either. That's enough, Patrick, we can get back to the house now. Oliver has the rest covered from here."

The van completes its turn and drives the opposite direction of the skirmish taking place. Glen shuffles to the back window and gazes at the cloud of smoke and hazy torch fires burning in the growing distance. He can swear he sees someone in the fog take a grenade to the face then pass out atop their own torch and gradually go up in flames.

"This is all because of me," Glen whispers quietly enough so nobody can hear him. His face remains stoic.

# CHAPTER TWENTY-SEVEN

"This will not stand," Eleanor seethes calmly with her jaw clenched, her emotions represented by the tip of an iceberg concealing her true rage beneath. She takes a pause with a sip of single malt to gather herself. "Vince and Carol are dead. Thompson was shot."

"Glen and I might both be dead too if it wasn't for Benny. One of them had a gun pointed right at us, but he snuck up and killed him."

Eleanor smiles at the young man and nods her head gently. "We are forever in your debt, Benny, so please accept my sincerest welcome into Brock's Babies. There is a brief, yet harmless interview process involved and I am certain you will pass. Thompson would typically oversee that process, but we will be giving him adequate time to recover from his gunshot wound. Until then, would you mind telling me how you knew about us?"

"Thank you so much for accepting me into the group. I will serve the cause proudly. To answer your question, I'm a member of an online forum dedicated to Brock Blackwood and there have been rumors of your group's existence for years."

"How many members are part of this forum of yours?"

"Thousands, at least. There are members from across the fifty states and a smaller number are scattered worldwide. They're absolutely thrilled that The Only Son has been found." Benny nods intently.

"Do you mean to say that you have all known Glen was Brock's son this entire time?"

"Yes, well, I mean ... there was one user who posted a long and detailed thread about it ten years ago, but he is inactive now. Nobody took the idea seriously at the time, although the thread has been resurrected since the news spread last week."

"And how did this ... poster know? They specifically mentioned Glen?" Eleanor asks.

"More specifically Penny, but yes, he did say the name was Glen. He said he traced all of the past murders and found out that Brock had been seen several times with the same woman, something unusual for serial killers, and he discovered her name was Penelope. Though there was no proof and the theory was quickly dismissed as a farfetched conspiracy, just like most of the stories surrounding Brock. I read that post when I was eleven years old and found it fascinating that my neighbor's name was Penelope, though we all called her Penny, and her son's name was Glen."

"Fascinating, indeed. You and your network will be of great use to us, Benny, like our eyes across the globe. And we will need you to facilitate that through the forum. Be cautious not to draw the eyes of law enforcement; don't use any specifics names or locations yet."

His jaw drops slightly before he catches himself and regains composure. "I would be honored ... absolutely honored to help. I'm confident we will be able to assist you, and if nothing else, there are at least hundreds that would leave their lives behind to join you right now. They would die to protect The Only Son."

"It seems at least a few of them will. We are going to strike back and prepare to send all of these blue-collar halfwits and weekend warriors back to their holes. We have not come this far to be derailed so easily."

"For The Only Son!" Kathleen shouts.

"For The Only Son!" everyone else in the house repeats.

Glen stares at his new friends, allies, and family, feeling mixed emotions about the identity thrust upon him. Carol and Vince are dead because of him, as are Monica and at least one unnamed assailant, but it is difficult to imagine Oliver didn't kill several more. He can't quite find the proper words to describe these feelings, although remorse would not be one of them.

"Glen?"

"Huh?"

"I asked what you think we should do?" Kathleen repeats.

"I think we should relocate for the foreseeable future. Getting trapped in a back-and-forth with the protesters will definitely lead to more of us dying, and that will only hurt our main mission. Right?"

"Right." She allows a subtle grin to appear across her mouth as she looks down at the floor.

"That is a fantastic idea. Benny, I would like you to find a geographical area where we will be able to gather significant support for Glen and guarantee his safety. We will send a team with him as well and keep the remainder of Brock's Babies here to clear the distractions. We must also move quietly to not draw their attention once he has gone incognito. Above all else, I want to reiterate my undying devotion to the cause ... to Glen." Eleanor toasts with her glass.

"To Glen!" they all repeat again, raising their own, and downing their drinks.

"You are certainly free to do as you wish, Glen, as we are only here for your benefit. That being said, and perhaps it goes without saying, I highly suggest you don't leave the house for any reason until we find a suitable place for you to land safely."

"And when might that be?" he asks, exhaling sharply.

"It is nearly midnight now, but we may be able to make arrangements by tomorrow night or the following morning at the latest. The Defenders will lose interest quickly once they realize they are marching the streets endlessly for no reason. Oliver will see to it that they are properly persuaded to find a new hobby. We should all be sure to get some rest here tonight and work on escaping in the morning, if that is okay with you, Glen."

"Yes, you're all welcome to stay. You were here before I was, after all."

Eleanor scoffs, showing a surprising sense of humor for the first time. "That is correct, although it is yours by birthright. I will stay in the basement with Kathleen and everyone else can take rotating shifts on guard duty. Thompson, you should not fight, though I know you won't listen if the time comes. Please ensure that the guards are alternating properly and see to it that Benny has access to a computer. And so help me, make sure you monitor your wound and call the doctor if it worsens."

"Yes, ma'am." Thompson nods.

"There is a clear path out of this mess, but we must take each step with extreme caution. I'm afraid there is no more room for slip-ups, and we will need to move strategically from here. I am going to get a few hours' rest and return to work early in the morning. I suggest you all do the same as soon as you are able." Eleanor stands and gives them a faint nod before descending into the basement with her familiar half-floating walk.

"We'll leave you and Kathleen alone, sir." Thompson nods, smacking Benny on the back of the shoulder with his good arm. He ushers the rest of Brock's Babies from the room to assume their posts.

Glen remains in his seat with a radiating tingling sensation pulsing from his core. The feeling is a warning to heed, yet what's the message and why does he feel this way? He has no desire to move from the couch, sinking under the weight of an unwarranted witch hunt, suicide, buried secrets, and suddenly assuming a legacy he never wanted. Suffering through visions and reliving Brock's atrocities while losing everything once considered to be ... normal ... yet wading through a new bloodline and leaving the rest behind might be preferable to revisiting a lifetime of misgivings.

"I guess we should get some sleep." Kathleen interrupts his trance-like interlude to remind him that it is not Dana offering thoughtful advice now.

"Huh? Yes, I should be getting upstairs. It's been a long day."

"It has ... I should be going to the basement now."

Glen doesn't move. He continues to gaze forward with a glazed over expression that suggests he won't be getting up soon. The thoughts and emotions of death continue to cloud his mind as screams fill his memory, the last echoes of life escaping from Carol and Vince. His vision adjusts again, revealing the shrieks to be emanating from Brock's house like a snow front rolling frost across everything in its path. Dark and angular shadow figures stretch and float from room to room, although Glen remains at ease, even welcoming of their presence.

One of them descends slowly and places her phantasmic hands on his cheeks. *Or you could lie down here, and I will take care of you again?* she asks, sounding eerily similar to Kathleen. The touch even feels like hers.

"Yes, I would like that," he drones at a volume no louder than a whisper.

The shadowed hands embrace his face with a cool caress, and they begin to rub. Icy imprints of everlasting comfort tingle in his cheeks, and he smiles. *I can feel how far away you are, Glen. I know it must be a relief to finally escape.*

"Yes ..."

*Take as much time as you like. You will always be safe in my arms.*

Glen nods mentally, though his body doesn't move; it can't. The swirling of spirits around him closes off the outside world from existing in his brain. He feels a true sense of togetherness, as if he isn't utterly alone for the first time in his life, even when surrounded by a room full of devoted allies. These shadow entities don't need anything from him ... They exist freely without direction, a family of the dead within his own home.

"I feel safe ... with all of you around. I feel full ... Complete."

*Brock's Babies will always take care of you. You are safe at last, Glen.*

He doesn't answer, allowing the long, black, spider-like fingers to smoothly wash over him and implant themselves into his skin. Exhaling slowly, every muscle within his body releases decades of repressed agitation. The room is dark, though he can see them all clearly like floating and sharply highlighted outlines. Their murmurs are indistinguishable from one another, yet the collective melody is nothing short of harmonious. The one closest to him, the voice that resembles Kathleen's, has fallen silent for the moment, although the shadow it belongs to has latched itself into his core and he likes it … possibly even loves it.

*I have been meaning to ask you something, Glen,* the voice continues at last. *What was in the shoebox you found? I hope it was important for what it cost.*

"Yes … How did you know about the box? Were you with me?"

*Of course, I was. I will be with you forever, Glen.* The entity leans closer and brings with it the agony of a violent death, though the convergence of their essences more closely resembles a kiss on his forehead, followed by several more. *Forgive me. I should not be so forward.*

"But I like it. I want … *this* for the rest of my life. I feel the lost spirits circling, but yours has a certain warmth beneath the chill that the rest do not … You are the only one that has burrowed itself into me, and I don't want you to leave. The box was my father's … It once contained some of his personal belongings and even held a dagger he used to kill someone."

*Brock's lost dagger … Are you certain?*

Glen exhales sharply again as he absorbs the excitement and wonder through his skin. "Yes. There was blood still on the blade. It's in my bedroom, and I will carry it with me for as long as I live."

*Oh, Glen … you have no idea how happy that makes me. You will use that dagger to do great things.*

"Yes."

*You will use that blade to destroy anyone who stands against you … Anyone you wish!*

"Yes, I will."

*You will use it to carry on Brock's legacy! Don't you see that you were drawn back to your old house for a reason? This is destiny in action! Carol and Vince were necessary sacrifices to ensure you complete your transition!*

He lays still, staring up at the waves of black light circling his vision. "I will use it to channel Brock. I will use it to preserve this feeling I am experiencing at all costs." The shadow's chill grows colder as it crawls over more of his body, its reach extending throughout Glen's core, and he embraces it.

*Yes, you will ... I can feel it. I wish there was more to give you aside from my soul. Maybe I will give you a son.*

Glen stares at the distant ceiling clouded in darkness and watches a visualization of this spirit rushing into his veins through the puncture wounds it opened with its sharp fingers, their essences coalescing into one before his eyes. The mixture of two separate clouds of mist combine to create something new and unique that he has never seen before. He no longer feels quite like himself, but it doesn't matter anymore. "I would like that ... although I don't know the first thing about being a father."

*Neither did Brock. That's why you have me.*

The idea of an eternity with these spectral spirits excites him, knowing he will never feel alone again. After all the years of being bullied, raising himself, never having a true friend, it would be difficult to return to the loneliness of those times, and he suddenly wishes he could have conferred with the dead as a child when he needed their camaraderie the most. Their infernal wisdom would have come in handy during those moments he was forced to resort to the most basic instincts of violence. This being communicating with him now ... is divine. "I need you to stay with me. I have been wrought with fear for the darkness and the dead since birth, although they followed me like a shadow and finally feel comforting ... There is a sense of euphoria to the screams of corpses both old and new. I can hear their anguish, but I only want more."

Kathleen smirks sharply as she continues to caress Glen's head and cheeks. She has dreamed of contributing to the Blackwood bloodline since she was a little girl, listening to stories from Eleanor about how so many other girls would have given anything to be with Brock. She told her how only the luckiest women caught his attention, as he wouldn't even know that many of them existed. She talked of his personality and how he changed the world for the better. People acted more honestly and with more civility, humility, and gratitude than before or after Brock's reign. They were united under a common fear, to know that any of the women, or the women in their lives, could disappear at a moment's notice and never be found again. Sometimes it was worse when they *were* found, Eleanor said, but Brock also brought an intangible excitement to life depending on one's perspective. Those same fears were often seen as a reason to live each day to the fullest because no one could know when *he* might surface, the supposed boogeyman and fabled bringer of the apocalypse. As with any tragedy, everybody chose one side or the other—either completely abandon worry or be consumed by it. *You want more? Then take it. Take what you want, let no human stand in your way. You possess Blackwood blood, yes?*

"Yes," he answers, still caught in a trance between here and there.

*Then use it wisely. Lead. Conquer. Do what thou wilt. We do not know why Brock did what he did, although in hindsight, there always seemed to be an ulterior motive. Some might call it fate, or destiny, or the will of divine beings, yet we always trusted Brock's decisions to be the results of natural selection. You will uphold that responsibility now, as will our son after him, and hopefully many generations afterwards.* Kathleen looks down at his dilated pupils as the eyelids slowly flutter and shut without another sign of struggle. *Goodnight, Glen. May you sleep as peacefully as Brock lived, without a care except for that which he manifested himself.*

# CHAPTER TWENTY-EIGHT

"Wake up, Glen! It's moving day!" Thompson jokes through the bedroom door after knocking on it several times.

He jolts up in bed and can't remember getting there. Kathleen stirs from the large sofa in the corner of the room. "We'll be right down!" she shouts back. "Good morning, Glen."

"Good morning. I thought I fell asleep on the couch?"

"You did ... sort of. Strange things can happen to the body after intense adrenaline rushes, but I helped you upstairs and stayed here with you. I hope you don't mind."

"Not at all. I think part of me was wishing you would." Glen rises from the large bed, still in his clothes from the night before. Kathleen smiles and folds the blanket she used to cover herself on the couch.

"Thompson is right, though. We need to have you prepared to go as soon as we get the call. I'm going too, of course."

"Of course." He nods, giving her a second glance. Whatever happened last night left a deep imprint that he can't shake. "There was something else I have been thinking about, Kathleen."

She stops what she's doing to turn and listen intently. "What is it?"

"I understand the purpose of Brock's Babies and that we are supposed to ... have a baby together, but how did the group end up with a military wing? I don't see the connection between the children of Brock's victims and an armed unit to destroy the opposition."

"That is both a simple and complicated question to answer. Brock's Babies *is* Eleanor. The group began as a refuge to collect the shattered remnants of people still trying to disguise themselves as humans. She would host and fund support groups for people like herself, whose lives had been profoundly affected by Brock. The main difference being that the people she was gathering had relented into simply being broken while she had found a new life from the suffering. My mother taught them to embrace what they had gone through and use it to transform as she had which became the original Brock's Babies."

"That is fantastic, but how does it equate to grenade launchers?" he asks sarcastically.

"I'm getting there. She founded EcoHarbor with the same philosophy of funneling her past tragedies into fuel for success, though Brock's Babies was her passion and the two hands began to feed each other. The group, then called 'Survivor's Support', began to receive donations as a means of funding, mostly from some of the business contacts she was working with; tax write-offs and things like that. You know more than anyone about the smoke and mirrors in the corporate world. Over time, her insane work ethic turned the company into a major worldwide player in environmental and humanitarian efforts, along with communications and emerging technologies."

"Humanitarian efforts? Really?"

"Humanitarianism is usually code for military activity, so yes," she snarks. "Either silencing or arming rebellions, the dirty secrets of peace are never told in full. Couple that with a highly successful and mildly controversial female CEO and it becomes rather easy to justify exorbitant defense and security budgets which is how Thompson, Reginald, Oliver, and others fell into her lap. They're spooks, black ops type of guys now on her payroll to do whatever she asks of them, whatever is good for the mission. There's nothing in this world or the next that could stop my mother from getting what she wants, and there are some who believe we only found you because she caused it to be after decades of focusing on the goal."

Glen bites his tongue to not add any more on the subject but fails to hold back after yet another odd rumbling rises in his chest, though this sensation is different from last night's. "I just find it odd that Eleanor is a phenomenal woman, and my mother was a hopeless mess. It's hard for me to imagine Brock choosing her over Eleanor when they're roughly the same age."

"Don't forget my mom was an addict too, and Penny only fell into that hole after her time with him. Eleanor was the mess at that age while your mother was a young woman with a world of promise. Whatever the situation was, only Brock knows the right answer for sure, and we won't be getting that from him now."

He continues to think about the empty shell of a human that birthed him, the only person he spent time with for much of his life, though it was mostly redundant to speak with a living corpse. Her virtual absence shaped him, much like the tragedy that planted the seed for Eleanor to blossom. "You said she gets whatever she wants, but what is it? What does she want?"

"I'm not sure any of us knows that for certain, either. She seems to have the grand plan etched in her mind, and we're only progressing through the steps as expected. What does she want right now? A grandchild, but that won't be the end. Similar to Brock, she has a large-scale plan in place that seems to only make sense to her, so we just listen and fall in line. She hasn't failed us yet."

"I wouldn't be here if I thought she would." *No, you are here because you had nowhere else to go*, the voice reminds as Glen clears his throat. "I trust her. I was only curious what her plans are."

Kathleen zips her jacket over a white tank top and sits back down to put on her shoes. "She thinks big, and everything is carefully accounted for years in advance. That's how she became so successful, because the average person doesn't have the vision to think ahead to tomorrow, if they're lucky. She planned ahead for tomorrow ten years ago, and the day after, and the day after that, and has a plan B, C, and D in place for them too. All I've known my whole life is that my grandmother was Brock Blackwood's first victim and that event connected our stories on a sacred level. We had always hoped to find *anyone* with Blackwood blood, even a distant cousin or something similar, but they are all dead now and then we found you." She pulls her shoelaces tight with a zip and stands up, ready to go. "Shall we get to it?"

"I'll be right there. I need a few more minutes to make sure I have everything."

Kathleen nods and heads downstairs, leaving Glen alone in his room to sit on the bed and try to shake away the feelings he has been resisting since last night. Baptized in the fires of chaos and death, inundated in unwarranted bloodshed and violence, he can't stop thinking about Benny smashing the man with a baseball bat or the red firework explosion of Monica's head erupting. Why doesn't he feel worse about their deaths, even if it could be argued they theoretically deserved to die? *Because you liked it.*

Glen jumps from the bed and shakes violently for the first time in several days. He had begun to feel the first waves of comfort lapping at his mind, though the delusion of contentment now feels to be irreparably shattered. "I didn't ... Carol and Vince died because of me, because I needed that damn shoebox."

*You don't care. If you were so worried about their safety, you could have sent someone else in your place.*

"That's not true. They wouldn't have been able to find it without me ... I did it to protect us all."

*You did it because you wanted to and nothing else. Watching the destruction excited you.*

Glen falls back on the bed with an impulse to escape himself, yet the mattress prevents him from falling any further into the abyss. If Kathleen were still here, she would remind him that these feelings have returned because doubt has crept back in. *Spiritual sickness.* He was living a lie before and has begun to once again resist the natural evolution of change.

"I did NOT enjoy them dying," he whispers again as discomfort strikes with a cold chill. The fear of the uncontrollable, unfortunately feeling at odds with morals and desire. "I did NOT enjoy it."

*You are only repeating what you have been programmed to regurgitate,* Eleanor's voice whispers in the back of his mind.

His eyes dart around the room with uncertainty, unsure what to believe anymore. He should trust his instincts but that would mean owning up to conflicting feelings blazing inside him.

*You need to follow your heart, Glenny. That's why you were born, because I listened to mine,* his mother's voice reminds him.

He closes his eyes to drown out the differing thoughts that try to persuade him in one direction or another. Glen has only just moved into this fantastic new house and now must flee once he has accepted his new life. It won't be for long, he reminds himself, and Eleanor won't leave them stranded in poverty while they're out there.

*You will never be anything but a worthless, lazy piece of shit!* Monica screams, and perhaps she has a point. What has Glen ever done to deserve their admiration or Eleanor's money? Who is he that people should kill and die for him? It feels so strange after a lifetime of having so little to suddenly be handed everything for free.

Then the doubt disappears in a flash, as if a plug was pulled, and the voices fall silent. The corners of his mouth curl upward so slowly, it could either be the rickety floorboards or his lips creaking. Glen lowers his head as that euphoric cold chill washes over his face and neck again. The thought of Monica's expression as shotgun pellets tore through her skin and disintegrated bone and flesh ... the image of her smashed ruby grapefruit of a head as she crumbled on the ground makes him grin with more pleasure the wider it grows. He releases a chuckle that accidentally tumbles into a cackle, the literal last laugh to metaphorically spit on her grave.

"Who's the little bitch now, Monica?"

# CHAPTER TWENTY-NINE

"How does Colorado sound, Glen? We have plenty of supporters down there, and my assistant was able to find you a wonderful house on short notice." Eleanor approaches him with a warm smile and places her hand on his shoulder, the only person in Brock's Babies aside from Kathleen that would dare to be so bold.

"I don't know much about Colorado, but I would like that."

"Wonderful. It will be cold at this time of year, but you will have all the amenities you could ever need and more. EcoHarbor has a branch outside of Denver, so my assistant will be traveling there to ensure you are well supplied. This will only be temporary, but you will have Kathleen, Thompson, Reginald, Patrick, and a few others coming too. Benny will also be joining to help facilitate support from his online community. I am going to remain here with the rest of the group and solve our issues so you may return quickly. This house will be well taken care of, and protected, in your absence."

"Thank you, Eleanor. My gratitude goes out to everyone in Brock's Babies for your incredible support." He nods.

Kathleen grins from the side of the room, seemingly excited to make the escape, and begin her life with him. "It is our pleasure, Glen. We're here for you until the very end."

"The others will fight and die for you, but my daughter will be the one by your side in those private moments when no one else is welcome. Remember, even in his most savage moments, Brock never harmed your mother for that very reason," Eleanor whispers so nobody aside from Kathleen can hear her.

"Yes, I have it handled, Mother."

"I am sure you do, although it is important for him to understand that too. There will be many intense emotions in the near future."

Glen is confused, but he nods anyway. "Kathleen has been great. I will never let anything harm her."

"Of course, you won't." She smirks as she looks into his eyes. "There are times when you are a spitting image of Brock. His charm, his confidence and wit ... I see it in brief glimpses, but it has all been buried beneath so many years of trauma. Brock was similar, you know. He wasn't always the brash figure we have come to equate with him. He also began his life afraid of every dark corner until the shadows broke him and shattered his fears. He showed the occasional flash of who he would become, but it wasn't until he escaped from his own cage that he realized he could never be confined in a box again." Eleanor leans in and smothers him with a hug as he recoils at first but quickly relinquishes himself into the embrace. "It's time to finally break your cage, Glen," she whispers into his ear without even Kathleen noticing.

"We are ready to go, ma'am." Thompson interrupts as he enters the room and places a large duffel bag on the ground, though it isn't clothes inside that clank together. They are now several hours into the darkness and will be driving through the night.

"Keep an eye on this one, you two. He has a bullet hole in his shoulder but can't stop himself from working."

"You already know there's no stopping him. Right, Thompson?" Kathleen jokes.

"Not when there's a job to do. I am fine, ma'am, just a bit of pain."

"Thompson is going with you to *supervise* security, not to jump in the fight himself, although I anticipate very little conflict down there. No living soul aside from us will know you are there."

"Thompson, do you copy?" Reginald calls over the walkie talkie with a tinny voice.

"Yes, I'm here at the house. We were preparing to leave."

"Hold off for a few more minutes. I received word that The Defenders are on patrol in the area. I'm just down the street. I'll be right there."

"Bloody hell, it's always something with them!" Eleanor exclaims. "We will wait. Getting into another pissing match with them could blow the whole thing if they know where we are. Let's make sure we turn the lights off for an additional layer of safety."

"Should we wait to leave until the middle of the night?" Kathleen asks.

"That might be the smartest option at this point. We will hang tight to hear more, but there is no use taking unnecessary risks now. We just might need to wait them out."

"I can help with reconnaissance, ma'am," Thompson offers.

"You will do no such thing. I can't afford you getting any more injured, and they might have already seen you last night."

They wait within the dim house for the threat to pass like a family in the days of old taking shelter during an air-raid siren. Glen reminds himself to return upstairs secretly and grab Brock's dagger before leaving, but he doesn't want to make a scene of it now, not while they are all on high alert. Kathleen rests her hand calmly on the pistol by her side as she winks at Glen and he smiles back. They are nearing their escape to reclaim the long-vacant throne of Brock Blackwood.

The front door swings open as they all jerk into action, and Kathleen draws the gun. "Only me," Reginald calls out as he waves a hand from behind the dividing wall. "Although I found this one sniffing around outside the house." The grizzled older man shoves one of the Defenders into the living room, already bound and gagged beneath a burlap sack.

"How did they find us?!" Kathleen asks with a voice of worry.

"I'm not positive they know we're here, but we can't send this one back out there now. It would surely give away our position." The hooded figure grunts beneath the sack in protest, but Reginald has already tied both hands and legs together. "What do you say, ma'am?"

"The Defender must die here and now. There is no other way." Eleanor pauses to gaze around the room at each of them. "And Glen must do it."

"Me?"

"Yes. We have killed your boss and many others to protect you thus far, but this intruder was preparing to break into *your house*! Break the cage! Right?"

Glen nods slowly and swallows hard before thinking about how he has been nothing but a spectator as the members of Brock's Babies have done everything for him. Monica flashes in his mind again, and he feels a sharp chill cascade down his back. *Yes, excitement ...*

"I have something for you," Kathleen cuts in, opening her jacket to reveal Brock's dagger. "I grabbed this so you wouldn't forget it when we leave. I hope you don't mind." She unsheathes the blade and steps forward ceremoniously with it laid across both outstretched hands.

Glen stares at it with an expression of both bewilderment and stimulation. "Thank you, Kathleen," he whispers, sounding distant to his own ears while grabbing the bone white handle.

The Defender cries and releases muffled screams beneath the sack, but Glen pays the noise no mind. His every nerve ending stands on edge, feeling like he might combust in a pyre of immolation if he does not act soon. Patrick, Thompson, Reginald, Eleanor, and Kathleen stare at him solemnly without excitement or anticipation; they expect this to happen and won't accept any other outcome.

*What are you waiting for?! You want to do this!*

"Yes, I do ..." Glen whispers, grasping the knife handle firmly as he turns the bloodstained blade over one last time to glance at his reflection. What did Brock think in these moments? Did he savor the anticipation or rush to finish quickly?

*Do it! Right God damn now!*

The unceasing roar of the internal voice forces him into action with a powerful lunge and thrust into the Defender's chest. His quivering hand falls still as it holds onto the handle for a moment longer, feeling too attached to let it go. The air escapes him with a slow exhalation in conjunction with the victim's last breaths as his head falls back and his jaw hangs slack to release a beastly groan. The blissful influx of power coursing through his veins holds him in place to simply *feel* something truly pleasurable for the first time since he bashed those bullies' faces in as a child.

Glen rips the blade out as the victim whimpers and falls into a fetal position, yet he is only focused on the incursion of rampant emotions within. The dagger remains at his side and drips blood rhythmically to the floor while his consciousness flickers between the living room and deep inside his inner sanctum. He stares at the Defender curled pathetically on the floor and feels the sudden urge to stare into the face of his first victim, if only to forever remember this moment for being when he broke free from his Overton chains. He kneels down to pull off the burlap sack as her eyes flutter.

"Dana ..."

She lays on her side and stares up at Glen weakly. He gently peels the tape from her mouth and leans by her side while she struggles to remain conscious. "Brock ... you came back ..." Dana reaches into her pocket, causing the rest of them to draw their guns and aim.

"She doesn't have a fucking weapon!" Glen shouts to stop them. "For God's sake, she was my best friend!"

Dana removes the small dog figurine she brought from his work desk and drops it as her hand goes limp. He grabs the trinket and stares for several seconds with an alarmingly blank mind, wading through a silence he hasn't heard in quite some time.

"Congratulations, Glen," Eleanor speaks at last from the corner of the room. "You are now free of all your human ailments."

He stares at the dog figurine again and turns it over without answering her. His father was electrocuted, his mother ended her own life, and now he has killed his closest friend. He burned his house down, left his job, and can't step outside safely without fear of being ambushed in any location. Everything he has left is in this room, all of them staring at him with concern. Glen blinks hard to maintain his mental footing but finds the complete darkness to be more comforting than the realities of his life and begins to slip.

"Hi. Do you wanna play with me?"

He opens his eyes and stares at the eerily familiar face of a boy about eight years old. Dana and the rest of Brock's Babies have faded away. "What would you like to play?"

"Don't know," the boy shrugs and sits cross-legged next to Glen. "I like playing with toys and stuff like that."

He looks down again at the dog figurine he has already inspected several times. "Here, you can have this. A dear friend gave it to me, but I don't need it anymore. I fear it would only give me bad feelings if I kept it."

"Thank you. I like dogs a lot, but I never got to have one for myself. My mom wouldn't let me. Who gave this to you?"

"Her name was Dana, and she was my best—no, the only true friend I ever had. Those don't come around often."

The boy taps his chin multiple times with his index finger and looks upward as he thinks. "I don't think I ever had a friend. People always act funny when I try talk to them, so I stopped."

"That happens sometimes, but don't give up. Some people are so defensive, they will act that way no matter who approaches them. What's your name anyway?"

"Glen. Glen Overton."

"Of course, it is," he chuckles. "Well, Glen, do you know where you are now?"

"No, I've never seen this place before."

"This is your daddy's house, and one day it will be yours. You can feel comfortable here."

"I never met my dad. Do you know yours?" the young Glen asks.

"No, I haven't met mine either, unfortunately. I know who he is, but he went away for a while when I was very young."

"I'm sorry, you were probably sad."

Glen laughs and pats the kid on the back. "Don't you worry about me. Please, take this dog figurine until you're able to get the real thing one day. Maybe it will help you find yourself a Dana too."

"It's okay. I like to be alone. I'm used to it because my house is usually quiet anyway. My mom sleeps a whole lot."

"Try to be patient with her, okay? She might be going through some bad things that are difficult for a little guy to understand, not that you should have to. But maybe you'll do a better job than I did."

The child nods and looks around the house. "Do you have any food here? I'm starving."

"Yes, we have lots of food. Help yourself." He watches the child walk through the kitchen and notices he has no visible injuries or blemishes like the rest of the wayward souls, just an inquisitive boy who has obviously been neglected in several ways. "You can always come back here if you ever need anything else, and you can think of me sort of as a ... dad."

The boy continues rifling through cabinets without saying a word in return. Perhaps it's still the wave of euphoria he is experiencing, but the urge to father a child and actually remain *present* is suddenly the only thing he wants out of life. He will do a far better job than his own parents, though the standard is practically nonexistent. "I found some crackers to eat. They're my favorite."

"Have as many as you like. What's mine is yours."

He gives Glen a satisfied smile as he chomps down on a cracker after another extended period of not eating.

"Glenny! Glenny, where are you?" a woman calls.

"I'm sorry, but I have to go now. My mother just woke up and she needs my help." The boy drops the box as he turns and runs into the hallway, vaporizing as he hits the wall and disappears.

# CHAPTER THIRTY

A heavy thud on the front door shakes Glen back into his living room where Dana still lies dead at his feet.

"Shit! They must've seen me take the girl!" Reginald exclaims as he unslings the shotgun from his shoulder.

"What's the call, ma'am?" Thompson asks with a pistol in his good hand.

Another knock shakes the house as Eleanor dials a number on her phone without responding to them and waits for the answer. "Eric, I am going to send you my location. I need law enforcement cleared for two miles in all directions. *No police*, do you copy?"

"Yes, ma'am, I'm on it."

She hangs up the phone and places it back in her pocket. "We're all clear. They are breaking into *your house*, Glen. You aren't going to allow them to do that, are you?"

He shakes his head, still lost in the fog, but his grip on the dagger tightens.

Eleanor walks toward the hallway closet and grabs an old fire ax then shoves it in Glen's free hand. "You will need something a bit bigger than that knife for this one. Take the axe; it was also used by Brock. You will know exactly what to do with it. Break the cage, Glen. There are *so many* out there that need to die, but it starts now with these *Defenders*. Kill them. Kill them all."

The front door bursts open as Glen drops the dagger to grasp the axe handle tightly with both hands white-knuckled around it. Reginald aims his shotgun toward the entryway, but Eleanor signals them with a hand gesture to wait.

"Kill the killer! Kill the—"

Glen buries the axe blade into the cheek of the first man through and kicks him in his chest to free the weapon. The other three that made it inside immediately panic and turn to run, but Reginald now blocks the doorway with his shotgun aimed at their heads.

The lone woman in the group turns and swings her baseball bat prematurely, missing Glen and knocking into the wall as he brings the blood drenched axe head down between her shoulder blades. His black eyes reflect back through a mirror in the dark house as he breathes heavily and glares at the other two.

They raise their weapons with trembling hands and charge at him fruitlessly with a final battle cry before meeting their ends. "Kill the killer! Blackwood must die!"

Glen turns the weapon over and catches the first man in his neck with the pointed end and rips out his esophagus to swing at the last man standing with the throat still attached. The Defender attacks with a steel pipe, but Glen uses his handle to block and knocks him in the teeth with the wooden end of the axe. The man covers his face in agony as several teeth scatter across the floor, and he rolls from side to side atop them.

Glen drops the blade into his shoulder and drags him slowly along the floor to lay beside Dana. The man quivers and stares into her partially open eyes in horror, knowing that will be his own fate in a matter of moments. "I curse you, killer!" He attempts to spit at Glen, but the broken and missing teeth only make a bloody mess of his face. "We knew from the second we heard about you that it would only lead to nightmares in this city! You're just like your fucking father!"

Glen grabs the glistening dagger once more and holds it ritualistically over the man. "Imagine what they will think when *my* son arrives to join me?" He pierces the Defender's heart with the blade and pauses to inhale the pure joy of conquest before savagery consumes him and he stabs the man a dozen more times out of unchecked impulse.

"He's dead, Glen ... you did it." Kathleen steps forward gingerly, not wanting to surprise him. Thompson, Reginald, and Patrick all stare gleefully.

"Yes, these four are gone, but the job is not done," Eleanor interrupts. "We still need to get you to Colorado safely, and there will be more of them outside. Your window will be brief. Kill everyone you see at will. We can't afford to be merciful and face an ambush by someone in disguise. Do you hear me, Glen?! The world is yours, light it aflame and rule the ashes! Go! Kill everything that fucking moves!"

Reginald throws the front door open and immediately fires his shotgun into a group of encroaching protesters on their left. Thompson and Patrick follow with their pistols drawn and spray bullets into the right end of the street. Kathleen falls back to cover for Glen as he exits the house behind them with both bloody axe and dagger drawn, his eyes ablaze with vengeance.

Screams of chaos and despair fill the streets as The Defenders scatter in all directions to take cover from fire while others succumb to it. One of the men dives to the ground and shouts, "There he is! It's Blackwood! Kill him and this is all over!"

Another man draws his gun before Thompson blows a hole in his forehead and several others charge toward him.

"Glen! We need to leave right now before anything happens!" Kathleen shouts from the van. "Reginald will handle the rest!"

"With pleasure, sir! You need to go!"

Glen stands still in the street and sheathes the dagger. He has tied his own hands behind his back for decades to wear the abuse in silent suffering. No more.

He swings the axe ferociously through the open jaws of the first two Defenders that dare to charge him, one of them a young woman no older than twenty. Several others freeze in position as Glen pants and stares wide-eyed and ravenous.

"We need to go! Leave them! Glen!" Kathleen pleads while leaning out the driver's window.

He steps toward the terrified attackers, blinded by rage due in part to Dana's accidental death. They have to pay for everyone they hurt by hunting an innocent man and forcing this to happen. He grips the handle tighter as he thinks of his mother taking her own life to end her pain. They all must die in a manner more painful than humans should be made to suffer ... though it would still pale in comparison to what he has endured.

Glen takes a slow step forward to a round of shocked expressions. Then he takes another. Each successive step picks up speed until he is sprinting toward the closest Defender with a thirst far bigger for vengeance than blood. The man drops his weapon and turns to run, though Glen catches up to him and hacks the axe through his calf to incapacitate him before stomping the back of his head into the asphalt.

"Kill the killer, right?! Blackwood's son must die?! Why is it that so many of you have been cut down like swine and I am the one doing all the cutting?!" he seethes with his chest heaving dramatically as he stomps forward through puddles of blood in a trance of death.

"We need you alive, Glen, don't do it!" Kathleen shouts again as she shifts the van into drive.

Glen charges the next closest group as they all drop like flies, and the explosions of gunshots fill the neighborhood. A lucid interval overtakes him to bring him back to the present moment. Thompson, Reginald, and Patrick slaughter every other protester around them to force Glen toward the van for a safe escape. He leaps into the front seat before Kathleen floors the accelerator, peeling away from the chaos left in their wake.

"Godspeed, sir! We'll handle everything from here!" Reginald shouts behind them with his shotgun waving in the air.

"And what a mess to handle. Congratulations, Glen. You are now officially a free man. How do you feel?" she asks.

"Elated ... content. Every piece of me feels complete for the first time."

# CHAPTER THIRTY-ONE

Glen's alarm clock rings to wake him from a deep slumber. His eyes take a moment to adjust to the digital display, but he believes it to read October 11th, 2012. No matter, as it's time to awaken regardless of the date.

Sunlight pours through the closed curtains as a beacon of resilience, wherein it is impossible to stop the prevailing forces of life. He would have found the rays of sunshine disgusting before, but life has taken an unexpected turn for the better in recent times, and the light is a welcome change from his previous dark existence.

Colorado was good to them, and the getaway allowed the necessary amount of time to pass for the soldiers of Brock's Babies to clear any remaining threats. The Defenders of Virtue haven't been seen for nearly a year, although they also believed Glen to be dead or gone as well.

He rolls over in bed to see that Kathleen has already risen before him, as she usually does. Motherhood suits her well, and she has never once complained about her responsibilities taking care of their baby boy, Brent. No matter how many times Glen tries to tend to the infant at night, she insists on doing so herself. It is good for the baby, she always says, because a baby boy must bond with his mother first and the father later.

Glen takes a long stretch before rising to look around his bedroom. He couldn't be happier to be back in Brock's old house, and the ongoing renovations look stunning. Brent's baby crib sits in the corner of the room for nights when he is particularly disagreeable, although that is not often; Kathleen has been nothing short of incredible and seems to have been built to be a mother. Her efforts have only been that much more impressive when compared to the lone frame of reference he has for comparison, the late Penny, though he knows she is raising their son fantastically so far in his first few months.

Fatherhood has been a bit more difficult to master with zero positive influences. Kathleen at least has Eleanor to confer with as needed, but it seems Glen's best strategy so far is to only do the opposite of whatever Brock would have done. At any rate, he couldn't be happier after trying for so long to find peace that he wasn't sure truly existed.

The house is quiet downstairs, and the scent of coffee has wafted into his bedroom. *She always knows how to wake me*, he thinks while throwing on a shirt and shoes. Even though the morning is still incredibly young, he has never been able to break the habit of being dressed and ready to go at all times. Vulnerability issues, Kathleen tells him.

Glen steps out of his bedroom quietly, another old practice not yet broken, and tiptoes silently down the hallway. He passes by the door with multiple colored letter blocks spelling B-R-E-N-T and grins just knowing they are there. The door is shut with no sound coming from the other side, leading Glen to believe he is still asleep. The time is only just after seven in the morning, and he might've needed a bit more rest than usual, being the growing boy that he is.

He nearly calls out to Kathleen but quickly bites his tongue to not wake Brent. She would have his head for waking the baby, and he laughs just thinking about it. Walking down the final few steps, Glen pokes his head around the corner and sees that their sofa is empty. Unpleasant memories resurface of a bygone era when he used to always check throughout the house for where his mother had passed out so he would know where he was able to sit. He shakes away the negative thoughts and returns to the pleasantries of family life.

"Kathleen," he whispers from the bottom of the stairs. She might be outside, where she sometimes sits with her morning coffee. Glen shrugs and walks back upstairs to check on Brent, where she has also been known to fall asleep occasionally. Some nights, though not often, their baby boy is particularly restless and will only calm down in the crib if he can see her sitting in the rocking chair beside him. Glen would walk in to check on them and find both infant and mother in a deep sleep with his sound machine playing for comfort.

He grabs the doorknob and twists it as slowly as possible to not make any noise then pushes through at the same pace. The chair, sitting in line with the doorway, is empty. Not the strangest morning they have had so far, but it would be unlike Kathleen to leave the house entirely without telling him, especially this early in the day. She might still be sitting on the patio.

Glen finally opens the door wide enough to slide through, and he takes only a couple long strides toward the crib. Brent isn't there either. Maybe they both fell asleep downstairs? Or maybe she took him outside to get some morning sun with her? That would be something Kathleen might do. *Not everything has to be a pattern*, a familiar voice reminds him as his cascading thoughts begin to bottleneck quickly.

"Kathleen?" Glen calls out again, this time a shade below shouting. Brent obviously isn't in a sound slumber in the house, and he doesn't have to be as cautious. "Where did you go?" He takes the steps two at a time going down and rounds the corner into the living room before stopping cold in his tracks.

Flickering light distracts him as the sound of their old VCR loading and clicking into position takes him back to his old living room that he burned down last year. The screen casts the death of Tiffany taking an unlucky gamble from Brock's revolver, followed by Betty, Rhonda, and Tara all spliced together and blowing their brains out without sound. Finally, his mother appears again, and she fearlessly pulls the trigger as if she already knew the outcome. Brock's grin is genuine, perhaps even full of relief, something that Glen failed to notice the first time.

"You know, I always admired Penny," Eleanor says from the kitchen table. She sits comfortably with a cup of coffee as Thompson looms over her shoulder with a shotgun in his hands. "Have a seat, Glen. Would you like a cup? I made plenty extra."

"I didn't know you were back in town. What happened to Kathleen? Where is Brent?"

"They are gone. You will never see either of them again."

Glen opens his mouth to speak as he takes an aggressive step toward her, but Thompson stops him in position with a lightning-quick spin of the shotgun.

"Sit down, Glen," Eleanor continues.

He approaches the kitchen table with his eyes trained on Thompson and pulls a chair out several feet. "Where's my son?"

"With his mother. As I said, they are gone now, and you won't need to worry about them anymore."

"*Worry?* I love them! You pulled all the strings for us to be together!"

"No, I put you in a position to give me a grandchild, remember? And for Kathleen to birth Brock's heir at last. The rest was nothing more than happenstance." Eleanor sips her coffee without changing expression throughout the conversation.

"So, Brock's Babies was all bullshit? All your false promises and manipulation?"

"We are *Brock's* Babies, not Glen's, and you are no true son of Brock. You are the son of Penny Overton, who was so insignificant she killed herself and nobody else even knew about it. You are not ruthless or powerful; you are still just a scared little boy with the occasional tendency for outbursts of violence. Glen Overton, true to your name, you would rather hide yourself from conflict than conquer it, just like your mother. She never did find the bottom of that bottle, did she? No matter how drunk she got, Penny had to wake up knowing she could never fend off her demons that way, and they inevitably consumed her. You are *weak*, Glen, but instead of liquor, you chose the comforting shrouds of family life. Who could possibly be afraid of The Suburban Serial Killer? We had monumental hopes for you, but unfortunately your blood is far more of the anemic Overton brand than Blackwood. It is terribly ironic that your mother's lame genetics could overpower Brock's."

Feelings he hasn't experienced in nearly a year begin to resurface at his core. Eleanor's silhouette goes hazy as tunnel vision closes in. Glen fights through the darker urges and scoffs instead. "You've got a funny way of showing admiration."

"Oh, but I DO admire Penny. I admire you too or else you would be dead already. These are only facts and really, they reflect my own overestimation more so than anything you have done wrong."

"Sorry to disappoint."

Eleanor smirks this time and pauses before taking another sip of coffee. "No use in apologizing. You and I are more similar in some ways than you might think. Brock killed both of our mothers in one way or another, although I used the pain to transform while you stalled. As for Penny ... I cannot imagine the anguish she suffered and for that, I truly respect her. She flew too close to the sun and that type of drug would be impossible to overcome. Brock could have had any woman he wanted, for a time at least, yet he chose *her*. Other girls idolized him like a deity, we *loved* him, but we were all cattle to slaughter while Penny received the same admiration we gave him. Why?"

"I don't know. We never talked about Brock until just before she died."

"Well, I'll tell you why. Penny was the only woman he ever encountered that wasn't immediately afraid of his presence, and that *excited* him. Sure, the rest of us idolized Brock and hoped he would fall for us, no matter how delusional that may seem now, but we were all terrified of him deep down. Penny's bravery was not an act either, and Brock knew it in his venom-soaked heart. Who would the beast at the tip-top of the food chain fall for? The only woman who would dare to challenge his authority at that position without flinching."

Glen bites his bottom lip as thoughts swirl within his mind. He never thought of his mother that way, as he only ever saw her as a defeated and broken woman without knowing why. What was seen as selfishness was in actuality something else entirely. "Hmm, so it seems the Overton line was not so weak after all? Is that what you're saying?"

"Ha! You caught me there. Very clever, Glen, although that still does not make you fit to wear Brock's shoes, let alone wield his weapons."

"Forgive me if I'm wrong, Eleanor, but are you suggesting I should have murdered Kathleen? Is that your idea of strength, me beating and bludgeoning your daughter to death until she was unrecognizable?"

"Don't be naive. Brock possessed more than strength to be who he was. I am strong, but I could not be a Blackwood, or I would have been already. Your mother was strong, but she broke once Brock was taken away from her forever. He held *power* and that can't be faked, no matter how long you rehearse the motions. Brock was a demigod." Eleanor closes her eyes for effect and breathes in deeply to imitate his influence.

"It seems I have nothing left to lose at this point, so please tell me ... why is it so important that there is a serial killer on the loose? Why the hell do you care so much?"

"It is not serial killers I am after, Glen. There are countless degenerates out there lurking in dark alleys, cutting up prostitutes and the homeless to satisfy their thrills. Brock was otherworldly, and society will always crave someone of his ilk around us, as I'm sure there were others before him. You may have heard of cultures that worship the angel of death ... well, he brought *balance* to a lopsided world. Brock Blackwood was the answer to a cosmic question that science has been unable to answer since humanity could study it. You carry his blood, however little, and we will be forever thankful that it allowed us to repopulate your family line on your behalf."

"So be it," Glen states solemnly. "All that being said, I'm sure you're aware I will not simply allow you to take my only son away from me, not to mention Kathleen."

"I'm afraid you don't have much of a choice in the matter. She left with him willingly, knowing you would never be able to live up to expectations. Please don't worry, we will take care of young Brent and raise him properly ... the Blackwood way."

Glen's eyes roll back in his head for a split second as the dizziness of sensation overtakes him. His tunnel vision goes dark, and Eleanor remains in position with an outline of dark light that smirks smugly in his direction. He can't stand it. She mocks him from her position of influence and now they have kidnapped his son ... the burning rage builds within until it boils from his pores. Brent is gone. Glen leaps from his chair as a cluster of rubber bullets peppers his abdomen in mid-air. The all-consuming desire to reach Eleanor's throat and crush it is cut short as the projectiles spray across his stomach and chest, dropping him to the tabletop just as he scrapes her skin with his fingertips.

Thompson cocks the shotgun and prepares to fire again until Eleanor holds up a hand for him to stop. Glen rocks back and forth on the table, unable to move further. "Do not search for us. You will be alone against an army."

He grasps his midsection with all his might, the bags under his eyes glowing red with hatred as the searing pain burns into his soul. "I'll kill you for this, bitch!"

"Looking forward to it." Eleanor rises from her chair and pushes it in elegantly before exiting the house with Thompson close behind.

Glen gasps for air as the first wave of adrenaline passes. He has taken riot pellets at point blank range, and his vision softens considerably along with his willpower. Thoughts of Brent propel him to push through the immense agony, though he can only crawl forward until falling from the large kitchen table and lying still at last.

# CHAPTER THIRTY-TWO

"I'm so glad you could make it," she said from the doorway as he approached through the pouring rain. It soaked his white tank top and revealed the vibrant colors beneath.

"This is all I've been thinking about since you told me. I wouldn't miss it for anything."

She caressed the baby at her chest to keep him warm but held him out proudly for his father to see. "This is Glen. I'm sure he's been dying to meet you."

"How could a fucking baby know I was coming?" he asked sharply, as was his typical tone. Brock took the boy in his heavily tattooed arms and stared into his face as the baby slept soundly. "Glen Blackwood, you will have more potential than you can handle."

"*Glen Blackwood*. I can't believe it finally happened. He's such a happy and healthy little boy, I hope you know."

Brock ignored the statement and grasped the sleeping baby's hand in his own as the infant instinctually closed his tiny fingers around his father's. They stood in the doorway for a moment longer, rocking gently with Glen in the shadow of the porch light. "I can't stay long. Don't want to draw too much attention here."

"Yes, I saw it on the news. The police are looking for you."

"*Everyone* is looking for me. Police, federal, private. You know me, Pretty Penny, I won't let them catch me. They've been after me for years."

She looked at him longingly as her eyes filled with tears. "I know, but ... what are we going to do if they actually *do* catch you, Brock? How will Glen and I get by?"

"He has my blood within his veins. Don't ever let him forget that, as he is a Blackwood forever more. And you'll be fine, Penny. You have already cheated death once." Brock smirked from the corner of his mouth as was his signature.

She nodded tearfully, already having known the truth, but she decided to play along anyway. "I'm glad you came by tonight, at least. It would be a shame for a boy to never be able to meet his father at least once."

"I already told you I ain't going anywhere."

"Regardless, I'm happy he will always have this moment, the first of *many* times with his daddy. Look at him ... He's your spitting image."

Brock stared down at his son's fluttering eyes and felt a connection he had never known before. There was no such thing as love in his world, but the tiny reincarnation made him feel things he wasn't ready to embrace. "Here, take him. I have to go now."

The tears began to fall down her cheeks as she grabbed baby Glen and held him tight. "When will we see you again?"

Brock leaned in and kissed her forehead. "As soon as I'm able to return. It may take a few weeks before the pigs calm down, but I will be back." The same dark instinct that had led him to butcher so many women then compelled him to look down at Glen again and kiss his forehead too. He whispered many promises of giving his son the world during the brief embrace, but only one of which Penny heard. "No matter what, may you carry my determination with you. Do you hear me? You will never give up no matter if the entire world has turned against you. Fuck 'em all."

Penny snorted through her tears and leaned forward to kiss Brock on his cheek. "I'll wait for your return. Glen and I will be right here, but I know you'll be back soon."

He nodded, knowing within it was not true. The police were hot on his trail and even traveling there that night was a massive risk he should not have taken, though it was worth the lives of anyone standing in the way to meet his baby boy for the first and final time. After all, Glen would be the only son left to carry on the Blackwood bloodline.

# ACKNOWLEDGEMENTS

Thank you to the Adams cult. You know who you are. Thank you to everyone who read early copies and gave me feedback. We all pitched in to create *Son of a Serial Killer*. And thank you to each and every reader who picks up one of my books in any form. Your support is invaluable.